Keith Turnbull:

Initially, Keith ran Europe wide defence sales teams traveling internationally, almost daily, before returning back to take up new challenges. He has worked at 'Top Secret' classification with the British MOD and Foreign Office, working alongside special forces, law enforcement and Intelligence services. Today, he dabbles in that field and with OSINT.

Philip Ingram, MBE, BSc, MA:

Philip is a journalist specialising in the security, counter terror, cyber and intelligence arenas. His knowledge is built from a long and senior military career as Colonel in British Military Intelligence, a strategic planner – who has helped take over a couple of countries/regions. Philip runs his own media company, Grey Hare Media, and specialises in delivering informed content.

To all those casualties of organisations whose role it is to make the world a little safer for us all, whether living or dead, with visible or invisible scars, simply thank you.

For those whose only crime was to seek a better life free from poverty, but who fell prey to the evil of human trafficking, may you now find peace wherever you find yourself, alive or otherwise.

Keith Turnbull and Philip Ingram

THE COMMITTEE

AUSTIN MACAULEY PUBLISHERS™

LONDON * CAMBRIDGE * NEW YORK * SHARJAH

A CIP catalogue record for this title is available from the British Library.

ISBN 9781398488496 (Paperback)
ISBN 9781398488502 (ePub e-book)

www.austinmacauley.com

First Published 2022
Austin Macauley Publishers Ltd®
1 Canada Square
Canary Wharf
London
E14 5AA

"The authors have truly captured the environment, emotion, and the anguish of the migrants forced to flee from poverty and war, and the suffering and horror that can follow at the hands of human traffickers'. The book raises the real and traumatic consequences of human exploitation, and brings to the forefront a real need for education and for us to be more vocal in our disapproval of these evil profiteers."

Miranda Coppoolse, Behavioural Analyst and Security Risk Advisor.

"This fast-paced novel brings out the international links between serious and organised crime, and terror organisations, illustrating how greed can and does lead to the entitled exploiting the desperate lining the pockets of the criminals, often in seemingly legitimate circumstances."

Roy McComb, International consultant on Transnational Organised Crime and former Deputy Director with the National Crime Agency.

"Both authors are spot on regarding the link between organised crime, terrorism and the plight of the weak and fearful. I have seen this first hand and this book further raises awareness of this vile trade."

Anthony Stephen Malone, Elite Operator and former CIA Agent.

Chapter 1
The Doctor

Early 2020:

When the first incision of the surgeon's knife went in, the patient was not fully anaesthetised.

The doctor had no incentive to wait.

No longer driven by his loyalty to the Hippocratic oath, stronger and more financial emotions now influenced him.

The second cut pierced the abdomen of the man laid out flat on the operating table.

Deeper went the knife, easily through the dermis and downward into the subcutaneous tissue. It should have been along what is usually called in female patients, the bikini line but was slightly higher and slightly bigger than the usual 10–20 cm, and this was a male patient. He would not care. He would not be aware. Post-surgical aesthetics were the least of his worries, currently.

The doctor did not take his focus away from the slicing of his knife into the flesh. He did not see the eyes of his patient suddenly opening and the instantaneous realisation that he was being carved up. His body was being opened up in front of his very eyes. The expression of immense shock changed to horror and excruciating pain.

The patient tried to move his arms in an attempt to stop the knife but nothing. So many things ran screaming through his mind and *why are my arms not moving* was just one more to add to the thousands of others mixed up in the moment.

Hearing a rapid increase in the patient's pulse rate through the beeping of the state-of-the-art monitors and sensing that his patient might not be fully under the influence of the aesthetic, the doctor temporarily took his attention off the scalpel and instead looked towards the patient's face.

In the moment he saw his patient awake, the face contorted in anguish and pain, he would know that his heart would, for a while longer, be beating much, much faster than was safe or good for the organ he was targeting.

The Succinylcholine in the IV drip had rendered the patient's limbs paralysed. No matter what happened, he couldn't move. This was not what the doctor had wanted but he had not waited the few minutes longer to start the procedure. Had he waited those few extra minutes, the anaesthetic would have been doing its job. The fluid drips would be fully circulating, and his patient's heart would be beating at a manageable sixty beats per minute.

"Guard, you, come here. Be prepared," he said to the powerfully built man now standing at the edge of the surgical table.

He would show no emotion towards the man lying in front of him, *even if he remembers, if he lives, it will do him no good*, thought the doctor.

Instead, the doctor got angry and frustrated that he may, after all, have to wait a short while and possibly let the anaesthetist back into his operating room, his workplace, to have a second attempt to settle his patient. Waiting was never a trait he embraced easily. *What to do?* His mind raced, it always did.

Not wanting anyone outside the door to know that he may have a problem, he decided to carry on with his cutting and keep on track with the agreed plan. The same plan that he had carried out emotionlessly and robotically many times before. The same plan that facilitated the rich and influential lifestyle he now enjoyed and expected.

Anyways, he knew the stress being caused on the donor would raise the cortisol levels in the organ. This was a good thing for the waiting recipient. He had written and presented many papers on organs donated from non-heart beating patients and cortisol, the stress hormone, was always an important factor. This unwanted action would strengthen the heart's immune system and the likelihood of a successful transplant.

So with a quick check to ensure the Succinylcholine was still working and the drip had sufficient fluid, the doctor nodded to the guard who stood by the table. It never felt strange to see a guard in surgical scrubs but the bulge by his waist wasn't caused by medical equipment; the guard was armed with the latest Glock 9mm semi-automatic pistol, not a regular piece of surgical equipment.

The guard duly obliged. He had seen this happen before. He had witnessed the doctor's impatience before and this time was no different. He knew what to do.

Moving up to the patient's shoulders, he looked down into his frantic eyes and smiled.

He felt for the second drip going into the arm and took the small syringe set on the stainless-steel trolley beside the donor's head and injected it into the back of his hand, through the venflon. Moments later the 'beep, beep', of his heart rate calmed down as the pain subsided as he now slipped into proper unconsciousness. Ten years with Special Forces had more than qualified him to give an injection to the wounded without much care and attention for procedure.

The guard placed his hands on the patient's shoulders. There was likely not much need for this now, but both men had also seen moments from victims with massive surges of adrenaline and the fear of imminent death bringing about some form of superhuman strength.

This would not happen this time. Instead, the doctor returned his attention to the now partly open wound across the patient's abdomen, small rivers of blood seeping out and down the side of the man onto the operating table.

This time, grunting under his surgeon's mask he went back to work lengthening and deepening the incision in the patients' body.

Reacting promptly to his grunted instruction, the only other person in the room, his long-serving and long-suffering nurse, threw some pads onto the floor and began to wipe the blood away from the open wound and the man's body.

The patient, the forced donor, the victim, was now in the sanctuary of unconsciousness. Perhaps the effects of the anaesthetic now doing its job would render his memory of the incident as merely a bad dream. However, the doctor did not care. All he wanted was for the relative calm to return and for him to go about his deed and towards his next pay check.

It would be a few minutes longer and several more deep and angled cuts before the doctor would call on this nurse to help him with the next gruesome task.

In order to have clear sight of the kidney and have unobstructed access to it, the doctor wanted the wound opened up as much as possible. He needed a clear sight. He wasn't concerned about post-operative discomfort.

The nurse would spend the next few minutes preparing the clamping equipment while the doctor sat and sipped water.

The nurse raised the mechanical winding clamp into place and, together with the doctor, positioned it horizontally across the patient's body and tight up against his lower ribs. It was forced into position.

Beginning to wind the cog anti-clockwise, the crude devise lengthened slowly before reaching either side of the unconscious man's rectus abdominis on both the left and right-hand-side. The cavity widened. Bones snapped and tendons tore.

Continuing to turn the cog, the tissue and muscle mass began to stretch wider.

When the doctor was satisfied that it was tight enough to support its own weight hovering above the now open cavity, he waved his left hand towards the nurse. She stopped turning the cog and let go of the device.

For a tiny moment in time, all three stood motionless starring at the grotesque sight that lay in front of them. The sight of another human being who had been surgically opened up while awake and who now lay in a strange peaceful manner, his abdomen now exposed to the flickering ceiling lights.

Then the next task to perform. To move the entrails aside, allowing access to the money prize still filtering out impurities from the hosts blood.

With a glance from the doctor, the nurse got to work. She had worked with the doctor on so many occasions before executing this procedure dozens of times before.

It would be so much easier just to cut it all out, thought the doctor, *it's not as if he will be eating much again soon, if ever.*

Slowly and carefully the nurse and doctor worked together, being careful not to cause any tears or ruptures that could cause cross infection. He may be needed again.

For now, at least, the easy part had been completed.

Nothing now lay obstructing the doctor from initiating the second and key phase of his ugly work; the illegal and secretive removal of human organs from unwilling captives, and their onward passage into desperate but very wealthy recipients.

The reluctant patient, motionless and unaware, would be 'donating' a kidney to an 81-year-old Russian billionaire who neither cared where it came from or from whom. Instead, this wealthy customer wanted only to extend his own life longer so that he may have that last cruise on his super yacht or see his teenage granddaughter graduate from a cliquey British University.

The doctor was under pressure.

His boss was waiting for news in the rooms above the subterranean operating theatre.

The customer was waiting, surgically prepared, grumpy through nil by mouth, somewhere inside the countryside manor from which they operated.

The money had been exchanged and hands had been shaken. Failure would bring more than just death to the awaiting guest. It would bring a violent end to the lucrative venture working in the shadows of this grand hotel.

The doctor was now under growing pressure to deliver the prize and he knew it. This customer was not to be let down. The doctor knew the consequences for him and his own family if he could not deliver a healthy kidney.

The Russian was notorious for his ruthlessness against his deemed enemies. He had accumulated his immense wealth through bribing corrupt government officials to allow him to win massive infrastructure contracts. There were even rumours that driving the Russian motorways that stretched for thousands of miles, one would be passing over the dead bodies of those who dared to disagree with him and his requests. The doctor did not want himself or family to be the next to 'fail' and lie forever under the concrete of his next project.

He deepened his breathing and for a few seconds watched the movement of the patient's heart. It beat slowly and rhythmically.

The guard, watching intently from where the anaesthetist should have been, likewise looked into the man's body. Being no medical practitioner he thought of his own beating heart and how it must be moving in a similar manner.

Fuck, this whole thing is weird, fucking weird, he thought to himself as he imagined the effects of injuries he had inflicted on his enemies, must have torn up the flesh he was now looking at.

The doctor, however, did not think anything similar. Instead, he visualised the pending procedure and it being a successful and speedy one.

"Right, let's go. Don't want to fuck this kidney up and have to go for the other one. That one's probably already sold to the highest bidder, and this lucky guy is going to be going through this all again soon."

So it began.

The doctor began clamping key arteries and other vessels around the target organ so as not to fill the cavity with blood. The bypass valves were pumping blood away from the kidney and returning the oxygenated blood back into the patient's circulatory system at a new and temporary location.

He needed the patient to survive, for a few more days at least.

It would be a further ninety minutes of work inside the cavity of the patient, with the occasional helping hand from the nurse, before he was ready to make the final cut and separate organ from host. This was the point of no return, however, this doctor was not for turning and the key moment came and went with a quick and deliberate cut.

The prize was carefully placed onto ice in preparation to move to another state-of-the-art operating theatre right next door.

Having carefully sealing off the ureter, reconnecting the vessels and closing his patient, he couldn't help picking up the organ again, deflated, and dull from its normal pink. Now a pulsating solitary state. No matter how many times he did this he looked in awe at what he had in his blood-soaked gloves.

"Sir?" His nurse looked on strangely calm and reassuringly.

She readied herself to support the doctor, should she be called upon but while she waited and watched, she also opened the iced storage box. The kidney could not last long without its own blood supply for long and would be physically deteriorating each and every moment it was out of its host body. He carefully handed her the organ, the prize, and then looked back to the operating table.

The patient could die from catastrophic internal haemorrhaging and related brain trauma and the doctor risked losing the other organ and any future pay out as well as future work. He wanted to make sure he was fairly stable before leaving the operating theatre. He set about with speedy basic and temporary aftercare.

The clock was ticking.

The current patient could wait for now, he was stable. He would be wheeled off to the recovery room, being kept in a state of unconsciousness. His safety was not about life or death, but about profit so he still had value and must be preserved.

The prize was packaged and the team of two ruthless and unemotional medical practitioners left the room to quickly transition for their next and more important task.

The guard glanced back at the detritus on the blood-stained operating table before himself exiting. The smell of blood as in every operating theatre, assaulted his nostrils when there was nothing else to concentrate on. He closed the door behind him and went after the doctor to stand by the door and safeguard the pending action from interruption once again.

Thirteen hours after he walked into the first operating theatre, he would walk out of another and off to his bed for much needed sleep. The transition of the kidney into his powerful Russian customer was done. Now it was a waiting game.

Would the organ 'take' to its new host. Would the Russian survive? Would he have to make a second attempt with the donors second kidney?

The doctor had many thoughts running around his head as it hit the pillow. But falling asleep was today not a difficulty for him. His conscious cleared and rebooted each night, ready for the next gruesome and illegal act the following day, his long game of ultimate riches and retirement was one further step closer to fruition.

Chapter 2
Grave Situation

1992:

She slung on her winter coat and skipped with purpose down the stairs. Rarely did she take the lift. Instead, she preferred the freedom of the stairs. She exited and entered the UN building in Vukovar, not risking more the electricity power cuts, and being stuck in a metal box freezing to death.

It was cold as she headed towards the waiting car.

"Fuck, I hate this place in winter," she said out loud.

The fact was that Vukovar was always cold. Croatia, or more properly now 'The Republic of Serbian Krajina', was always cold at this time of the year. She longed for a new placement to perhaps the heat of Miami or the civilisation of London. However, for the next few weeks and months, Victoria Fleming was where she was. A UN investigator getting into a marked car enroute to what was believed to be yet another mass grave site.

"Ready, Ma'am?" said her driver inquisitively.

He had been assigned to her for around a month now and had already forgotten the number of times he had to U-turn and return to her base as she had forgotten this or that. Today, he decided to question her.

"Do we have what we need today?" he said in a quiet, non-confrontational manner. He waited for an answer.

Not taking her eyes of the small screen of her mobile phone she made a small grunt, taken as 'yes, let's go', the driver engaged first gear and the UN vehicle moved off with a tiny skid of the wheels on the slippery snowy road.

It had been a strange assignment for Fleming to get. New to the International Organisation for Migration, she was a career professional within the UN. Previous assignments had been investigating illegal whaling in international waters by Japanese trawlers and before that she had led up a small research team in Geneva focusing on women's rights and equality abuses in China. She now had a new assignment.

Only seven weeks into the role, which she had been told was supporting the UN effort to manage displaced persons, refugees and mass migration out of conflict areas or extreme drought, she was on her way to witness the second mass grave discovery. Reports had surfaced that a whole hospital of around one hundred and fifty people had simply vanished. That the patients had been seen being forcibly taken away at night in a convoy of trucks and off to an unknown location.

She felt this was out of her remit, but her boss had sent the telex giving her the instruction to investigate this development. An instruction she did not really want but had to follow up on.

The car moved steadily along the slippery roads. Not suited to this type of terrain, she felt she had been singled out for 'special' treatment by Richards, her boss. Instead of the usual all terrain jeep, he had seen fit to assign her a reconditioned long frame Ford which tried hard but struggled as soon as the first snows fell. And in Croatia, Fleming felt, snow fell constantly.

It was a Tuesday in February and like any other day Fleming utilised every minute of every day. She could not change her assignment this day, neither could she order her driver to drive faster on the treacherous roads, so accepting her current fate, she reached inside her warm winter coat and pulled out her note pad.

Fleming kept a meticulous notebook, like children kept their focus on their card collections, longing for that one missing footballer or Disney character that would complete the collection.

She flipped through the notebook until she reached the next blank page and started to scribble.

Erdut. Sixteen miles North of Vukovar. A shit hole of a village with one way in and one way out, but strangely untouched by the war.
Why?

She stopped and looked out the window and lost her thoughts staring at the snow-covered fields and occasional wooden huts with smoke coming out from the chimney as the inhabitants' huddle around a fire and look to survive another day in this 'paradise'.

Who comes here, to Erdut?

What is this place known for apart from Drako?

No airfields, no sustainable crop yields, telecoms get a crap signal. Isolated from the developed world.

Why here and what? Mass grave? Genocide?

Not religious?

Not ethnic? – Bollocks.

Fleming put her pencil inside the notebook and closed it before pulling on the rubber band and placing it around her treasured notebook, her own form of private diary that she used to keep herself sane, focused and make good of a fucked-up world into which she had been dropped. For the rest of the journey, she let her thoughts wander gazing out of the car window and watching her snowy world go past.

The large yellow digger was relentless. Its mechanical claw tore into the side of the bank and lifted ton after ton of cold partly frozen soil before rotating on its axel behind its giant caterpillar tracks and dumping the soil in a growing secondary hill several feet away. Each time, a group of charity workers would quickly close in and rake the recently freed dirt looking for something, but what, even they did not really know. Then as the next claw load of earth swung around, they would retreat and repeat the action once again.

Again, and again the large mechanical claw would crash down into the soil and shovel up the frozen mud and whatever or whoever was caught in between. There was no delicacy about this operation.

The locals of Erdut had been hardened from years of corrupt and strong rule from the war lord residing just a few miles away.

Unopposed by any legitimate law enforcement or rule of law, Drako, who had his headquarters and training base on the outskirts of the village, controlled an area, the size of a large city and his powers, as well as his arrogance and confidence, was rapidly expanding. The villagers knew this and had chosen submission and survival over resistance and disappearance. It would prove a strategy which would bring longevity to their small town.

As a result, many watched on, unemotional as the yellow beast tore into the frozen earth, looking for something that only they knew was under the ground and likely about to be exposed in all its horror.

Fleming's car was still a way off and the charity workers, the village locals and the digger operator knew this. Order and structure were coming to the find soon enough but for now they had a free hand at conducting the dig in the manner they wished and at the speed they wished. If evidence was destroyed, or worse, if it was itself made to disappear, then now was the time and quickly was the manner.

When the UN marked car finally arrived at the excavation site, Fleming was back to her focused self. Notebook in hand, together with camera and authorisation documents, she sprang from the car and after slipping on the ice and recovering her balance and dignity, she immediately set about seeking out the likely leader of this motley crew she found herself with.

Showing her UN pass and calling out for the lead participant, she walked and watched as the mechanical arm continuously threw itself into and out of the deepening and widening hole.

That's so wrong, she thought to herself, *if there is anything there, evidence, that beast is going to destroy it, never mind if it is human in nature.*

Stopping her search for the group's leader, she decided to let him or her find her instead.

"You," she yelled into the operating cabinet of the large digger. "Stop now and get out. That's an order," soon followed. She was finding her inner strength now and was ready for whatever happened next.

What did happen next however, surprised her a little.

The digger operator smiled back at her and simply turned back to the hole and continued. The next claw went in and the next ton of broken soil came out and spun around to the eagerly awaiting charity workers to sift quickly through.

Taken aback and with no obvious command structure showing itself currently, she turned from confident to angry.

"Hey, fuck, stop that digging or I will," she yelled back at him now walking towards him as best she could on the wet mud.

"Stop now! I am in charge here and we do not destroy any evidence…" But as she spoke the mechanical arm swung back around and back towards the pit. She was in its way and the operator didn't seem like the type to care.

Fleming ducked as low as she could while everyone else, it seemed to her, simply looked on to see what, if anything would happen, if it hit her.

Standing once again, she clambered quickly onto the caterpillar tracks now with total disregard for her clothing or wellbeing and reached up to tug on the door of the glass shell which housed the operator.

When she threw it open, she stood fully and again yelled at the man inside.

"Stop this madness. Last fucking warning, my friend."

The operator looked at her. He was a large man and could easily have pushed Fleming aside. Strangely he did not. Reaching for the ignition key, he turned the machine off and the arm came to a sudden halt, no longer feeding from the hydraulic pressure. The area fell quiet.

The operator stood up as best he could inside the cramped glass housing and pushing his way past Fleming, jumped down onto the frozen ground. Lighting a cigarette, he walked off to stand with the others watching and waiting.

Fleming turned to face them, still standing aloof on top of the machine tracks.

"Right, you lot," she began, "before you totally destroy this UN evidence site any further, which one of you is supposed to be in charge here?"

The silence continued.

"Ко је главни?" she shouted again in her limited Serbian. "Who is in charge?"

Stepping down, trying hard not to fall face first into the muddy ground, she made her way over to the group.

"I said, who is in charge, Ко је главни? Speak up."

From the corner of her eye, she saw a young woman wearing a branded jacket of the 'Slavic Care' charity. Finally, this might be someone more approachable.

"You, tell me who is in charge? Is anyone here in charge?" Fleming asked.

Reluctantly the young charity worker spoke up.

"Them," she said in perfect, accent-less English, pointing in the direction of a fast-moving, all-terrain, black vehicle speeding up the road.

The group's focus turned from Fleming to the black car. Fleming's hair on her neck stood to attention. The fast-moving car did not seem to have any recognisable markings on the paint work. It did seem to have blackened out windows and driven with purpose unlike her inappropriate Ford.

The large jeep came to a halt after an uncomfortably long number of seconds. A few long moments later the engine was cut.

Fleming had the sense that she was being studied from inside but could not see for herself through the blacked-out windows, who was inside.

The back door of the car swung open.

A man stepped out and looked around, familiarising himself with the surroundings, temperature and vantage points. Then a second door opened and a smaller stocky framed man stepped out. He was wearing army trousers and boots with an out-of-place designer shirt. His receding hairline partly covered by a burgundy-coloured cap.

He did not acknowledge the group of locals and charity workers, attention now fixed upon him with fearful eyes. Instead, the man smiled and unimposingly walked over to Fleming, stretching out a hand.

"I run things here and I see, Miss Fleming, that you have taken control of the situation."

Too many questions entered her mind. *How did he know who I was? In charge of what, the site or the town or more? Why is he smiling and not concerned about what is happening here and who can see this place being dismantled?*

"Miss Fleming, I feel obliged to thank you for your timely interruption at the dig site. These fools show no respect for the dead and it will be taken care of later. For now, I wish you to take command of the situation and my UN friends to gather all the evidence that remains here," he said, before turning back towards the vehicle. He swivelled back to her for a moment. "But for tonight this site is off limits even to the United Nations. I will have my men secure the site to ensure no more contamination of any evidence of wrong doings, and in the morning please do return at any hour you wish to begin your crucial work."

Fleming knew that she had just received an order and something in the back of her mind told her that, on this occasion, she should follow it and leave this gloomy wet place until the next morning when she could return with reinforcements.

When she eventually returned early the next morning, Fleming found the area filled in and flattened. Heavy machinery had been busy the previous night and now in its place was hazard waste barrels, many of which lay on their side. Their contents having spilled out onto and into the soil.

Around the site were numerous signs in both English and Serbian. They simply read 'Keep out; contaminated ground' and underneath the words was an image of a skull and cross bones which seemed to be staring straight at Fleming and smiling.

She took out her notepad and started to write down her initial thoughts of what she now saw in front of her, just as she had done returning back to UN regional headquarters in her car the day before. A few quick snaps from her camera to record the scene.

She knew it was him, she knew he had done this. He had destroyed what he could of the evidence and that was why he had been so keen and demanding that she return back early the day before. But she also knew that the locals would be of little help in her search for the truth. She suspected that whoever he was, he owned the village and the lives of those who lived within it. They would not likely talk for fear of repercussions, but she also knew she had to try.

Together with the two UN colleagues she had persuaded to join her, Collins and Durham, she walked the short distance from the site onto what appeared to be the main street through Erdut.

It was a tiny village, but the thing that stood out most was, it was like a time capsule shielded from the horrors only a few kilometres all around it. This centre of the village had been virtually untouched by the conflict. The town's leadership had certainly done well and stood out from others in the region gaining favour with the local infrastructure builders.

The three women decided to split up and move from home to home hoping to find answers to a series of agreed questions surrounding the rumours of genocide and mass burials. And also what people had heard about the hospital and to find out why the bodies were transported to Erdut and placed in a mass grave right next to them.

Each would spend a fruitless two or so hours walking and knocking on doors. Some doors would be closed in their face while others would remain unopened despite the noise of family life inside. Sometimes they would also be confronted with the aggressive chained dog whose purpose in life was to protect the home and the 'pack'. Those properties would be avoided.

Collins and Fleming would bump into each other, close to a tiny coffee shop, the only coffee shop, and decided to wait for Durham to join them. They had agreed that each had sole discretion on when to continue the round and when to call it a day and these two colleagues had called it a day with nothing to show for their efforts.

"Should we go looking for her?" said Collins.

"No, not yet. It's fine. Nothing out of the ordinary. Maybe she's on to something and needs more time," replied Fleming.

"Anyways," Fleming went on, "I'm enjoying this coffee and it's not fucking snowing, let's give her thirty more."

Thirty more minutes came and went and Durham had still not shown up at the agreed rendezvous point.

"Should we be worried, Vic?" asked Collins.

"Nah, she's fine. Bet she's got the local rakija and she's downing it with some family right now. Sure, she won't be driving back to HQ as that stuff's strong, but let's give her another fifteen," Fleming tried to sound positive. She'd started to think back to the day before and the man from the black jeep. She had not yet figured out who he was but would in time. She hoped he wasn't going to become problematic.

Fifteen more minutes passed. The two coffees, unfinished, now stone-cold. The two colleagues sitting in silence both wondering what to say or do next. This was not like Durham to leave them hanging without proper reason.

Being unable to wait any longer, Fleming pushed back her chair and stood up. Collins instinctively did the same. The noise of the metal chair legs on stone caught the waiter's attention.

Collins pulled out several Dinar notes and placed them under her cold coffee cup. The women then walked briskly away in the direction where they had suspected Durham had been knocking the doors.

Before they had reached the edge of the square, they saw her.

Durham was walking purposefully towards them. She was slightly silhouetted by the dimming sun in the sky and the streetlights, but both knew it was Durham and likewise Durham knew instantly she had found her two UN colleagues.

Coming out of the street shadow and into the open square, Collins and Fleming could now see their friend's face.

Durham was blank. Her face was neither friendly or relieved to see them nor was it in any shock or anguish. Durham walked right up to Fleming and with a slight acknowledgement to Collins, grasped her colleague's wrist.

"Vic, not sure how to say this. Not exactly sure what it is I have just seen and heard but…" Durham was interrupted by Fleming who instantly realised her friend and colleague was in shock.

"Jane," said Fleming, "Jane, its fine. We are both here. Slow down and tell us what it is, take your time."

"The graves, the mass grave we came here for, it's gone."

"Yes, Jane, we know, we saw the rapid make good together remember. Something or someone spent a lot of time last night making sure we could find nothing today," she went on.

"No, sorry, you don't understand. When I said the graves were gone, I meant most, not all," she replied.

The three women sat on a nearby wall. Collins and Fleming held their colleague's hands in a reassuring manner but said nothing.

"They were not all gone, you see," started Durham, trying to find the logical order for her words.

"The family you see, the one I knocked the door on, they have a grave. Not all have gone."

Fleming looked at Collins. Both knew not to speak but to wait.

Durham started again, her lips quivering a little.

"The family had a young son, a teenage son who worked the fields. He went missing and so they went to search him. When they found him, he was in a shallow grave. He had been strangled," Fleming interrupted,

"Yes, Jane, take your time, why is this important here and now to our investigation?"

"You see they showed me the body. They cannot bury it yet because they don't have it all. The mother wont properly bury her son until they find all of him," she forced out.

"They killed him, they seemed to mutilate him and then simply dumped him in a shallow grave for the beasts to eat him."

Durham continued one last time, "I saw the body. They keep him in the house in a wooden box while his father searches for something…peace…or something. But he searches every day and won't stop until he finds something. It's fucked up, it's truly fucked up here and I want out," she said with sadness and fear sounding in her voice.

"They said he was not the first. They said it was him. The man you met yesterday!"

Chapter 3
The Road to Damascus

1983:

To become a highly qualified doctor came as a big surprise to his parents. Growing up they never thought their young son, Frederik Hofmann, had either the ability or the desire to become a doctor for he showed little motivation through his teenage years.

Born to middle class parents, Frederik was the surviving twin. His identical brother dying within hours due to birth complications. Frederik would become a loner with few friends.

His parents spoiled him. Perhaps out of feelings of guilt for the dead twin or perhaps from a desperate desire for him to rise above their own average living existence.

His father worked long hours at the local railway station while his mother set up a home baking business and would sell her produce to local shops and anyone else who would take some. This sounds more working class than middle class so perhaps change the middle-class thing. Both loved Frederik very much, but as he grew up, he would more and more distance himself from them. He would become independent enjoying his own company more than that of his parents and few friends he would find.

The early teenage years were a struggle for he was often ill and missed school. His small frame and pale and weak complexion often made him a target for bullies and laughter.

Perhaps it was the loss of an unknown brother at birth or the false drive and ambition pushed into him by his father who only wanted the best for Frederik, but either way, he grew apart from them. They grew to resent his independence and lack of respect which made family life ever more difficult.

Pushed around at school, seen as a waste of time by his teachers and now resented by his parents, Frederik Hofmann left home at seventeen and ran off to Munich, ironically from the very rail station his father worked at. The family would keep in touch periodically and their calls and letters would be friendly enough but never again would the family be close.

He had just turned eighteen by only a matter of weeks when the call he had expected finally came.

His mother had been ill for a while and Frederik had ignored pleas from his father to return home to be by her side.

Ending the call from his father and with the news that his mother had died, his head spun. *Had he contributed to her illness and worry? Had he broken her heart? Could he have done anything had he returned home as his father had wanted?* That night he lay awake and pondered what he believed now to be a mistake in coming to Munich and not seeing his mother during her last moments alive.

Overnight, however, this changed. He became even more focused and determined. He worked long hours as a labourer during the day to fund his evening classes. He was determined to prove his former teachers wrong. He became solely focused upon his task and reason for not being with his mother and his leaving home against their wishes. He would now become the success that both he and his father wanted. Month on month, his grades slowly began to rise.

The more success he had, the more it drove him to work harder and study longer. He did not need friends or any social life. There would be time for that later. For now, he studied hard at Munich University and that was his life.

When Frederik Hofmann finally graduated with a leading degree in Medicine, he became free from the shackles around his neck. Free from those teachers prophesising his life would come to nothing. Free from the feelings of inferiority that years of bullying had forced into his consciousness. He was twenty-three and the world was now his for the taking. Nothing was going to stop him from becoming the success he craved.

He spent less time labouring and more time planning how to get the opportunity and path to self-respect. Something that had eluded him in his teenage years.

Then one very ordinary day in February of 1992, the opportunity he had waited for presented itself to him.

In a café in the student area of Munich, Frederik sat down at a table recently vacated by a group of university employees. One of whom had left behind a copy of that day's 'Die Zeit' newspaper. Moving the paper aside to make space for his coffee, his eyes became transfixed on a photograph of a bloodied little boy on one of its pages.

For a moment his mind flashed back to a time when he himself came back from school bruised and bloodied after a particularly troublesome bullying incident.

He picked up the paper and folded it smaller, focusing on the image and article and sat back to read the story trying to figure out why this image resonated so vividly with him.

Battles were raging in Yugoslavia between the Serb Army with its various splinter groups. Serbian paramilitary groups and the militias and supporters of the breakaway states seeking independence battled their neighbours, then would fight each other. The majority of the dead and injured were not soldiers but unarmed civilians caught up in indiscriminate barrel bombing and gas attacks. The world stood by and watched. Occasionally, the world leaders would ask for a ceasefire but no one listened…

The newspaper article focused on the town of Vukovar and how it was being systematically dismantled through ethnic cleansing on one front and random bombing on another. In the middle were families from both sides being squashed into smaller and smaller safe havens. The UN had been slow to react, and these targeted civilians relied heavily on the few charity organisations that had the courage to send workers into danger zones and a stronger reliance on those very representatives themselves, who risked their own lives to help strangers in desperate need.

Finishing the article, he scanned the remainder of the page for further commentary and was this time attracted to a small advertisement from Médecins Sans Frontieres, appealing for medical professionals to travel to Vukovar and work in makeshift field-hospitals.

Frederik Hofmann's calling had arrived by chance, the casual discarding of a daily newspaper. His life's turning point was staring him directly in the eye and it was an image of a bloodied and terrified little boy stuck in a war zone. He stood up and exited the café to plan for his trip to Yugoslavia. Hofmann's calling had found him, both willing and ready.

Returning from his father's home he was set to travel. Goodbyes done and wise words said; Hofmann would not yet know that it would be the last time he would see his elderly father who would die soon after, of a short illness. He would not return for the funeral but promised himself that he would visit the grave soon and explain to his dead father why he had stayed away.

It was a cold and wet morning when he lined up at the charities centre with the other volunteers. They all waited for the buses which would take them and their limited luggage to the Yugoslavian medical camp and the horrors waiting for them. Each of the sixty or so volunteers had signed up for this trip for their own personal reasons. Some would share stories on the buses, others would try to sleep and dream of the good that they would bring to the suffering people. Hofmann did neither. He read journals and kept himself to himself.

Most had heard rumours of terrible atrocities during this war. How captives and villagers fleeing the bombing had been caught up in mass executions, only after being butchered for body parts and organs which had become a prized commodity.

The world had turned a blind eye, and for those volunteers waiting to get thrown into the 'deep end' of the current war and the current shameful situation, the United Nations and world leaders either were reluctant or simply failed to grasp the magnitude of the situation once again.

When the buses did eventually arrive, the drizzle had stopped and the sun had come out. Stepping onto the second coach, Hofmann took a double seat near the back of the bus and stayed silent. He would not acknowledge the others taking up places around him nor would he respond to those who spoke to him. Frederik Hofmann had been a loner when he was younger and now, starting his new life, he kept the demure appearance of the quiet and shy individual.

The engines appeared to start up all together and, as his bus started to gently vibrate under the strain of the aging diesel engine, he looked out the window. *Good riddance*, he thought to himself.

Several hours later, the buses would arrive and enter the gate of the medical refugee camp.

The camp representatives, who had accompanied the volunteers on each bus, had insisted on the window blinds be pulled right down before they entered the camp. But some volunteers tried to peek outside with growing excitement and anxiety of what awaited them.

Hofmann did not attempt to look out his window.

It is what it is, he thought to himself. Sensing their journey was at an end, he stood up and grabbed his oversize rucksack, which for now held all his worldly possessions and waited until he could move out. He walked down to the front just behind the driver and stood and waited. The camp representative looked up at him from his seat and said nothing.

The next few hours involved their processing into their new medical professions and paperwork, followed by an introduction talk about the camp set up. Each was assigned a bunk in a designated dormitory and one by one escorted to their new sleeping quarters. Hofmann's second life would start for real the next morning. For now, he would try to sleep and get ready for the toils that lay ahead of him in the morning.

Chapter 4
Accidents Happen

Durham and Collins decided to stay indoors and have a quiet time with colleagues at the British Medical Centre, just South of Erdut. They showered and made their way to the cook house for food, but neither spoke of the events of that day.

Fleming had returned to the camp with her colleagues, but she needed to get out. She was restless, she needed something to help her process the brief encounter she just had. She was also furious. Her lithe appearance was kept trim through running and her Taekwondo black belt she had worked so hard to get whilst in South East Asia. She feared further interference with the site, and while she would not 'guard' it, being close by she felt she was doing her duty to whatever and whoever may still be there under the soil.

Walking into the operations room for the British Medical Battalion East Detachment, responsible for emergency UK medical cover over the Eastern United Nations Protected Area (UNPA) in the self-styled Republic of Serbian Krajina, she was looking for a running map of the area.

"Richard, fancy seeing you here, I thought you were back in Zagreb."

Over the few weeks she had been posted in the Vukovar, she had befriended a senior charity worker, Richard Livingston. This tall slim American had taken her under his wing as to say when she first arrived. He could see the disbelief in her face around her posting to such a place and remembered similar when he had first arrived at a former posting in Somalia. The poverty and suffering he witnessed there were a real shock to him. Now, months later, Livingston found himself in a different posting but with the same old symptoms, poverty, death and suffering. He remembered telling himself 'same old, same old but much bloody colder here' when he stepped of the charter plane upon arrival.

"Fleming! Somebody has to keep an eye on the Brits to make sure they are all doing good and the right thing. I'm just doing a bit of liaising," he said as he gave her a friendly hug and held her slightly closer than he should and definitely slightly longer.

"I'm doing the same as you, looking for a running route, fancy joining me for a bit of a jog?" He added, "Ten minutes, front gate, I'll bust your ass, but you are navigating, Fleming," he said with a grin slightly bigger than it should have been and an extra beat of the heart that made her think *maybe today won't be that bad and I'm only looking.*

Booking out at the little guard hut they turned right along the road heading past the houses. Most were untouched by the conflict, however, every now and again they passed a burnt-out shell. This could have been anywhere in Europe, Austria, Germany, Switzerland but no this was Croatia, and a Croatia where friend turned on friend, neighbour turned on neighbour just because they were from a different ethnic group.

They were officially in the Republic of Serbian Krajina, only formed a year before in 1991, when the rump of the Yugoslav National Army were supporting Ethnic Serbs in Croatia, a country that had just declared independence from Yugoslavia helped displace ethnic Croats from ethnic Serb strongholds. The battle of Vukovar had become infamous with the Croat defenders being beaten and driven out of their city.

Jogging in silence, Fleming reflected on her day, wondering what the morning would bring. She couldn't shake it off, but she had a feeling of impending something, she stopped herself thinking the word death, end, even doom.

"Hey, this is too easy," she yelled towards her companion, "let's try and find the river."

"No problem, there is a small trail coming up in 300 yards on the right, well, take that, I think they have lifted all the mines," Livingston yelled back with a wry grin. He had this uncanny ability to remember a map and find his way from memory.

Fleming glanced briefly down at his shorts, 'Navy blue Ron hills'. She noticed he has been in the British Naafi shop in Zagreb.

Livingston disappeared down between two walls heading down a muddy path. The dew heavy in the evening cold, and with the light fading, she shivered as she followed him. She almost didn't see the black SUV drive past, then turning slowly just in front of them, but nothing suspicious registered.

"We keep the river on our left for about two miles and then right, back up on the other side of the village from the camp," Livingston called back to her over his shoulder.

"I'm looking forward to a beer later, the Brits always have a well-stocked 'liaison facility' as they call it and although it's a school night, they will happily liaise with us," he puffed. Livingston's breath suspended in the still air, along the riverbank. "You OK back there? All I can hear is puffing and wheezing," he laughed, for a moment just before he felt himself sliding to the ground, like his legs had collapsed, which is exactly what had happened.

Fleming giggled. "A little manoeuvre I learned," as she tripped Livingston, "and when you can get your ass out of the mud you can try and catch me! Good luck."

It was like she found another gear, covering the next mile without being caught, her slight build didn't slip and slide as much on the mud-covered path and at the turn, just where Fleming said it would be, she pulled up laughing and pointing back at him.

"Right, that's it, you win," he said in a snigger, "don't you say a bloody word in the bar, sorry liaison facility, later."

Although it was only three in the afternoon, dusk was already beginning to descend, and with it a feeling of heavy dampness in the still air. They slowed to a jog, side by side along the river.

"So what are you doing in this backward shit hole?" Fleming asked. She had also wanted to ask, 'and how long are you around' but stopped herself. She had just met up with someone in Zagreb before having to be sent to Vukovar for this task, she shouldn't be 'keeping her options open' but there was something about Livingston that intrigued her. He was more than he made out to be and she wanted to know what.

"I was just checking reports of aid coming across from Vojvodina on the bridge, just south of here and to see if the railway was still operational. We get so much conflicting information in Zagreb," he replied. "We need to know what is coming in so we can deliver the stuff that is missing like medicines and medical supplies, that's why I came to see the Brits."

Finding the track meeting the road they turned right back towards the small British camp, jogging along the road. Both wanting to talk but keeping silent, deep in their own thoughts, and now a little out of breath from the run. They both missed the SUV parked in the driveway of a house under the remnants of the vine-covered car port. Why should they have noticed it, there was nothing unusual in this area except it was newer than most and behind the tinted glass there were two figures watching the joggers go by.

32

"Revenge time, race you the last mile back to the camp," yelled Livingston and he took off at pace. Try as she might, she couldn't catch him, he was just too strong, and his longer legs gave him an advantage.

"We're even now," he shouted as he pulled up by the gate to the camp, he had won by a good 150 yards.

Fleming was raising her hand in a defiant gesture, middle finger proud, when she saw it, speeding around the corner, she started yelling, "Richard…"

The sound of the thump, the breaking bones, the metal of the SUV denting slightly, the sight of this 6' 2", fit athletic American being thrown in the air, the change of gear in the vehicle as it sped past her, its wing mirror almost brushing her arm. The thud as Livingston hit the ground. Then the silence. It seemed like an eternity. It felt like watching in slow motion.

Suddenly there were lots of people, in uniform, shouting, the noise, the confusion and then it became deafening. Soldiers with red crosses on their arms were surrounding Richard Livingston's broken body.

"He's breathing, just," someone shouted.

The figure huddled over him yelled, "OK people, listen in: a) clear, b) laboured, possible tension pneumothorax, right side, c) pulse 97, BP 90/60 we have a possible bleed, no sign of external bleeding, d) spine seems clear, but we have multiple fractures, possible pelvis, full splint kit please, now! GCS 7, we need to work fast, e) the road isn't the best place for him, primary survey complete, let's get him inside as quickly and gently as we can; Sgt Major get ops to request a 'Medevac', he isn't going anywhere in one of our wagons, move people."

The shout had come from Livingston's first piece of luck, Major Bill Cash. Major Cash, a reserve officer, called up to deploy with the British Medical Battalion for Operation Hanwood, was in his real job. He was an emergency consultant in Swindon, a town next to the busy M4 motorway between Bristol and London, and he had seen many RTAs in his years as a doctor being recognised as one of the best in the field.

Inside, the small treatment room looked like it was out of the 1960s, an advanced first aid centre at most, certainly not a modern accident and emergency. The door swung open.

"Can I help Bill?" Major Jane Fieldhouse was the detachment commanding officer, a dentist by profession, she asked as she poked her head around the door.

"We need to get him to a hospital, he has internal bleeding, fuck knows how many fractures, he needs surgery and I need X-rays and blood now, but he is too unstable for a road move," came the reply, calmly and without panic.

Everyone was doing their job, they had just been training resuscitation in that very room when the sound of the SUV impacting Livingston caused them to stop and run out.

Fleming had walked the final 50 yards, watching what was unfurling in front of her. The shivering started, uncontrollably.

"This way, Ma'am."

She vaguely heard as a blanket was wrapped around her shoulders and she was led into the base.

"Tea, Ma'am, two sugars, get that inside you and I will go and find out what is happening."

"Bill, the hospital in Vukovar is a no-go and its facilities are crap – we will try and get the new US MASH in Zagreb, but they are an hour's flying time away at least. Let me see what I can do," Jane Fieldhouse said calmly and strode into the operations room that axially looked more like a large janitors' closet covered in maps.

The operations warrant officer, Sgt Major 'Chalky' White didn't stand up as she came in. "Roger that ETA 45 minutes, we will mark the HLS with green smoke," he was heard to say.

"Ma'am, we have a black hawk 'Medevac' inbound with advanced trauma team, they were burning and turning before I had finished my 'methane' report, keen to get here is an understatement."

Poking her head around the treatment room door again, she said, "Bill, major trauma team ETA 45 minutes, Medevac helicopter inbound, just keep him alive."

"I'll try," came the reply. "This is a bit of a challenge, but I'll try," he said again.

Major Fieldhouse then went to find Fleming, sitting in the ambulance bay on an old sofa wrapped in a blanket cupping her mug of tea, she was just staring at the wall.

"Thanks, Corporal Davis, you can go back on duty," Major Fieldhouse said as she sat down beside her with another cup of tea appearing as if by magic from Davis.

"It came out of nowhere, he didn't stand a chance, too fast, it drove at him." The words tumbled out of Fleming's mouth, she started shaking again.

34

"He's stable for the moment and there is a trauma team and 'Medevac' helicopter coming from the new US field hospital in Zagreb, it will be here soon, he is in good hands, if anyone can keep him here, Bill Cash can," Fieldhouse said. "How close are you two? Do you know his next of kin?"

"We keep bumping into each other like the proverbial bad penny, that's all. I know nothing about him except he is American and one of the best-informed aid workers I have met. He always seems to be just where it's at, it's like he is following me," Fleming croaked, choking back the urge to burst into tears, but she didn't cry, she never cried.

"Well, there is nothing any of us can do at the moment, he is in good hands with Major Cash and the 'Medevac' should be here soon. Come and help us clear any FOD from the HLS, we are only a small team."

Outside in the yard at the back of the camp, the vehicles had been moved to create a temporary helicopter landing site. Durham and Collins were already walking slowly across it in a line with the other off-duty soldiers and medics, looking for anything that could fly up and damage the helicopter. Falling in line beside them, Fleming scanned the ground in front of her for litter, loose bolts, bits of wood, anything that could cause 'foreign object damage, FOD'.

Inside the treatment room, the frenetic activity had calmed down a little. There were no beeping machines because they didn't have any. Livingston had three IV drips running into him, two with just fluid and the third with intravenous haemostat, designed to try and stop internal bleeding.

"Pulse is weak but steady, boss, and his BP, although through the floor is holding just," said the young sergeant, a combat medic class one.

His advanced trauma experience was as good as any A&E nurse and probably better in a combat situation. "We need this helicopter."

Chalky stuck his head into the treatment room. "Medevac five minutes, Sir, they have a full trauma team on-board and will stabilise him for the flight, I can confirm they have O negative blood on-board too."

"Thanks, Chalky," Major Cash muttered back. "Right let's get this place tidied up, we have visitors incoming, push that bag through as quickly as you can, it will be replaced with blood soon," he added.

The low frequency beat that was unmistakably a helicopter coming in fast, could now be heard by those outside. Inside silence had descended again.

"Stand back folks."

Taking a radio handset from out of the back of a Landover Chalky spoke into it, "Lifeguard 20, Lifeguard 20, this is Medbat 11, this is Medbat11, over."

Crackling back, the response unit relayed back over the vehicle speaker, "Medbat 11, this is Lifeguard 20 inbound your location in two minutes, throw smoke, over."

"Roger, Lifeguard 20, popping Green now, out," and with that Chalky threw a smoke grenade to the end of the landing area, noting where it was to pick it up as the helicopter came into land.

The green mist billowed up from the grenade hanging in the still damp air, its only movement caused by the chemicals mixing in the grenade to produce the smoke.

"Medbat 11, I have you on visual, 20 out," came the call.

Chalky donned two orange forearm sleeves, retrieved the spent grenade and stood on the HLS with his arms raised, indicating to the pilot where he should land, for wind and clearance reasons. Seconds later the black hawk touched down, doors already open and four people jumped out, the trauma team.

"This way, sirs," Chalky yelled over the whine of the helicopter engines, now shutting down as the pilot knew it would take a short while before the patient would be on-board and they wanted to conserve fuel. It was also getting dark and that made the crew nervous. Chalky led the trauma team into the treatment bay.

"GCS was 7 now 10, BP is a steady 105/60 but he is bleeding somewhere and I'm not happy about head injuries, it would be easier to tell you what isn't broken, but with no X-rays I can't tell, oh, and I'm Major Bill Cash, the duty doc here."

Handover complete, Cash stepped back a little in awe of the kit being unpacked from the boxes the trauma team brought in.

"Thanks, Major, I'm Colonel Wilson of the 212 MASH, we were getting a bit bored in Zagreb, so thought we'd come and give you a hand," he said in a deep Texan drawl.

The beep of a monitor started, the saline drips were replaced with whole blood, O negative, the neutral blood type that anyone can have.

"Great work here, once we get him prepped for flight and are happy. He'll make it. We're outta here," barked Wilson.

It was clear this team knew what they were doing and carefully moving into a flight-ready stretcher, they were out with all of the equipment hanging off the stretcher, helicopter rotors were already turning and without time for goodbyes the black hawk lifted off into the dusk at first nose down picking up speed as it climbed away.

Silence fell. Bill Cash pulled off his plastic apron and gloves.

Fieldhouse shouted, "Show's over folks, let's get this place cleaned up and ready for the next one. Back to work."

And she headed off to her office to write her report. Fleming headed for the accommodation. The water was on and apparently hot.

She needed a shower, she sniffed back a tear.

"I don't cry," she told herself firmly.

Letting the hot water blast her weary body, Fleming once again thought about her day, writing the words in her head that would fill the pages of her journal, she noted everything in that, she always made an assessment with her notes, an interpretation so she could understand what she was thinking at the time. She had an uncanny ability to spot the reality of many situations quickly. Her notes over the years were testament to that.

However, there was something about today that made her nervous, she couldn't put her finger on it.

How did he know my name? she thought. *Was Richard deliberate and linked, was I the intended victim?* Dried, dressed and diary written, she felt hungry; she hadn't eaten since early morning and she could hear the clattering of plates and activity from the room used as a dining hall.

The hum of conversation in the cookhouse was all about the day's events, supper was what was known as 'range stew' and mash.

She sat with Durham and Collins.

"Just what I needed," she said and quickly finished the plate, running her finger on what was left and licking it off, not to miss a morsel.

"Thank you, for saving him," she said to Bill who was sitting opposite her.

"He's not out of the woods yet but is in the best place, if I get any updates I will try and let you know," Bill replied, sounding tired yet matter-of-fact.

"Come on you two, I'll buy you a beer, it's been a hell of a day," chirped Fieldhouse. "Right, five beers?" And without waiting, Fieldhouse held her hand up to the JNCO behind the bar, five fingers outstretched.

"How long you been here, Victoria?" asked Fieldhouse.

"Reached day fifty today," she replied.

"Still in days then. Christ you must still like this place. When it becomes 'weeks' you know you hate it and want out," Fieldhouse responded.

"Well, apart from the incident with Richard, it got very interesting today," Fleming said.

"No, shit, Sherlock, the site and the lost evidence," said Collins while looking around for the beers which promptly arrived.

"Crikey, that didn't touch the sides."

Fieldhouse laughed as Fleming necked the bottle.

"I needed that," she said, "feeling a little better now. Did anyone get the details of the SUV?"

She wasn't much of a drinker and knew it as she listened to her disconnected voice.

"Sorry, but I just can't get it out of my mind, and after the incident this morning, I can't help thinking there was a link."

"Leave that till tomorrow, the SIB are sending Sgt Major Gabriel from Zagreb tomorrow to carry out an investigation. He is with the logistics company there, so we will get to the bottom of it," replied Fieldhouse. "Have another beer."

As the banter flowed, Fleming put the events of the day to the back of her mind and settled back into her chair.

Why can't the UN have banter like this, she thought as another beer appeared by her side. She felt totally integrated into this military group, and as it did, her confidence grew.

"Well, Chalky," she started, trying to copy Fieldhouses' manner and accent. "I think this beer 'em Piva is fabulous," she continued, picking up the empty bottle and reading the label.

Bill Cash winked and Fieldhouse had a smirk on her face.

"So the Piva is acceptable, my dear?" said Cash. "Does it have your approval, good choice?" he continued.

"Yes, Bill, very good. I must remember this brand for when I get back home to the UK. They have so many foreign beers now, I am sure they sell Piva in the supermarket," she answered in as logical manner as her current sober-less state would allow.

"Beer, yes, they sell beer back in the UK, positive they do," said a sarcastic Chalky.

Fieldhouse chirped up, "Beer? Yes, I think I have had that once. Prefer wine myself however but needs must so beer it is then."

Believing her new friend was weirdly unsupportive with her last comment, Fleming turned to her and felt it necessary to reiterate her point.

"Jane, I meant this beer, Piva, not just any beer."

Bill could not help himself. "Shall we ask the Chalky if he knows if Piva is sold abroad?"

Again, without waiting, Bill yelled to Chalky whom he suspected knew what was coming.

Bill spoke up, "This beer we have here, 'Piva', is it sold abroad, for our UN friend here is rather fond of it?"

"Piva is sold abroad, yes. I cannot think of a country that does not have Piva," he replied. Then, contemplating for a moment he spoke again. "Not sure but I believe Piva is not encouraged in certain Muslim countries in the Middle East however," he went on.

"Wow, OK, why does 'Piva' have some special meaning in Arabic or the Koran," barked up Fleming truly believing she was onto something interesting.

"No, lady, 'Piva' means 'beer' and beer is not allowed in public in some countries," and with that he got up and walked off. His smirk returned to his face.

Fieldhouse put a reassuring arm on Fleming's shoulder.

"Yup, me too, months back. It happens to us all, it's an initiation right. Welcome to the stupid gang," she said with a smile.

Fleming lowered her head for a moment before her defiant retort. "I knew that! I was messing with you lot."

"Yup, we also responded like that," said Fieldhouse before again turning around and putting five fingers up in the air in the direction of the bar. "Last round," she mouthed.

Soon enough, five more Pivas were thumped down on their table along with the customary complimentary plate of fritule, left earlier by one of the local staff.

"Careful, Fleming," started Fieldhouse, "these doughnuts are very boozy, not Piva, but boozy all the same."

"Warning taken," she replied as she reached out to grab her first liquor-filled dessert.

Another hour passed with the five, now, good friends chatting about a number of work-related subjects and others totally unrelated.

The chat was only interrupted when Bill came over and whispered into Fieldhouse's ear. They both glanced at Fleming, but she blissfully didn't notice.

"Sorry team, I need to make a call," Fieldhouse said as she stood and walked off to the ops room.

"Time for bed, I want to be at the site early tomorrow," said Fleming.

She also stood and walked the short distance to the female dorm. Exhausted, she undressed quickly and climbed into her sleeping bag on her US Military camp cot, a sought-after piece of kit in these parts.

The next morning, over eggs, bacon and beans with what could have been tea, Fleming met with Durham and Collins. They were joined by Phil Gabriel, the Special Investigations Branch Sergeant Major, who had travelled overnight from Zagreb to be there. He agreed to journey to the possible grave site with Fleming to add weight to the UN presence just in case the 'black off-road vehicle' appeared again.

"Victoria, can I have a quick word upstairs before you shoot off," said Fieldhouse as she sat down with them.

Fleming didn't need the chat, she knew immediately from the look in Fieldhouse's eyes and this time a small tear formed and ran down her cheek.

"Sure," she said with a sniff.

Fifteen minutes later, upstairs in Jane Fieldhouses office, a map of UNPA East on the wall behind her desk, crisscross tape across the windows that had sandbags up the wall to window height.

"Victoria, I'm really sorry. He didn't make it, I have just had confirmation this morning but was told last night that he had slipped into a coma, I believe you may have been close, my deepest sympathies." Her well-practiced patter showed this wasn't the first time she had broken bad news.

Fleming hadn't heard anything after the word sorry, she let out a huge sob and stopped.

"I guessed this when I saw you this morning," said Fleming. Stifling the tears, she stood up, shakily and wiped her eyes. "I have work to do now, thank you for last night."

Less than two hours later, Fleming was at the cordoned-off site again, this time with her UN reinforcement. She felt angry now. Something inside her wanted the man in the black car to return. She didn't really believe in coincidence.

The number of disappearances spiked, and Fleming was curious. She was at her third reported mass grave; this one was supposed to have 25 bodies but again the ground was freshly bulldozed. She measured, photographed, noted all she could about the site and then got back in her car, something wasn't right, this wasn't just atrocities of war, her gut told her there was more to it. The rumours talked of mutilated bodies, of bits missing; she noted it all.

The man in the black car would not, however, return that day to the now UN designated work site. He would not need to. The site had been secured in the manner he wanted. No further excavation work could be carried out for weeks due to the requirement to fly in specialist equipment to counter the toxic waste that had suddenly appeared on the soil.

The next few days would be a wasted time for Fleming and her colleagues. Unable to fully investigate the site, the locals had shut up shop and would no longer accommodate the presence of the UN and even now the charity workers. And the man in the black car had disappeared. Fleming would be unable to look him in the eye and gauge his involvement in Livingston's death.

Night-time back in the camp was increasingly becoming a frustrating place to be. Fleming was again questioning her placement and what she may have done in the past to deserve this boring and uneventful tasking.

Her routine would become mundane and automated. Rise, breakfast, the car journey to the site, unhelpful townspeople and a wish for the equipment to arrive that was needed to begin the dig again. Then she would think, *I can get the evidence and leave this shithole back to a new tasking with real value.*

This day was like all the others except for one specific interruption to the routine. Returning to the camp after what appeared to be the hundredth wasted day on-site, her driver was halted from entering the perimeter security of the camp.

"What's happening?" she asked her driver.

"Some new special party arriving, Ma'am…We have to wait," came the reply.

"Special party, what or who the fuck's that then?"

"Likely the American CIA, they tend to close stuff up on arrival. Instead of being discreet, those lot love to shout about their arrival. After all, only the CIA can save the world, right?" he replied to Fleming. "Well, the CIA or the British lot, you know the lot from '6' who unlike the Americans prefer to sneak into places. So I guess there is one angry spy blocking the guards and camp commander about his public arrival. We will soon know."

Fleming was curious. She looked past her driver, hoping for a glimpse of this possible spook, but after the car moved off with a slight jolt, she refocused her thoughts on her task. She took out her notebook and scribbled down notes on the day and the arrival in her camp of a new stranger.

Later that day sitting down with Collins for food, the two listened to the chat about the new arrival.

James Abernethy was a Captain nominally assigned as part of the British Medical Battalion, BRITMEDBAT, operating across Croatia, but he spent most of his time working for who he believed was the Head of Station in Zagreb, the senior MI6 officer in the Embassy in Zagreb. Abernethy was in Flemings's camp and she was determined to know exactly why.

A few days passed and no further sightings of Abernethy but the gossip around the place grew. Being a decorated undercover soldier from many operations in Northern Ireland, he had had to fight his way out of a sticky situation in South Armagh and was credited with numerous kills after he singlehandedly brought down a terrorist cell minutes before it was about to execute its kidnapping of a senior British politician who had just driven across the border as he traced his family tree.

The details were never made public. He had been sleeping with the girlfriend of a known South Armagh terrorist and was spending the weekend with her…Unbeknown to her she was running an agent inside the IRA cell, her boyfriend was a member of. When he heard about the plot he knew his antics would either make him a hero or get him court-martialled. He was lucky. The IRA team weren't. The politician dropped his genealogy hobby and it was all swept under the carpet.

It was this level of detail that got Abernethy noticed by MI6 and from then they kept an eye on him, not knowing that he would be working for a group, one with no official name or title but one that this time worked for the legal institutions not against them. This group was a highly secretive collection of specialised individuals from around the world powers and at this time he was being tasked, not by the Head of Station but by a shadowy figure, known to the Head of Station but infinitely deniable; when people talked about it, they only talked of 'The Committee'. He was on a task, related to Northern Ireland, but again he was being played to develop a relationship with 'him'.

Abernethy was now himself in 'Fleming's camp' and not even he could foresee their imminent meeting and the outcome of it. A few more uneventful days passed and Fleming was calling her boss twice a day demanding he pull her out of the tasking and reposition her somewhere else. He, on the other hand, knew more than he would tell her and refused her demands. He too was being tasked through his embassy. He too knew nothing of what was going on but was just following orders.

As events unfolded, Livingston was becoming a memory. She hated not knowing what was going on, she hated mystery, she hated all the spook that seemed to surround her. Today which like many others before, was a cold, wet, dull excuse for daytime, she had a job to do. Collins and Durham had accompanied her to the site and together they would yet again try the locals, going door to door.

This day, however, would prove to be a little more interesting than those before it.

Fleming and her colleagues were having their usual unsuccessful face to face with the locals, who would either slam the door after seeing them or more often simply not open the door despite there being lights on, music playing and the smoke of the wood burner exiting the open windows.

Around one corner and out into the small main square, she walked not expecting to see him but there he was.

A short distance away, Fleming saw Abernethy talking to a tall slim man who looked like he had won the local lottery. The clothing, brands, sunglasses on a dull day, the glint of jewellery against the limited sunlight, it all stood out and was just wrong. However, there he was, Abernethy causally chatting to this man and one other who had his back to her.

She watched the three men.

The tall man touched the arm of the smaller heavier man and looked right at her. All three men turned and looked directly at Fleming.

Fuck, he's with him, she thought to herself. Her expression must have changed to one of shock and surprise.

The smaller, bulky man smiled at her and lifted a hand to acknowledge her in what was a sarcastic tone. It was him, the man from the black car, and he was smiling at her while talking openly to the British spy. Fleming was at first confused and then started to feel strangely betrayed. He was a bad man, an evil man and most likely responsible for both Livingston's death and the burial site being tampered with, and this British know-it-all was speaking with him.

Abernethy frowned at her and grabbed the shoulders of both men, turning them away. All three men walked away towards a street across from where she stood. None looked back. She heard the start-up noise of a powerful car. They had simply just left.

Fleming looked around her. *Somewhere to sit,* she thought.

Taking out her mobile phone and perching on a small wall, she again called her boss.

"No, Vic, you're not coming home yet, stop this," came from the phone immediately upon answering.

"Boss, no, listen, listen," she snapped back, a sense of urgency in her voice, "this man who arrived at the camp recently. The British spy one, or that's what the camp chatter says anyway, anyway…" She was cut off abruptly.

"Fleming, stop. Breathe, tell me, slowly."

"Yes, sorry, boss. I saw this man, right now, speaking with the man in the black car. The one everyone's scared of. The same person who I am convinced sealed and polluted the mass grave site here."

"…and the 'spy' chap?"

"Yes, well, I don't really know if he is a spy, it's just what others are claiming. He's someone, however. Turned up a few days ago with much pomp and ceremony. Now, he's talking with the bad guys. Really, what's that about?" she asked out loud, as much to herself as to her boss on the end of the phone conversation.

"Vic, stop. Listen to me. Leave this man alone. You hear me? The British one. I am aware of his presence in the camp. Just leave him alone, do you understand?" Came back down the phone line in a strong and forceful manner.

"…but who is he and why…"

"No one that concerns you, Vic. I am ending this call now. Do what I have said. Leave him."

And sure enough the line went dead.

Fleming looked down at her phone now even more confused than when she had first seen the three men. She looked back up trying to make sense of what had happened in the last few moments. Reaching again inside her coat, she pulled out her notepad and began to record what she had seen.

Collins and Durham joined her at the agreed meeting point and she told them both what had happened. This was much more interesting to the three women then chatting about doors being slammed in their face. Walking back to their waiting car, all three were silent. Each contemplating what it all could mean.

An hour later, they arrived back at the camp. There had been little chat in the car. Everyone was tired; with the pointless role they were carrying out and with the cold and the short daylight hours.

It was late afternoon and now dark outside. Heavy rain added to the state of gloom felt by Fleming. Blanked by her boss and wasting her skills in some shithole in Balkans, waiting on some equipment and clearance so she could restart her purpose. Start the dig, get evidence of a mass grave, and leave this forsaken place. However, nothing seemed to be moving back in the UK.

It would be a further hour later that Fleming would re-join her two female colleagues and several other colleagues for beers before they went in mess for food. Sitting with her friends, more relaxed and less on edge after her first beer, Fleming started to smile, chat, and laugh, and for a moment she forgot where she was and why she was there.

A few of the group left for food after the first drinks were done while Durham went to the bar for round two.

Drinks duly brought to table and the chat resumed. This time, the topic of the mysterious man in the camp was raised. This immediately brought back Fleming's curiosity and some anger at that day's events.

"Right, what are we doing team? Sneak in one more?" said one of the group.

This brought Fleming back to the present. "I'm in," she replied. "But first, I need a visit."

She left towards the direction of the toilets, exiting the community area out into the hall.

The hall was dimly lit as it always was at night, the camp engineer preferring to utilise the limited electricity supply on heating, rather than lighting, at night.

Further down the corridor, she saw a shadowy shape of a man. He appeared to be talking on a large phone as he moved towards two large fire doors which led to a small room occasionally used for private calls, back home to family.

As he pushed open the first door, a beam of light illuminated the immediate area. She could for a second, see his face. It was him. The 'spy', the man who had befriended that man who had killed Livingston. It was the man who her boss had said 'leave him'.

Fleming was in no mood to leave him.

Putting her bladder on hold, she followed him into the room, just as the door was swinging shut.

The slight delay in the door closing behind had alerted Abernethy to the event occurring behind him. He was busy on a satellite phone but had still been aware that he had been followed into the room.

"Right, you, who are you and what are you doing here?" she said, assaulting him with her verbal tirade. "And what were you doing with the two locals earlier in the town and who the hell are they?"

Abernethy stopped talking down the satellite phone and smirked slightly at the woman in front of him.

"So you close roads because you think you're special when you get here, then you sneak around my site and don't introduce yourself to the official teams on camp?" she continued, furiously.

Abernethy's smirk widened. He admired her brash confident interruption. He raised his phone to his face again.

"General, as I'm sure you heard. I am going to have to call you back," and receiving an acknowledgement, he ended the call and put his satellite phone down on the table next to him.

Waiting for a third tirade from out her mouth, he sat down on the table, facing her with crossed arms.

An awkward silence fell. Fleming having heard the word 'General' now felt uncomfortable.

Abernethy broke the silence.

"So, Miss Fleming, which one of those 'questions' do you want me to answer first? I will tell you anything that I can."

He knows my name, she thought. *Shit, of course he knows my name, he's a fuckin' spook, he knows everything.*

Trying to regain her composure and dignity, she waited a moment before responding.

"Your name's a good place to start. You seem to know mine."

"Abernethy, Victoria. James Abernethy. But I like you. Just call me James."

Christ, he does know my name, she thought, still slightly anxious about her earlier interrupting his call to a 'General'.

"Why are you at my camp, and why did I see you at the town square earlier?"

"That I cannot say, I'm afraid." Was the answer to her follow-on question.

"Those men you were with. Who are they? Gangsters, thugs, who?"

"Hmm, another question, I am afraid I cannot answer, Victoria."

"So, it's a name only?" she asked.

"I did say I would tell you everything I could. So I guess you're right, name," Abernethy replied unfolding his arms placing them on the table by his side in a less confrontational pose.

"Let me see, Victoria," he went on not waiting for her to come back with some smart quip response. "I work with the British Government and you likewise are here indirectly because of that very same wonderful institution. So I guess, we are partners."

Abernethy knew he was winding her up some, but he had taken to Fleming and was enjoying the conversation even if it was slightly gladiatorial in nature.

"We are not the same and we are certainly not partners…" Fleming was interrupted before she could finish.

"So dinner tonight is out then, Victoria? I really need to call the General back urgently so shall we carry on with this chat tonight?" he said, with a wry smile. "My treat."

Fleming didn't respond for she was taken aback. She wanted to say yes, but felt after her outburst, she couldn't as he would then win. She need not to have worried, however.

"Right, that's settled. Meet me at the guards' hut at the main gate tonight. Let's say 7:30 pm."

Without looking at her again, Abernethy stood up from the table top and started dialling on his phone. As he did so, he strode to the door and opened it to her, indicating for Fleming to leave.

She duly did, curious. *There is no restraint in this shithole*, she thought.

The next couple of hours were a confused mess for Fleming. *Do I actually want to go out with him tonight?*

Her mind was full of counter and cross arguments and statements, however, during all of this she found that she had indeed showered and dug out her best casual trousers and top that the primitive location allowed. Then, hair done, well brushed, she left her small quarters and went towards the guard hut. It was seven thirty at night and it was neither raining nor particularly cold.

Fleming stood just inside the small hut with its only other occupant and made polite conversation, interrupted only when a black hatchback Ford pulled up at the exact same time as he arrived from behind her.

"Perfect, bang on time. Shall we, Victoria?" said Abernethy.

Without waiting for an answer, he stepped forward and opened the back door for her, before getting into the front passenger seat. This, trivial but highly provocative action bothered her. A sudden doubt returned into her head.

She sat in the back, seatbelt on and waited for some introduction or invitation to get involved, *hell,* she thought, *acknowledge I'm here you tosser,* but instead, he spoke quietly to the driver never looking around towards her.

Soon enough, the car pulled up at a dimly lit building and thanking the driver, Abernethy leaped out and grabbed the back-door handle, opening it for Fleming.

She had fumed to herself the whole journey, feeling that she was being used but that soon disappeared, and a warmth replaced the coldness when her 'date for the night' spoke.

"Victoria, sorry about that, you know in the car. I had to confirm a few details with the driver and also he may talk, so thought it best to blank you so he never really thought anything."

He directed her towards the only door in the building which she now saw as a very large open room in someone's house.

Hesitantly, she let him take her hand and lead her inside. It was only when inside that she realised that not only did she let him hold her hand, but that she had rather enjoyed it.

"Mister James, we are waiting for you."

Welcomed the pair as they were noticed by the host.

"Welcome you and Miss Lady you come with." He went on as he reached them. "Sorry, my English, lady but I am happy you here in my home," and with that waved his hand and arm around the room inviting her to see where they would 'dine' that night.

Fleming didn't know what to do or to say. He had taken her to one of his contact's homes a for dinner, yet she was liking it. She was liking it a lot.

For the next two hours neither Fleming nor Abernethy were on the outskirts of the God forsaken Vukovar. Instead, they were in a place of their own making. Somewhere warm, a happy place and well-fed and looked after. They would talk about her past assignments and her family life. Abernethy would share what he could, and she knew not to push hard. She was just happy that he was telling something.

When the plates were cleared and a number of small warm slivovitz, the local plum liquor, appeared at their table, she asked the one question she had feared doing earlier.

"That man, James, the one from the square, who was he? It's just, I think he is a bad man and he had something to do with the spoiling of the evidence at the mass burial site."

That was fair and not pushy, she thought.

"Which one, Victoria, there were two," came his reply but he already knew who she meant and was simply stalling a few seconds to formulate his answer.

"I think you know, James. I really want to know," she said with a smile, appealing to his honest softer side.

"His name is Drako and he is a bad person. A really bad person. I would say you're best away from him. I would even say that I insist you stay away from him but telling you to 'stay away' from someone doesn't always work Victoria, does it?" Abernethy said, knowing full well that she had been instructed not to contact him and yet here they were, dinner and a pleasant chat later.

She paused for a while, taking in what he had said.

"So if he is such a bad man, why were you with him? Does that make you a bad person, James?"

"Friends close and enemies closer type stuff. I have a few things to chat to him about," he said while picking up a second warm slivovitz shot and downing it in one.

"Yes, fine, but why him and why at that time, oh, and why so close to my site?" Fleming was confident enough to push him a little but held back from changing her friendly tone.

After all, she was having the best time she had had since she arrived in Vukovar on assignment.

"I am doing something for people back in the UK."

Fleming knew there was more, so she waited.

"People believe that Drako has been contacted by an Irish group and it isn't to exchange addresses for Christmas cards, so I need to know if this is true."

"So why would he agree to see some British…person."

Fleming wanted to use the word 'spy' but restrained herself.

"Why wouldn't he, Victoria? He's a bad man but he's also a shrewd businessman and politician. No doubt he thinks he can get some better offer from the British or play one off the other and get both agreements at the same time. He also wants to know what we know about the cigarettes, prostitutes and drugs he smuggles into Europe and the UK."

"So you're here to do a deal with Drako?"

"I am here to find out what is happening, and I would prefer to end this part of our chat now if I may."

Abernethy was not angry or disappointed that she had raised the topic. He had expected her to do so at the beginning of the meal and was pleasantly surprised when she did not.

"Yes, James, of course, sorry I raised it," she said reaching out to touch his hand.

He allowed her to put hers on his, then looking up into her eyes he knew something very wrong was happening. He knew that he liked this person and he also knew that on assignment he had no time for anything or anyone but the assignment. Yes, something very wrong yet strangely very right was happening this night and for now he would let it continue.

Several days would pass and Fleming looked forward to her chats with Abernethy. They would enjoy their nights much more. Sometimes he could only spend minutes with her but would always give her as much affection as time allowed. On other days, he would spend hours with her. They had become very close and when she spent the nights in his cramped quarters, where she would often stare at the green armoured boxes in one corner and guess to herself what might be inside. She never asked him, nor did she ever feel tempted to open one. Being with him was enough. She was happy knowing that he was thinking of her and being with her. She started to feel safe and the horror of Richard Livingstone's accident had stared to subside.

Scribbling away in her notebook, she wrote down everything. Notes, comments said and even a few pencil drawings. Fleming would not forget anything. Her notebook made sure of that. Abernethy also noted her regular, almost obsessive approach to note taking. He was curious, perhaps even nosey, but never asked to see what she wrote nor tempted to steal a glimpse when the book was left unguarded.

Fleming felt happier in her work at the camp and the site. Some specialist equipment had finally arrived and work on the site had begun again. This had caught the attention of the locals and word was spreading that digging had started again.

Abernethy was very careful not to be seen with Fleming outside the camp but someone inside it had begun to notice and talk. Their friendship was becoming noticed and soon it would be talked about outside the boundary of the camp.

This cold and wet day, Fleming and Durham were leading the dig at the site. They, like the others, were covered fully in special protective white suits and were very noticeable.

One of the local helpers come over to Fleming and politely interrupted her.

"Miss Victoria, the car, it's back again," he said, turning around to show her the location but hesitant to point directly at it.

"Yes, I see it is, is it the same car as yesterday?" she asked.

"Yes, Miss Victoria, and they just seem to be looking, although I did see a flash which may have been something else," he said before moving off, anxious that he was not singled out.

A flash, so they are recording or taking photographs of us here, she thought.

For the next hour, everyone carried on their slow meticulous work, moving small amounts of dirt and stone away from their inspection site and placing it into rubble bags to be taken away when full. No one spoke but everyone occasionally looked over to the car which remained motionless perhaps three hundred yards away.

Another hour passed and her team were beginning to pack up their equipment for the day when they heard the noise of an engine starting up. She looked over towards the vehicle, its full beam lights flashed twice.

It's not dark enough for lights. What am I being told, she thought. *Is it in fact me they are signalling or am I getting paranoid?*

The car moved off out of sight and Fleming felt like a weight had lifted from her shoulders. She had forgotten her notebook, and this annoyed her. She failed to capture the registration before it moved off. *James could have perhaps found out who these tossers are if I had just got the bloody reg,* she thought.

She was very keen to get back to the camp and tell Abernethy about what had happened.

It was dark when Fleming and Durham arrived at the camp. Fleming scanned the parking areas for his car, but she could not see it. She decided to freshen up before coming back out to check for it again.

Fleming would have her usual chat with Abernethy on the cell phone that night and would eventually go to bed pondering his whereabouts.

The next day was like most of the others. After breakfast, Durham, Collins and Fleming would brief the team and they would make their way to the waiting transport to take them to the site.

The sun was shining and she enjoyed the warm rays on her face as she neared the site. It rarely rose above freezing temperature during the Spring months, so she was determined to max out on the day's gift of vitamin D.

Durham and Collins chatted freely as they walked the short distance to the equipment hut. Fleming, however, wandered off.

"Guys I am just going for a short walk. I won't be long. Enjoying the sunshine you know." And with a wave of acknowledgement Durham and the others turned back and entered the equipment hut.

She didn't know where she was going nor did she really know why she wanted to walk alone with her thoughts, but she did all the same.

Along one smart narrow street turning into another then another, she had no idea where she was going but she was not scared. She had wandered the streets of the town so many times that she knew, when she was ready to, she could easily make her way back to the site and her colleagues.

This next street had particularly strong sun rays and she decided to sit on a wall and enjoy them. A local passed by and said something to her. She smiled back at her not knowing what it was the old lady had said.

A few minutes later, a second elderly couple walked down the street in her direction. She moved her legs in so to give them space to pass, however, the second old lady did not at first seem to want to pass. Instead, she gestured to Fleming to move away. She nudged Fleming on her arm as if to say "Move along now.' Then when Fleming stood up, the elderly husband said something and the couple walked as fast as they could down the street in the direction she had been encouraged to go.

Confused as to why this had happened, Fleming did indeed move away but in the opposite direction than that of the elderly couple. Hands in pockets and pondering the strange confrontation, as well as if she would spend time with Abernethy that night. She never really noticed the man standing smoking by the door when she went around the corner.

The man almost dropped his cigarette when he saw her. Fleming on the other hand walked innocently towards the building he stood outside.

Standing on the cigarette to put it out, one hand went instinctively into his jacket searching for what rested in its holster. Then just as he did that, he withdrew it again. He turned and entered the building, careful not to again look directly at her.

When it happened, it did so fast as if rehearsed many times before.

The first man together with now a second larger man burst out of the door and knowing exactly where she was, grabbed Fleming before she could react. Her vision went instantly dark as a cloth bag was forcibly pushed over her eyes.

She felt her left wrist forced behind her back violently. She seemed to float off the ground. The second man lifted her legs and together moved her quickly and easily away from where she had been walking.

Despite the bag over her head, Fleming could distinctly smell of sweat mixed with what she instantly thought was hospital antiseptic. Now more confused why she was being taken, and now away from the cold, inside to a hospital or similar, her head spun around.

Gathering her senses as best she could she called out.

"What is happening, where have you…" but her words were interrupted by a firm hand feeling for her mouth over the bag, finding it and covering it to stop her speaking.

Fleming was helpless and she knew it. She stopped resisting. She felt herself shoved onto a chair, hands still firmly holding her arm and mouth, a second pair of strong hands bound both her arms together.

A third man seemed to enter, for she saw shards of light through the bag as a door must have opened then closed again.

The bag was lifted from her head at the exact same moment, she felt a sharp pain in her neck. Desperate to get her eyes to focus, she thought she saw a man in a white overall standing in front of her.

This smell of hospital and those white overalls? There are no hospitals for miles, she thought.

It would be her last thought. Everything went dark again, this time without the need for a cloth bag as the drug kicked in.

The camp would miss Fleming when she never returned that day. She did not return the next day either and the disappearance was reported by her colleagues. Her colleagues would not visit the mass grave sites now fearing they too may become a victim if indeed, this is what Fleming had become.

Collins waited as long as she could before approaching Abernethy.

"Are you going to help her? Do you even care that she has not been seen for two days now?"

Abernethy looked up from his coffee and reading material. He knew she would confront him but was unsure as to its tone.

Collins stumbled a little. "Well, Mister, are you able to help, for we all know you two were well, you know together and…"

"Yes, I also know we were as you say together. I am also aware that she has neither called me nor answered her calls from me. Like you I am concerned, however, it's Collins, isn't it? I have an assignment here and this is taking up more of my time than I had anticipated. Moving a resource here or there or focusing my own time on this mystery would not be the best use of government money," he replied.

Inside Abernethy was hurting. He did not wish to be formal and steer the policy path, but he also knew he had little choice but to do so.

Hearing his monotone, even practiced, words made Collins angry but she knew she had to leave it there. She turned and walked off, leaving Abernethy to his slightly raised heartbeat not caused by the coffee he held in his hand.

Then, out of character, he called out to Collins. It took her by surprise as much as it had surprised himself over the apparent weakness of mind and character.

"Look, I have to cross the river tomorrow morning and visit some people but after that I will try to find time, I will make some calls, see what I can find out. OK?" he said, now expecting a thank you smile or something similar from her.

"Lucky, Fleming," muttered Collins as she turned and walked away out of the room.

Abernethy felt deflated. The burden was weighing heavy on him. His mind switched between the assignment and her and then back to the assignment but never too long before he found himself wondering what had become of her.

The next day, with limited sleep, Abernethy's driver took him back over the only passable bridge for miles over the Danube and onward into hostile territory. Located just a short car ride from Erdut, over the river on the Serbian side of the Border, lay a collection of run-down towns and villages. Each seemed to have a militia and a strict command hierarchy, and getting to grips with all the locations and town leaders was proving too difficult for Abernethy.

Everyone recognised the car and the registration plate, and the driver and occupants were allowed to progress unchallenged each time. In fact, Abernethy often noted how he would be shepherded forward and prioritised through the queues of cars and tractors trying to pass and make a living, one way or another.

No one would complain when his car was moved quickly forward and through the checkpoint by armed men in slightly outdated military fatigues.

Abernethy was meeting Drako's second-in-command that morning. There were rumours of a rogue Serbian field hospital in the area, and it was his job to determine its legitimacy and more so, its real purpose. Not sanctioned by any authorised charity or health organisation and with no Western volunteer medical workers, he smelled a rat and was determined to get to the bottom of it.

A few miles after passing Border Control, two cars drove towards Abernethy's car. This was usual. His driver flashed his headlights to acknowledge their presence and moved into a position that would allow the two advancing vehicles to head and tail them.

Duly obliging, this small three-car convoy drove on through the next small town and back onto the dirt tracks that made up the road network. Occasionally, they would slow to manoeuvre around a small mortar crater or similar but usually the convoy would show limited care and move at speed towards their end destination.

When the dust settled and the three cars had stopped, Abernethy was first to exit. He was a little anxious but knew that not even Drako, with all his local power, nor his Nationalist Serbian 'football' hooligan mob, would dare threaten a British military officer. More, as long as he held out the carrot of possibility of British aid, then he was perhaps the safest person in all of Serbia.

A tall, slim man in a freshly pressed military uniform approached Abernethy. He looked out of place amongst the ruin and dirt of his current surroundings.

Stretching his hand out towards Abernethy, the man spoke.

"James, I am happy to host you today. My name is Goran Aleksa, and I can guarantee you free passage where you need to go."

"Pleasure, Goran, nice to meet you." Still holding onto the handshake, Abernethy went on. "Anywhere I wish to go, Goran?"

"Yes, James, I have been given instruction to provide you passage to anywhere he allows you to go to." Came swiftly back but this time Aleksa had a smirk across his lips.

"Hmm, right, anywhere he lets me go, you will take me. Right my new friend, let's test that right here, right now." Abernethy was a little irked by the last comment and that he had been promised free passage, but this had meant 'free passage within reason and not likely to where he wanted to go'.

"Take me to the hospital. Do it now please!" Feeling more confident while also in a challenging mood suddenly, he stared straight into Aleksa's eyes.

Aleksa prepared his reply. "Would it do any good for me to ask you what specific hospital you refer to James? I am unaware of any said building close to here."

"None!"

"Right then, let's get going then. I remember now, there is a 'hospital' not far from here and we can walk."

What the fuck, thought Abernethy. *That fucking easy?*

The small group of men set off. Abernethy's driver was instructed to stay in the car and to forget both the location and the direction they now set off in. He had a family. It was very easy for him to forget things in this part of Serbia.

Abernethy, flanked by several young men, perhaps in their early twenties and clearly concealing some form of weapon under their out-of-date football tops and loose clothing, watched him as he walked. They had their orders to leave Abernethy alone and none would break that order for fear of terrible repercussions. However, as long as they did not know who this 'British man' was, they felt brave enough to occasionally bump him and look aggressively into his face from close range.

Abernethy knew that he had to ignore this. It would only take one drugged up or drunken hooligan to feel pissed off and the order would go 'out the window' likely leaving him bleeding on the dirt track with no help close at hand.

Several minutes passed and the men walked on. Aleksa knew exactly where he was going but would no longer be the friendly host, he had been upon meeting Abernethy. Instead, he had become 'functional' and what Abernethy interpreted as 'worried'.

Worried about what? James Abernethy thought.

Then, turning yet another corner passed yet more closed and boarded up windows, they came to where Abernethy had been promised.

"Your hospital, Abernethy," said Aleksa not dropping the first name and using a slightly threatening tone.

Goran Aleksa went on. "What then do you want to do now, British?"

"I want to go inside. I want to see if my government can assist you with medical supplies and equipment?" Abernethy knew that no aid had been offered by the British Government. He also knew that his Serbian hosts knew this, but he wanted to try the approach anyway.

"I'm afraid my British friend that today we are able to go no further. We have some virus outbreak, and the hospital is in quarantine. Perhaps next week once it has been sorted out," said Aleksa but both men knew there was no next week.

Abernethy wondered why he had been brought all this distance and so close to what was clearly a suspicious facility only for them to stop him at the front door. *Were they showing strength, rubbing his face in it or teasing him to act*, he thought. Nothing made sense.

"We leave now," said the man, curtly.

The pleasantries had stopped once and for all. A firm hand was placed on his shoulder and Abernethy was led away from the facility back towards his driver and the car back across the Danube river.

As he left, he thought he saw an old Praga terrain troop carrier at a side entrance to the building and what looked like a wounded soldier being taken off it on a stretcher. One further thing that he was sure about was the smell of burning flesh on the occasions the wind came their way. Abernethy had smelt this before, and it was an experience that he would never forget.

Two hours later, his driver left him at the camp and drove off. Abernethy went back to his quarters to freshen up. He was frustrated and a little puzzled at the events of earlier.

Something did not sit well with him. However, for now, as promised to Collins, he made the call. A moment later, he ended the call and lay on his bed wondering what would happen next. *He had been promised police investigators but was it too late for Victoria Fleming?*

Chapter 5
The Irish Connection

A few days had passed and still nothing. No sign of Fleming, and he still showed little interest or willingness to assist.

Collins was furious with Abernethy.

She could not hold it in any longer. She wanted to shout at him and tell the camp that he and he alone was responsible for the disappearance of their friend and colleague. She wanted to confront him, but something stopped her. Something stopped her from actual physical contact with the man that had emotionally taken the heart of their friend.

Abernethy could sense her anger towards him, her body upright in a confrontational manner, but while he kept his gaze upon Collins, he knew she would back down. He knew that she wanted to know what had happened to Fleming. He too wanted to know what had happened to his Victoria. He wanted to talk with them. *Had Victoria said anything that day when she left to soak up the little sun that was in the sky? Had she said anything out of the ordinary when she left the dig site and never returned to the camp?* It was forty-eight hours after Durham and Collins had waved their friend off and no one knew anything.

The UN were sending two uniformed officers to investigate but they would take a further forty-eight hours to reach the camp. They would likely be wasting their time as always thought Abernethy. Who says this, is it Abernethy thinking?

Abernethy had a call to make to the General. It was scheduled for seven forty-five that night. He still had twenty minutes.

Right. Fuck it. He will have to wait, thought Abernethy, rising to his feet, and forcing the last of his dinner into his mouth. He set off towards Fleming's quarters.

Her door was locked and a 'Do not cross' sign was displayed upon it.

He pulled the tape away on one side and forced a thin metallic strip into the lock between the frame and the hinge. Applying a little pressure, the door swung open. He had done this many time before, usually in foreign hotels.

Replacing the tape to the frame, he closed the door behind him. Easy. He was in.

He breathed in deeply. Searching for her scent inside her room. He had been in her quarters many times before, however, this time was different. This was a lonely visit. He knew she was not in the room, but his nose and his imagination looked for her, nonetheless.

Coming back to the present after a few moments, he began to scan the room.

What am I looking for...? He looked at his watch. He had less than ten minutes before he had to call the General but had already decided to himself that this, whatever this was, was more important. The General would have to wait.

Instinctively he went straight to her clothing drawers, opening and quickly closing each as nothing of interest caught his eye. Then the small wardrobe. Opening the one door, he saw the dress that she wore when they first went out and he had told her why he was in this place. She had looked very attractive in it. Now it hung lifeless in this small wardrobe in her small quarters.

Nothing here. Then it struck him why he was in her room. It was not just to *feel her one more time. It was the notebook.*

The notebook had drawn him in. That notebook could be the key to her disappearance.

He scanned the room again.

Now he knew what he was looking for, he could quickly establish its likely hiding place. He looked up to the ceiling and around the edges. Nothing seemed to be out of place. No secret storage panel. Perhaps too clever, but he was used to establishing hiding places. Walking slowly around the room, his left hand traced the wall. Occasionally, knocking it in a manner that weirdly comforted him.

Again, am I trying to be too clever as to her hiding place, he thought. Is he saying he doesn't think Fleming is clever...?

These places are rapid-made accommodation, so the walls will likely be hollow because of that, nothing more. He stopped when he reached her bed. The single bed in one corner that they had both shared one night before agreeing future liaisons should be held in his larger quarters.

He smiled to himself. He remembered them both struggling to stay comfortable on the narrow mattress.

"Clever or obvious?" he said out loud looking at the bed.

He bent down and lifted the mattress.

"Yup, obvious."

Again out loud. There it was. Fleming's notebook, with her pen forced down inside the page ring binders.

He picked it up and then lifted the mattress higher to make sure he didn't miss anything else. Then he lowered and dropped it back onto its frame.

Notebook in hand, he looked one last time around her room. Suspecting he would never again see her belongings or sense her presence, he reversed his entrance procedure, roughly and instinctively wiping his prints. Everyone knew he had previously been in her room but training was training. Locking the door, he looked both ways along the corridor and then replaced the tape once again.

For now, Abernethy did not fully appreciate the extent of his findings. Thumbing through the pages randomly, he promised himself a thorough investigation of it soon. For now, he had a call to make with a General he had left waiting.

The SUV stopped in a house with very large grounds. It could easily be mistaken for a farm complex on the edge of an old barracks. The door opened and Frederik Hofmann stepped out. He was welcomed and shown in like a VIP into the house. He was warmly greeted like an old friend at the door by Drako. They had never met before.

"Come, come, I have heard so much about you. You're just the person I need. We can help each other," Drako said, showing him to a chair in the lounge and not letting Hofmann reply.

Coffee appeared. Getting straight down to business, Drako outlined his cousin's medical history and explained a business relationship that would unfold when he saved him.

"Let me see the patient," Hofmann asked curtly and he was immediately led to a room behind the lounge, set up like any private hospital room. It was fully equipped with everything a post-surgical patient could need. Nothing like what was in the hospital in Vukovar.

The doctor didn't blink an eyelid, nor did his heart miss a beat, but he simply got on with his examination. He examined his new patient for a few minutes.

"Without blood tests, I can't be certain but I'm pretty sure his one remaining wounded kidney is failing. He will need a transplant to save him and that is impossible here. He may have a week, he may have a month, no more."

"There is no chance of a transplant here. We have no dialysis. This is your home and so it is slim to get him out of the war zone, to a hospital, and hope the donor registry can find a match," he added in almost flawless English.

Suddenly the colour drained from Hofmann's face as he looked at Drako expression, he knew the only answer, to save his skin, was to say a transplant was possible. Quickly changing his tone,

"Well, with a tissue typed organ, a transplant is possible here, but…"

He never got to finish his sentence as Drako interrupted.

"I can guarantee an organ within the week and you will perform the surgery. He will live and that is non-negotiable and you will be a wealthy man and that is just fact."

Drako's voice became more distinctive and more authoritative. He was losing patience; he didn't like this doctor saying 'but', he was used to things just being done.

"Doctor, one more indulgence at this time if I may? Please stay a while. I have another small operation for you to perform. The lab in Belgrade has matched another, how shall I say, colleague with a donor. Your skills will be needed again and how fortuitous, two for the price of one as they say."

Drako stared at Hofmann.

Hofmann was very confused.

Organs to order? He knew he had little choice but to do as Drako asked.

Brendan McCann was born and bred in South Armagh, on the border between Northern and Southern Ireland. It was known affectionately as bandit country. He was not a well man. His legs were swollen and his breaths short. He thought on the flight to Belgrade he was going to die. The car journey to this hellhole was even worse.

He was not good chasing the Brits in Crossmaglen, but his knowledge of the cause and his influence, was second to none. He was still very valuable.

He had been the quartermaster for some years now, but since he became ill, since his kidneys were packing in, his doctors had told him he was dying. He knew that in Ireland he had little chance of a successful transplant. He had reconciled his fate with his maker but wanted to first finish his work for the cause. So he was prepared to travel and try every opportunity.

McCann had come on a mission. Since the Libyan weapons route had stopped, the cause needed new supplies. They needed new friends and they knew the Serbs were not fond of the British.

For months, talks had been going on and now it was time to close the deals. McCann was the dealmaker. Drako knew of the cause and knew the Irish were good for cigarettes, tobacco, fake booze and drugs. They had been supplying them for a while and profits were good.

Guns and explosives were the next logical stage. But Drako wanted a hold over his customer and then it arrived on his lap in the form of a sick Irish negotiator. He knew that if he could keep real control then not only could he develop business opportunities long after this war had finished, but he could feed the British with enough to ensure he maintained influence with them and also so that they kept out of his business.

Drako knew everything about McCann's illness and knew the lab results for his cousin had said the donor was as close to someone who could be compatible with many in a similar way. The donor was a one in 100 million chance, but the lab knew not to ask questions and just operated on and with what they were supplied.

"Irish, my friend," Drako almost sang, "our deal is signed but I have a present for you. I have a surgeon with an organ from a casualty of war, only alive because of the machines. I like you. I want you to live, so we can do more business."

It took McCann only moments to agree and the next evening, thirty-six hours later, a new-functioning organ was pulsing in his body. The pain was nothing compared with his feeling of being alive again.

As McCann was transferred to Belgrade and a safe house to be used as his recovery location. Drako called a number and spoke when the call was answered.

"The Guinness was fantastic for a pint that isn't supposed to travel."

It was a phrase Abernethy had left him as a code for the Irish being in touch and one that he never truly thought he would hear.

While lying in his makeshift bed, sore and a little woozy from the aesthetic, was day dreaming of being back in County Donegal owning a luxury hotel. He thought of all of the field hospitals the IRA had and all that spare equipment stolen from hospitals all over Northern Ireland. He had a use for it, he too would set up a facility like Drako had here. One with the best equipment, staffed with people whom he would blackmail to do as he wanted. Drako had shown him the blueprint for extending life and making money and now he would replicate this in Ireland, right under the noses of the British Military Intelligence.

The thought of this made him smile and as a faint laughter pushed its way out from his lungs escaping through his mouth, McCann grimaced in pain.

Yes, I will have my medical hospital, but it will have to wait for a while, he thought. Then, without invitation, his eyes closed, and he went back to sleep.

Finishing up in Zagreb, briefing the Head of Station on recent events, it took him no time to be on the motorway heading for the crossing point as Osijek into UNPA East and onto Drako's headquarters. *Maybe he will know where Fleming is,* hoped Abernethy as he drove.

1998:

"Why the fuck does Mo Mowlam need a briefing from me?" Major James Abernethy, Operations Officer with the Joint Support Group Northern Ireland, (JSGNI), shouted. "Where is the bloody CO when this happens, that's his role?"

With the motto 'Fishers of Men', JSG(NI) ran human sources in the IRA, INLA, UVF and UDA as well as some of the Northern Ireland so called political parties. They had a handle on everything that was going on. Abernethy oversaw all of the operations but was seen by the CO as a bit of a maverick. But then the CO saw everyone who didn't hero worship him as a maverick or just useless. So being labelled a maverick was better.

"Ma'am, welcome back to JSG, Colonel McKeown, the CO, apologizes for not being here. He is on leave in Scotland," rattled off Abernethy. He had briefed Mo Mowlam, the Secretary of State on several occasions.

She had the Chief Constable, her private secretary, and the General Officer Commanding, with her at the private briefing.

"So, cutting to the chase, Major Abernethy, what do Tony and I need to remain worried about when we sign the 'treaty', and I don't want the normal PC bullshit which is why it's just you, me and my trusted." Mo was not known for her subtleness.

"Ma'am, cutting to the chase, South Armagh PIRA have effectively split from the rest and with elements in Tyrone, Derry and Belfast are ready to form a splinter group. They have access to money, plenty of it, and have smuggling routes from the Balkans through Ireland and back out to mainland Europe. Drugs, counterfeit goods, including tobacco, people and of course weapons and explosives. They are now supplying organised crime with weapons."

"None of this, Ma'am, is in any official report in any detail as it is from unassessed sources. We also have indications of some PIRA members spending time in some conflict zones sure but actually in refugee camps, posing as missionaries and we can't yet work out why. I have personal experience of this a couple of years back, in Croatia during that war."

Abernethy cut to the chase and took the opportunity to outline some of his work that McKeown kept putting him down for in public.

"Ma'am, the link between the terrorists and those involved in serious crime is clear, they are one and the same. We can't separate this into a military task and a policing task as some want and because of that we are missing opportunities to hurt the criminals and terrorists in their softest spot, their pockets."

"When you sign, Ma'am, elements will already be outside the Republican leadership and they have the capability and connections to make the Russian Mafia look poor and weak. You will launch a path to the globalisation of a dissident crime gang, the likes of which we haven't seen before," he added. "They have money, a lot of money and that buys a lot of influence. We just don't know where."

"Thank you, Major, to the point as ever. On a scale of 1to10, how worried should I be?"

"15, Ma'am," Abernethy replied. With that the Secretary of State left the room.

McKeown immediately turned on Abernethy, his voice seething with anger. "You are just a fucking half-baked maverick. You know what the fucking GOCs priorities are, you know my fucking briefings, yet you wait till I'm out of the country and you brief the fucking SOS on what is police shit, nothing to do with us. We just want terrorists; your thoughts are just shit. I have been here hugely longer than you, sonny, and that is just bollocks," he barked. "You think pussy footing around in Germany with BRIXMIS and the Balkans with the UN qualifies you for this job? Well not in my fucking books. You think with a few successes in the Balkans you can be a JSG operator? You have another fucking thing coming, get out…"

McKeown returned to duties now back from leave a few days after Abernethy's meeting. He was a small, nearly bald man with 'little man syndrome' and a pop star ego. He always knew what the right thing was, as that right thing was only his thing.

That was the moment when James Abernethy, MBE, decided a blinkered military lifestyle wasn't for him anymore. Full of self-centred, egotistical sycophants, he wanted a proper job. That is when his move to the Secret Service, to MI6, became inevitable. He knew McKeown should eat his words one day, but also knew, he never would.

Present day:

Checking around him for one last time and seeing no one, James Abernethy pushed the steel door on the wall of the carpark. A hidden palm reader verified his biometric data against the facial recognition map that had been collected as he walked into the carpark. The door opened and led to yet another at the end of a short corridor.

In the corridor, he was being scanned by millimetre wave radar, peeling layers off him electronically, looking for metallic and ceramic objects, looking for wires, checking it was him.

"Abernethy," he said into the wall unit, and the final voice print check opened the door to the lift. Ten floors underground, beneath one of the largest nuclear civil shelters in Geneva, unknown to the public, was the operations centre and headquarters for The Committee.

Exiting the elevator, a semi-circular, stainless-steel door slid open silently. Air condensed slightly as it met the moist outside air giving a wisp of a cloud.

In for the final briefing, all permanent members of The Committee were required to be present as operational sign offs had to be unanimous. The briefing room was on the left and to the right was the bear pit of desks of analysts with computer screens showing 3D relational maps of different groups and geolocations. The walls were covered in huge screens with satellite data from all the nations being displayed. Nothing moved in the world without The Committee seeing it, well almost nothing.

Nodding down to the pit, Abernethy was the last to enter the briefing room.

The Chinese were chairing the meeting and Xi-Koh was waiting.

"James, welcome, we are just about to start."

Xi-Koh indicating to Abernethy to take a seat, turned to address the room.

"The China Tribunal, a group that is investigating the claims of organ harvesting from groups including Uighur Muslims and members of the Falun Gong religious group, is blaming the Chinese Government and given what it calls evidence to a meeting of the United Nations Human Rights Council. Of course, the Chinese Government denies any involvement and I believe them as they have tasked The Committee to prioritise an independent investigation into this practice and the global market."

"We have indications that the Sneakhead groups have been kidnapping people to order and send them through the people smuggling routes into Europe. Those selected get fast tracked and don't have to pay," he added. "Vitaly, you have some information also?"

Valeri Petrov was a huge block of a man. He was GRU to the core but the Spetsnaz military side rather than pure intelligence. The Russians would never let a true spook be part of such a deniable organisation.

"Da, we have been following reports of individuals being selected for 'golden passports' to Europe from the refugee camps in Syria. This is similar to rumours we could never pin down in Chechnya and Georgia years ago. They would just disappear. Numbers aren't high but they all have had recent medical tests with the charities in the camps."

Pierre Melville, a wily DGSE man who had lived in Africa most of his life, spoke next.

"We have been monitoring similar disappearances from camps in North Africa and nearby. Nobody stays silent when people are fast tracked to Europe. Everyone wants to get on that gravy train."

"Same beef with rumours from the refugee train from Central America that was heading for the US. It's why the President was so vocal. We thought terror groups were getting people in," piped up Roz Cherrie, the American member of the group, and the only woman in a top position.

"And of course, we have just had those refugees from South East Asia found frozen, then suffocated to death," added Abernethy. "We have a global pattern and horror stories building on some I even heard in the Balkans in the '90s. Gentlemen, what are we missing?"

Chapter 6
The French Connection

Summer 2019:

Pierre Melville could sit anywhere unnoticed. Today it was in the corner of Rue Pelleport on the avenue Gambetta in the 20th arrondissement in Paris. There was something about the coffee in Paris. No coffee anywhere else in the world smelled or tasted the same. At a little under six foot and wirily built, he didn't look like a spy, *but then what should a spy look like and why was a spy having coffee in Rue Pelleport?* Pierre smiled to himself.

He pulled his phone out again. Everyone else around him in the café was staring at their mobile phone screen, so he would not look out of place.

What did people do before smart phones? He wondered.

No one was chatting.

Swiping open the screen, he tapped the icon for the sandbox and entered another pass code. Opening the encrypted mail app, he had another quick read of the message.

Manipulation spéciale uniquement (Tau): Le réseau identifié se réunit demain: Traitement spécial uniquement (Tau).

He knew by the 'Tau' designation, it was for him and could only have come from one person.

Just around the corner from where he was sitting was the CAT, the *Centre Administratif des Tourelles*, the headquarters of the French DGSE, the French 'MI6'.

Pierre had been stationed there for four years so knew the area well and the owners of his favourite little coffee shop. He never received details of where a meeting would be or at what time when his boss needed to see him. It was unusual, it was in person as Pierre was officially off the grid and no one else in the DGSE knew of The Committee or his involvement with it.

"Un autre café mon ami et peut-être un croissant?" asked the waitress.

Pierre had known Sasha for many years, and they were like old friends, but never saw each other outside the café.

"Dans un instant mon vieil amie, j'en aurai probablement besoin de deux, j'ai une femme embellie qui me rejoint," he replied with a wink.

"Comme toujours." Grinned Sasha and with that was gone.

She was indeed beautiful, but Pierre was waiting for a more elegant and powerful woman.

Sophie Roye was the first woman to have been made a deputy director in the DGSE and currently heading the 'Division Action'. She would likely be the next director.

He caught her confident stride as she crossed the road before she saw him. His drills would have been terrible if she had in fact seen him first inside the café.

He gestured to Sasha as she entered. Sophie walked up to him and they hugged like old friends.

Two coffees and two croissants; smelling of fresh butter, were waiting on the table. Sasha knew not to say anything.

"So good to see you again my friend," whispered Sophie.

"And you, beautiful lady," muttered Pierre as he held her hand in both of his.

"My friend, we have a breakthrough for you. We have broken an organised crime communications network using the EncroChat phone network and the amount of intelligence it has yielded is enormous. It is much more than we have ever gotten from a single source before. Here is the file for your eyes only." She handed over a green covered document to Melville.

"Read it now, I must take it back, but I can brief you on more detail as you need. You just need to know the key detail now, and the details for your 'Tau' colleagues," she said to him.

She then handed him a red folder.

"You have a couple of months to do what you need with this as it will take that long for the police forces across Europe to get their operations planned and take these people off the streets."

As Pierre picked up and read the green file, Sophie sat in silence, watching his expressions closely, trying to read what he was thinking, reprimanding herself for lingering too long on his eyes.

"Fascinating," he said. "What a coup for your team. So we are reading and tracking almost everything across a number of international organised crime gangs, but the tacit support from certain governments is worryingly low," he said.

This was acknowledged with a smile.

"Here is your file back."

He handed the green folder back to Sophie who stuffed it into her bag.

"Take care my friend and keep safe. The Tau team have an interesting job now!" she muttered and with that she was up and out the door, but not before a quick air kiss as she left.

Pierre sat looking at the red file. Picking it up, he signalled to Sasha for another coffee, then he began to read.

Surprisingly, there was more detail in the releasable file, not less as is usual, but it was different detail. Names, links, organisations, locations, routines were all carefully mapped out. There was an API for a live feed.

Merde, the rest of The Committee will be eating out of my hand with this, he thought.

Then the next page made him sit up and read a little more carefully.

Wow, James will be interested in this. It keeps mentioning underground medical capabilities, he thought.

'The Facility', the title of the page read, a supposed torture chamber but it is a crude medical facility to test tissue types and more. It is within easy flight time of a wide area of Europe and, on the major people smuggling routes, especially through the Dutch ports. Melville was fixated with the document. 'The packing boxes, ice and fast motorcycles along with some specialist equipment suggest it is not just for cutting off the fingers of those who have crossed the gang'.

"The Facility has been saturated with covert surveillance capabilities all uploaded to a satellite feed at this API," he said out loud and then instantly looked around him to see if anyone had heard him.

Christ, he thought to himself as he continued to read. *Another coup for me and for France.*

With that he was up and out, a €50 left on the table. Sasha was busy with another customer and never noticed him leave.

Strolling through the Paris streets, Pierre had pangs of longing to come home. Even though in the past twenty years he had spent less than a year in France, he had a bond with the city.

Instinctively, he wandered towards the Gare De Lyon. He had lost count how many times he had trudged this route alone. He loved walking, looking and just listening to the surroundings. This reminded him of his hatred of 'Le Metro'. He loved the train to Geneva, however, the TGV Lyria. That train would whisk him back to the office in just over three hours. This was so much better than fighting through airports, especially as he was armed and this made passport control a bit tricky despite his authorisation if border control wanted to be awkward.

But then he caught himself dreaming too deeply and he came around.

Geneva will have to wait until after Amsterdam. Need to sort Amsterdam first, he thought.

Strolling into the Gare de Nord he bought a return ticket on the Thalys train to Amsterdam. Melville always carried a 'rush' bag or an 'exit' bag with him everywhere just in case he needed to travel at the very last minute. It would include one of his many passports, one set of completely different styled and coloured clothing so he could be a different person when exiting the toilets if need be and the basic toiletries. Nothing more was needed that couldn't be bought as required.

I need to see what else the Dutch know, he thought as he took his phone out and smiled as tapped in a name.

It was answered on the first ring.

"Miranda, Pierre. I'm coming to see you so book a table at our usual, perhaps you should be there for say 7:30. It's on me but I want something from you."

He heard a quiet "yup" and with that, he hung up.

He bought a paper before heading onto the platform. It had been so long since he had bought and read a daily paper in Paris. The writing style was so different from most other countries and he was looking forward to the down time on the train.

Once boarded, he booked a room in the Artist House hotel, his regular, as it was a short walk from the station but with rooms named after famous Dutch artists. Art was a passion for him and he liked the escape of sleeping in the Rembrandt or Vermeer rooms. Food, however, was a bigger passion, and he enjoyed the Dutch approach to tasting. So his usual restaurant was the aptly named GUTS. His mouth was already watering at the thought of its ever-changing menu and he was looking forward to an evening in the company of Miranda. They had been on the same 'Interpol' team in the past and hit it off immediately.

The train pulled into Amsterdam Central and he quickly made his way to the hotel. A quick shower and change of shirt. He knew she would look stunning so he spent a little longer than usual getting ready.

Melville took a stroll along the Kloveniersburgwal, along the edge of the canal, drinking in the atmosphere of people, bicycles, laughter and, of course, the smell of cannabis, wafting up into the air.

He wanted to be at the restaurant early to find a quiet table however with the throng and bustle of so many people, that may now prove unlikely. He quickened his pace towards his dinner date.

"We will have the table in the corner by the window if that is possible please?" Melville asked in English. He knew everyone spoke English and locals did not care if the tourists didn't even try the home language. He had been lucky.

"Yes, Sir, this one?" said the waiter, as he walked and pointed to the exact table Melville had wanted.

The warm evening sun was still heating the heady atmosphere. He was early. Melville always arrived early. He wanted to get the lay of the land before Miranda arrived. He studied the other diners, the waiters' behaviour and the passers-by on the street, paying particular attention to vantage points in the park across the street.

Nothing. Fine. Relax now, he thought to himself.

"Great minds as always."

He turned quickly to see Miranda strolling through the doors towards him smiling. She was wearing figure-hugging jeans and a revealing white blouse. She would have turned more heads than just his if this were not Amsterdam in the summer and such glamour was everywhere.

"You know me, Pierre," she said, as he kissed her on both cheeks, "like you, I hate being late and hate not knowing who else is around me."

She sat down at his table and finished her own scan of her environment. Both smiled with what could have been embarrassment at their routine actions or their joy at being together again after a few months away of operations.

"The five-course surprise menu please and we both like anything," said Melville not waiting to get his guest's approval. "A bottle of water with gas and a bottle of Chablis, please."

He knew the place well and he knew what Miranda would like.

As the waiter wandered off and small talk subsided, their mutual smiles were clear evidence of their closeness, a professional closeness, but both secretly wondered if there was more than this to their relationship.

"So, my friend, I have been reading about the Encrochat's success, but what is the detail behind The Facility?" Melville's voice was low, and he moved slightly closer to her over the table.

Miranda glanced around and leaned across the table a little more also. There was no 'personal space' between these two colleagues.

"It is as fascinating as it is horrible, my friend," she replied, mirroring his hushed tones. "We are openly referring to it as a prison and torture chamber but it has a more sinister role. We found one container set out as an operating theatre. From what we can make out, there is some form of Latvian link, possibly also Estonian, and the OCG who are running it don't know we are investigating them yet. We are still analysing much of the intelligence but your teams have all of that already. You may have cracked it."

She sat back as the waiter brought the water and wine.

"It will be fine," she said as the waiter enquired who wanted to taste the wine. "Just pour please."

Miranda carried on. "We know the gang is moving people from refugee camps in Turkey, likely Syria, and have reports about Chinese Uigars and others being smuggled out through Vietnam to Singapore and then into North Africa. It seems that there is some form of fast track for people and we assume it is a premium price route into Europe illegally costing a lot more. We don't yet know what qualifies as 'premium' but from what I can gather, these types tend to be the younger age group."

She paused for a moment and sipped her wine. Melville waited.

Wuhan, China:

The food was good, there were no political classes to attend, but it was still over 2500 kilometres from home. Phones were banned, the internet non-existent and speaking Turkic was outlawed.

Doctor Yusf Sabir was unusual. He had a PhD in genomic sequencing from Huazhong University of Science and Technology, having been one of the few Uighurs allowed to attend mainstream education. But that was why he was really where he was. Originally from Xinjiang Province in China, Sabir had been lucky to be allowed to study and to work in such a prestigious research centre, the Wuhan Institute of Virology.

Since the crack down on the Uighur people started in 2009, he was 'advised for his own safety' to move into accommodation in the institute grounds. He used buses to and from the University for his academic work but his research always remained in the Institute. Bats. His research. He hated bats but their physiology and more important ability to resist getting sick from many unusual viruses fascinated him.

Like the twenty-five others who were effectively prisoners, all had Masters degrees or PhDs in biological sciences of some description and all were originally from Xinjiang Province. Sabir was tired after another 14-hour shift in full Level Four Bio Suits with little time to eat properly or drink when he got back in the sparse accommodation. Six to a temporary room, five rooms all, in one temporary block and only one toilet and shower between them with only one small kitchen area.

As he walked past the kitchen, he wondered, *how can a bunch of biologists leave food preparation areas in such a mess, someone will get very sick...*He chuckled to himself...*but not me as I'll be gone.*

However, neither food nor sleep were on his mind at that moment. He had a small bag with a change of clothes. The others, Doctors Abdulla Malik and Gulmira Omar were already behind the accommodation block. They were seventy-five metres from the fence. Seventy-five metres from the workers' side gate, monitored by CCTV and needing a pass to get out of which none of them had been issued. But they were leaving.

Sabir had taken the pass of one of his co-workers from the disrobing room outside the bio lab. He knew that tonight and for the next few days the CCTV on the gate was broken. He knew the opportunity they had waited eight years for was finally here and they weren't going to miss it. Their plan was just to walk straight out.

Normally the CCTV scanned everyone with automatic facial recognition software and tracked everyone's movement, ensured people didn't tailgate through opened doors and gates. But there was a blind spot. From the back of the accommodation to the path. And the CCTV covering the path and gate was now broken. Nothing could be easier.

For a while now, Sabir had managed to get letters smuggled out to his mother in Xinjiang through a friend he had made at the University. This friend brought in extra food and hidden within, replies. But all for a price because his 'friend' was part of '14K', the second largest Triad Gang in the world. It had tentacles across not just China but the globe, from its bosses in Hong Kong. *14K would be my saviour*, he thought to himself.

The cough was nothing. Too much dry air into his bio-suit, he thought to himself as he nodded greetings to Abdulla and Gulmira. He also ignored the regular headaches and heat spasms that had been developing recently.

No talking. No noise. They had rehearsed this together many times checking if the CCTV would pick them up and it always did. But now they had an opportunity. He had got a message to his friends at 14K and they had confirmed the receipt of $75,000 to get the three of them to Europe. They knew of the plan. They were integral to it. Bold as brass, the three Doctors walked towards the gate like any other workers leaving and with a tap of the stolen key card; the reassuring beep allowed them to open the gate. Once through the first gate there was a second that could only be opened after the first shut. Yusf put the sweat on his forehead down to nerves as he swiped the card on the second gate, then 'click' it was open and they were out. Their journey to freedom was just beginning.

Across the concrete path then through the landscaped gardens at the side of the institute. They walked slowly to the large boulevard to the north side of the complex and right on time the side doors of a silver minibus, just like those used as taxis, opened and silently in they got. There was honour amongst the Triads. They had accepted the contract. Sabir knew they would get them to Europe as promised.

Timing was everything. The plan was for them to take a leisurely ride on a small cargo vessel, owned and run by 14K, on a routine run down the mighty Yangtze to Shanghai where they would get another cargo vessel, again run by 14K, to Hanoi in Vietnam. The authorities often monitored the vessels but rarely intercepted them, choosing instead to watch, wait and report. Here new identities and new papers would be waiting for their onward trip to Singapore and then to Genoa in Italy before finally being driven in lorries across Europe to their target location.

Their final destination was to be Ireland.

Sabir smiled. He knew some of the research professors from University College Dublin and in Queens University in Belfast. *Ireland will be good*, he thought.

Amsterdam:

When Miranda was ready to talk, she did so with a strange uncertainty. Melville had not seen this type of Miranda before. He could see she was struggling with something. He knew he could not help her currently.

74

"It seems that the routes continue into the UK from Rotterdam, to Tilbury in London, so we are working our surveillance around these assumptions," whispered Miranda. "The key is this Latvian link. Christ, I have even heard about Chinese gangs being involved, but we know little about it yet," she added.

"So what is this Facility for? Does everything go to London and what happens to them then?" asked Melville as Miranda shrugged her shoulders.

"We have increased covert surveillance," Miranda stopped and contemplated for a moment, hesitating. She took a deep breath. "We think there could be a British mole somewhere in Whitehall and suspect that this person could be involved somehow with the trafficking or the free passage they seem to have had recently. It has been all too easy for their drivers to move through Europe and into the UK."

"A mole? In the UK Government? Have you spoken with James?" replied Melville.

"No, not yet. I am not certain yet. Still working on it. But there is something more," she said as she looked down at the table struggling to find the right words. "I think it is someone James knows. I cross-referenced the suspects career path with Military Intelligence and it seems the two worked together in 1998 in Northern Ireland."

Melville thought for a moment.

"James has mentioned a Colonel before. McKowen or McKeown or something," he said.

"Yes, Colonel McKeown, now a Senior Civil Servant having spent many years on the fast-track system. He spent time in the British Department of Transport and was key to securing good access contracts to countries across Europe. They included the Balkans, Latvia, Poland, and Turkey. We think this is where he made his network and from where the ease of movement is facilitated."

Miranda looked perplexed. Melville interpreted this as not really knowing her next step. The waters were muddied with the James Abernethy connection.

"Right. Good. Keep at it, Miranda. Get the evidence you need and when you have it, come to me first if this makes it easier. Together we can figure out how best to progress this. Do you agree?"

Miranda smiled.

She slipped a card across the table. The card had a jumble of letters and numbers and nothing else.

"This is the API code for the secure feed. I know your colleagues are not in Paris so use it wisely, but promise me, if you get anything you let me know first."

His smile and wink was all Miranda needed.

The realisation that this was too important for him to wait, hit him full on, or rather, the realisation he couldn't spend nine hours getting back to Geneva by train and would have to now fly, hit him. He hated flying. But that was tomorrow's burden. An amazing meal with a beautiful friend and another bottle of wine, with the now sinking sun warming them both through the window, made the moment certainly more than bearable. Pierre loved working with The Committee, especially tonight.

Wuhan, China:

The trip to Shanghai was uneventful. Just long. They officially worked as kitchen hands on the boat. Sabir's cough and fever seemed to have disappeared but then Abdulla and Gulmira got sick. The same, cough and fever. Abdulla self-diagnosed it as simply a bad dose of influenza. Gulmira couldn't say. He struggled to breathe most of the day. He even tried to help but suddenly collapsed.

"We need to get him to a hospital," Sabir pleaded with the captain, "he can't breathe, he seems to have pneumonia. He could die."

The captain knew that any deviation from his path and his lucrative contract with 14K would finish immediately and he would become just another body washed up on the banks of the river.

"No, we are not allowed, too many questions," he barked back sharply.

The rasping and rattling from Gulmira lasted through the night, neither Sabir nor Malik could sleep. Their anxiety and the noise of their friend's laboured breathing kept them awake. They knew they were alone with no help available.

Then it stopped. Both doctors had nodded off but woke suspecting something. The noise of forced breathing had stopped. Gulmira had died. The strange pneumonia had taken him.

Quietly praying, Sabir carefully washed his wracked body as tradition required before wrapping him in a sheet and stitching it up.

"Get him over the side quickly," the captain ordered. At that point the two doctors realised just what a helpless position they were in.

The wrapped body made little sound as it hit the water. It made even less as it disappeared under it.

In Shanghai, while they were smuggled into a shipping container, their money had at least bought them some comfort. Checking for port guards and seeing all clear, the guide quickly opened the containers doors, and pulling a couple of boxes aside, a small passage going deep into the container appeared.

"Quick, quick," he said, thrusting a torch into Sabir's hands and as they went between the boxes, the guide pushed the front boxes back in place and the doors closed with a resounding clunk.

The silence was now deafening. The smell of the boxes almost overpowering the two men. In the centre of the container, there was a space with three collapsible beds, three buckets, a big box filled with tinned food, a large water container and more torches.

"So this is what a $25,000 ticket buys you," Malik said.

The clunk reverberated through the container. The gentle swinging grew as the container was being moved onto a ship.

For the next three days, time seemed to stand still and silent while the gentle rocking of the ship made its way to Hanoi. They knew they had arrived when the clunking and swinging of the container off the ship started once again. A completely different sensation to the slow methodical movement over the water.

Hours later another clunk, then suddenly the container was filled with fresh air. They froze not knowing if they were about to be discovered.

"Quick, quick," shouted the voice, "time to move."

Moving fast towards the fresh air where it felt cool even though it was a muggy thirty degrees with eighty percent humidity, they felt alive again. Staying quiet, the group followed the individual in front of them past rows and rows of containers.

"OK, right, you will be in this next container for many days and when you see the light again, you will be met in Europe. These are your documents." Thrusting a packet into Sabir's hands, as another container door was opened.

A similar set up as the last container but this time there were four other people already in the space.

Being locked in a container for many days, in a small space, where you couldn't speak the same language, was just like being in suspended animation. A vile smelly suspended animation. But they were heading for safety and a new life.

Only a couple of days had passed when the others got ill. It must have been the stuffiness and lack of fresh air but everyone got sick with a temperature, dry cough, difficulty breathing but none so far as bad as Gulmira. One of the Vietnamese adults came close to death, they felt, but pulled through.

Day after day would pass but without the sun and the moon no one inside could tell just how many.

The relief of the clunking of the crane lifting the container, their enforced home, and then it hitting the land, signalled progress on their arduous journey. However, the strange movement and sound soon revealed to them that the crate had been placed onto a train carriage. At least there was new movement and sounds to concentrate on after the weeks of solitude and silence.

More days passed but again no one knew how many. The train stopped and moved on, then stopped and moved again. The occupants inside didn't know but it was making its way through Europe, northwards to Rotterdam.

The lift and thump onto the ground signalled arrival. Somewhere.

Suddenly there came the sound of the doors being opened. Then the rush of the cool night air. Fresh air, at last.

Adjusting their eyes to this new light, they saw the moving of boxes and then torches.

They all hid as best they could when a whispered, "Quick, quick, last leg, we have to move now," was heard. The voice spoke Vietnamese and Cantonese. Now moving was difficult after such a long time being cooped up. Muscles had become weak and jelly-like.

The smell was terrible but having lived with it for weeks the two doctors didn't really notice.

They hurried up to a lorry trailer, one of those refrigerated ones, but the mechanism was not working.

"Move now, inside here, next stop England past London. Doors will be opened just after you land – there is plenty of air for you all, but this way the immigration dogs won't detect you. Keep movement and talking to a minimum, you will need the air," the voice said.

Another voice with a broad accent whispered, "Fucking hurry up. I've got a boat to catch." The accent if anyone had known was broad Northern Irish.

The doors to the truck container were closed.

The two doctors both thought the same thing at the same time.

How can he say on the one hand there would be plenty of air and then say not to talk to conserve the air? Which was it to be?

Immediately the air seemed stale, there was nothing, not even seats or something to lie on. It was cold, so cold. There were over thirty other people huddled at the back of the lorry when Sabir climbed in.

This is not a good idea, he thought to himself as the doors slammed close and darkness arrived with the thump.

Later, maybe hours, maybe days, the movement and rocking would have indicated they had been loaded onto the boat.

Most could imagine exactly what was happening from the motion after so long isolated. The cold, the shivering, the headache, there were whispers amongst the others, all Vietnamese, all relatively young.

Sabir wished he could understand that they were saying.

Some had phones out looking for a signal, the pale blue light outlining the huddle of bodies, the fear on everyone's faces.

Not long now, he kept thinking.

His headache grew, the noise in the lorry had changed, there was panic in the air. Breathing became difficult. Then the crying started, the rasping, the gasping for breath. Malik held his friend. Both were scared and they tried to stay calm. Then the wail, the screaming as if someone's world had ended. Unbeknown to the two doctors, the first had died.

Their oxygen was running out.

At last, he felt warm. It was the warmest he had felt in many days. He closed his eyes. Suddenly he was back home in Xingjian. His mother was holding him, smiling at him. He was only six years old. Then nothing.

Chapter 7
Geneva Thinking

2019:

Schiphol Airport is one of the easiest European Airports to get to from the centre of the city it serves, however, the one thing it guarantees is you have to walk a long way once you get through the check-in. Pierre hated flying and airports, something about them he never trusted and, after a couple of near misses in the Balkans, when helicopters he was flying in had what were euphemistically called rough landings, he had lost that flying spark.

Ninety minutes is much better than almost nine hours, he thought to himself as he browsed the shops, not really taking in what was actually for sale. He was too busy doing what he always did, watching those around him. Always looking for someone or something out of place.

Even in the airport he would 'drill' his way around. He would walk into a shopping area and stop to look at something but he was really looking at the people. Then walk towards a departure gate and fain getting it wrong, having only to retrace his steps and look to see if anyone else changed direction. He liked the open nature of the walkways. The distances between everything. He loved people watching.

Always watching, always noticing and always inconspicuous.

All clear, he thought, *without being obvious.*

KLM 1927, Terminal 2, Gate B19, came up on the departure boards as he drifted off to get a coffee before heading for the gate.

It was only a short ride from the airport to his destination where he jumped off the bus and spent another half hour walking in and out of shops. Occasionally around the back of buildings, then going back on himself before he got to the carpark and checking all was clear he walked down the path to the steel door underneath the steps. This was no ordinary steel door.

He heard the usual click of the lock as he approached and quickly ducked inside, walking along the concrete corridor to the elevator doors. As he did, he heard the noise of the doors closing behind him.

He knew he was being scanned.

He had been electronically searched by millimetric wave radar looking for concealed objects, thermal imagery and 3D optical imaging doing a complete auto body and behavioural analysis of his short walk and gait. He never wondered what would happen if he chose to change his walking style away from what the artificial intelligence knew was his.

The lift doors opened automatically.

"The Pit," he said, into the wall mounted microphone.

The voice analytics software matched his voice print and the computer said in a gentle female voice, "Welcome back, Pierre, how was Paris and Amsterdam? I hope the flight wasn't too stressful, I know how you hate flying."

The AI-enabled security programme always spooked him, it knew too much. While it may just be following his passport at airport security and what was previously programmed about his character, it still spooked him all the same.

The Pit was the heart of The Committee.

The Committee as a name, to those that need to know, is the regular meeting with all of the senior officers from the P5 Intelligence agencies, assigned to head their delegations in this completely deniable organisation. They are the workers who man and run the intelligence production and monitor live operations across the globe with one mission, to make the world a safer place without the constraints of national borders.

Their working area is a series of workstations in a pit about two metres lower than the surrounding floor. The pit is surrounded on three walls by massive displays, giving newsfeeds from across the globe that is not available on normal news media channels. Instead, they are real time satellite feeds watching troop movements in Yemen, tracking Boko Haram, or shipping consignments of interest passing through the Suez Canal. They were a tracking feed for targets and agents.

A series of meeting rooms were off The Pit and each had an affectionate name.

The workstations ran the latest all-source intelligence analysis software and often analysts were wearing VR headsets as the data balls could be displayed and manipulated in 3D. It was very Jason Bourne versus Enemy of the State, but even made that look old fashioned.

The technology was all biometrically powered on and operated and would deactivate regularly when the assigned operator left the immediate proximity of the pod. Some screens along the walls predicted terrorist movements and AI generated algorithms pushed into commands that could be sent to any one of a swarm of reaper drones hovering above numerous sovereign states around the Middle East. Each one waiting the human touch and a missile would be sent to earth at breakneck speed landing where the target was predicted to be at that moment. The calculations changed in a millisecond but the incredible accuracy never did.

This was an advanced facility that to the outside world was regarded as both frightening in its efficiency and futuristic in its outlook.

"I even have the croissant, the way you like it," James greeted Pierre as they walked down the stairs into the side briefing room off the all-source analysis floor. The room was affectionately known as The Den, or more often James's den, as he used it more than most.

"Let's keep this Western European," said Pierre stifling a quip about Brexit.

"It's still very sensitive and operations are ongoing," he added.

Having pulled his laptop from his cell, what each of the senior members of the Committee called their strong room, the mini-dressing-room style room jokingly known as something more custodial. He plugged it in and then the same with the cable for the screen into the HDMI port. As he tapped the API code into the viewer the screen was filled with multiple views from surveillance cameras.

At first they made no sense, there seemed no logic. But the API wasn't just to a dumb set of camera feeds. It was to the senior surveillance analyst's master system. They could interrogate all the information that was known about each of the scenes they were looking at, including the intelligence that triggered the surveillance operation.

Damn, I owe Miranda more than dinner for this, thought Melville.

He handed James a red file with a single symbol on the front, the Greek letter Tau, the compartment that designated intelligence for or from The Committee.

Leaning back on the chair, scanning the file as Pierre flicked through different camera feeds and the underlying intelligence, James Abernethy let out a low whistle.

"This, my friend, is the key we have been looking for. This is the gold dust. I'll get the team to source some food for we could be here a while.

We now need to bring all of the threads we know together to work out our next steps, and I agree, strictly between us. At least the others are not here as this is sensitive, Xi is back in China, Roz off to the USA and Valeri somewhere in the Middle East. So let's keep this to just us for the time being," said Abernethy.

He walked over to the wall and called for the protective screens to be drawn back. Instantaneously, the walls moved, exposing an array of futuristic equipment. Abernethy still preferred using a white board and pin board combination to all of this new-fangled software. His brain worked better when not staring at a screen. Pierre smiled. They were both of that era.

Abernethy drew a circle around the word 'Latvian' in the centre of the white board. Branching out from it, he wrote on one line 'Netherlands' and extend an arrow line to 'Rotterdam' and then another to 'Tilbury'. Underneath 'Latvian', he scribbled 'people'?

"So, my French friend, what are we missing? What are the threads to this and how does it link to our wider investigations? Have we got anything from our other colleagues?" Abernethy said aloud as much aimed to himself as to Melville. He couldn't help himself, a page from the notebook, from Fleming's notebook flashed into his mind, it was a similar exercise, Ireland, Serbs, a German, were the three words he remembered.

As he finished the question mark the news ticker above their head, always on, always monitoring, caught their attention.

'Thirty-nine bodies discovered in the back of a refrigerated truck in Essex, one man arrested.'

"Pierre, what do you think? Coincidence? Get on to your contacts again and I will call London. I have this feeling," he whispered. "We need the link. There is much more to all of this and I feel we have a connection. We just need to find it," he added.

Abernethy paused and thought for a moment. *Oh, how I wish Fleming were on my team. She could see connections better. I miss her.* He caught himself thinking of her again and hoping Pierre couldn't read his mind. No matter what new relationship he was in, his mind always drifted back to Victoria Fleming, especially when he was problem-solving. Sometimes it wasn't problems, he kept daydreaming of. He found her memory comforting in a way and still wondered what had happened to her when she disappeared in Vukovar. They had become very close, very quickly, but so many years ago now.

A message flashed up on his computer screen. The usual header 'Tau eyes only'.

'Vietnamese refugees being smuggled' was next. The signature on the email was Xi Kho, the Chinese intelligence member of The Committee.

Koh had always been a leading supporter of the Chinese Communist Party. When he was in the military, he was part of the formation that put down the demonstrations in Tiananmen Square, commanding the unit that followed the tanks and dealt with the demonstrators. His ruthlessness was almost legendary, and he had been commended for it. His skills and tenacity quickly brought him to the attention of more politically motivated members of Chinese society and he was seconded to the Ministry of State Security (MSS), a cross between the CIA and FBI.

His ruthlessness was backed by his intelligence and linguistic prowess, and he was then sent to the Embassy in Hong Kong where he ran agents inside the Hong Kong Government and police authority tasked with monitoring for continued British sentiment and influence.

Hong Kong saw him absorbed fully into MSS and then sent to Japan for two years, followed by Singapore several years later to further widen his experience. Singapore proved his real strength. He ran an intelligence agent with links to the highest echelons of western high-tech business which was China's number one intelligence priority.

After Singapore, jealousy in the ranks of the MSS in Beijing started. Worried about the career part of Koh, those who were in authority but felt threatened moved him sideways to 'The Committee', thinking that he would be out of harm's way. Ironically this meant he now was the only person who could protect the Chinese Government before it even knew it needed protecting and before the world found out.

Abernethy knew all of this of course as MI6 continued to brief him in detail about each of the other members of The Committee, including his French and American counterparts.

Abernethy stopped for a moment and digested the message he had just received.

Tau – Eyes Only
Top Secret, National Sensitivities
"Ministry of State Security (MSS) have been tracking regional people smuggling operations coordinated through various Triad criminal gangs. This

has been a regional problem for many years and taking its regional responsibilities seriously, the Chinese Government has been doing everything to monitor and interdict criminal operations. A recent development is a link to a Western gang, no further details yet, but intelligence intercepts have identified the word 'Latvian', and also discussion around blood groups. More details to follow when authorised for release.

Xi Koh – Tau China. Stop.

"Pierre, by some strange coincidence we have a link to a Latvian from Koh in SE Asia. This is getting interesting," he said as he pointed to the message on screen.

A few weeks beforehand, late Spring 2019.

The two men stood at the table and neither was prepared to concede.

"But I need to give something to The Committee. We can control this, I can control this," Xi Koh of the Ministry of State Security (MSS) and The Committee member said angrily to his boss, Lee Ho.

He didn't wait for a reply.

"Why was there a camp by the facility in Wuhan anyway? Have we caught the gang that smuggled them out? If we can't keep people we call terrorists secure what hope is there for low-level criminals? This would never have happened on my watch. Luckily I am now in a position to make this go away," he barked, showing little of the respect his boss should have expected.

The report sitting on Lee Ho's desk that Xi Koh had just read, described how two days ago three workers from the scientific support camp attached to the Wuhan Institute of Virology had escaped. Apparently they had paid Triad people smugglers to get them out and away from China, disguised as Vietnamese refugees as they knew they would be sent into Europe. What the report didn't say but Lee Ho knew, was where they were working specifically, what they were working on inside the labs and that some of them were sick with respiratory illness.

"We have it worked out. We know the Triads smuggled them through Vietnam and on to Singapore before going up to North Africa. They were communicating with someone they referred to as 拉脱维亚语, the Latvian. We can find no trace of him. If it is indeed a 'him' and no related links with anyone who has been near Wuhan. That said, his name keeps cropping up in different communications.

Three days earlier there had been a break in at the labs. The truth of the matter was that it was actually a breakout from a holding facility within the Wuhan Institute of Virology. The facility was used for scientists from minority populations, mainly Uigars. They would be of no use in the normal re-education camps and clothing factories and so within the Wuhan Institute of Virology their 'retraining' facility, they could be of use to the Chinese state instead of being a thorn in their side.

Forced to continue their scientific research in the Labs and then take retraining programmes when not at work, they had a more comfortable life than many in similar but larger more standard facilities. They were, however, still prisoners. Food was better than their counterparts' in Xinjiang Provence in North West China. The accommodation was better and pay, if it could be called that, was better. They were all university professors or research doctors but they all knew they were actually prisoners.

However, the Uigar prisoners had things other 'free' Uigars didn't. As scientists they knew the black market well. Often it was the only way to get the resources they needed for their research, and success kept the authorities away from their families. They also had some available money, so buying an escape was less difficult. After all the Institute was never designed to keep the people secure, just the diseases.

"So, this is one of the communications we intercepted in a dark web chat, in a chat room we are monitoring. "每个B和O中的两个，至少一个AB,

'(Two of each B and O and at least one AB, preferably male and in his 20s)'. We have narrowed the B, O and AB down to blood groups but why?" Xi Koh asked Lee as he continued to read the file.

"That is unimportant," said Lee, "we have to distance any fallout from the party, from the Country," he added.

"Explain the Vietnam connection?" asked Koh now more calmly and a little apologetically.

"The Triads smuggle people into Europe and elsewhere under Vietnamese identities. They have false documents and are still exploiting processes they had in place during the war with America," Lee explained. "If anyone tries to suggest the people came from China, never mind were Uigars, we can easily pass them off as Vietnamese, but for that we have to ensure they can't talk."

The die was cast.

"Will they survive the journey?" asked Koh. "You know what they were working on, if it out there, will it kill them? Could it spread?"

The Wuhan Institute of Virology was known for its work into some of the world's most deadly viruses, including a new strain of Corona virus. Both men knew what this could mean.

"We have taken steps, our team in Holland is on it and know the stakes," came Lee's reply.

"So, what can I take back to my Tau friends? I need to keep giving something. We are supposed to be cooperating and the Abernethy one is too clever!" Koh exclaimed.

"Give them triads, give them blood groups and a Latvian connection. Mention nothing about our retraining schools or even the city of Wuhan. You have been around long enough to construct something. Just make it look good."

With that Lee left. As he walked back to his office he typed out a short message on his smart phone, 'Contaminated batch, destroy it', and hit send. He was not referring to any virus.

Syria, Spring 2019

Same time, different place, others were working on a similar problem.

Dawn was just breaking over the horizon and the sound of the traffic was already everywhere, as was the smell. The smell in every conflict zone is the same. Burning rubbish, an acrid soldering plastic smell that just hangs in the atmosphere and the undeniable smell of death. And then the call to prayer. The wailing from the speakers in the minaret of the mosque near his hotel. At least he had a hotel.

Ducking out of the staff entrance, Valeri Petrov's slight build belied his strength and abilities. He had started his military career in the Russian Air force as a helicopter pilot flying Mi8, in support of Special Operations. On one operation he crash landed in hostile territory and had to exfiltrate with the remnants of the Spetznaz troop he had been flying. They made it back, no thanks to his leadership and wider navigation skills. His photographic memory helped him remember potential routes from his flying maps and the praise that was heaped on him by the team came to the notice of the generals in the First Directorate, the GRU or Russian Military Intelligence. He had now found his niche.

I hate war zones. I hate Middle East war zones. I hate that fucking smell, he thought to himself as he ducked through shops often doubling back on himself. All the time watching, noting, observing. He was like everyone in The Committee. He had done the same course. It was second nature and anyone in The Committee would never think of taking a direct route.

Valeri Petrov, GRU, but attached to The Committee as its Russian operator, was back in Damascus in Syria, a city he knew well.

Finally moving into a café, he nodded to the waiter who brought him an Arab coffee and a bottle of water. As his eyes adjusted to the dark, he heard a familiar voice.

"Valeri, my old friend, have you come back to join the Slav Corps?"

A voice he couldn't mistake, Dmitry Rushkin, the erstwhile commander of the Slav Corps and colleague from Unit 29155 of the GRU. He had been responsible for all overseas direct-action operations. Of course the unit didn't exist, it was always denied, but somehow it kept popping up.

They hugged, big bear hugs.

"You said it was urgent, it must be to get a soft UN pen pusher to come to a proper fun conflict zone like this my old friend," said Dmitry with a grin.

"It is urgent. Is this place safe or should we walk?" Petrov made to get up.

"No we are safer here, I have secured it. You are getting soft if you hadn't noticed." Laughed Rushkin.

"I did, that is why we should walk," and with that Petrov got up and put an arm around his old friend moving him on. He had won this very small initial battle.

"We, no you, have an issue my friend with some of the business you are doing," whispered Petrov as they walked through the gate of the park."

"Your man, the Latvian, is drawing too much attention and my organisation will start to get curious soon. They may be already. There is only so much I can do. You need to rein him in," said Petrov.

Rushkin's brow wrinkled as he thought of his answer. "We have probably made enough money and now could be the right time to stop. Getting the right people is proving more difficult and those fucking White Helmets were onto us, so we had to deal with that Le Mesurier guy. He was too close," he replied.

Le Mesurier was the head of the White Helmets, a humanitarian group in Syria aiding President Assad's opposition. He mysteriously fell from the balcony of his apartment in Turkey whilst home on holiday.

"Anyway," he added, "he is not my man, we trained together, you facilitated some business for him in Croatia if you remember, when you were a young pup. All very messy with that Drako guy."

"I just exploited further business opportunities as they came up. Both our retirements will benefit from it." Laughed Rushkin despite his inner anxiety. "The Irish connection you made with him all those years ago has kept us busy and wealthy."

"Their haulage routes set up to smuggle weapons for their war with the British has given us so much more, we are using it for other goods as you know well my friend," said Rushkin, putting an arm around his friend Petrov's shoulders.

"I thought that had your fingerprints all over it and it just focused more attention on here. Did those fucking drunken bogtrotters ever turn up for the other stuff?"

"Ah our Irish friends, they must have Russian genes, they kept up with us on the Vodka when we met! And yes, they found some of what they wanted, the weapons, but what was better is they control much of the transport network, so good business all around," smirked Rushkin as he remembered his hangover. "The biggest risk is theirs."

"Be careful with them my friend. My British colleague, Abernethy, has links from his past into Ireland. We don't want them triggering his interest," replied Valeri, "and keep them away from the Latvian. When is your last shipment?"

"A couple more and that's it, two months max," came the reply. "The government here likes getting people into Europe, their troublesome people, so they can get Paris and Nice and London style disruptions going with terrorist style attacks the West believe were inspired by ISIS."

"OK my friend, but be careful," said Petrov as he gave his old friend a bear hug again and wandered off.

As he strode back to his hotel the familiar buzz of his phone in his pocket grabbed his attention. Petrov took the phone out and looked at the screen.

He walked over to the window and pulled the curtain back. Admiring the view of the ruined city he answered the desperate ringing of his phone.

"Something has happened in China. Drop into the Embassy before heading to the airport for the Menu," the voice said, and as the call ended another small explosion bellowed out across the city. The grey smoke rose slowly over the Eastern half and he waited to see how high the smoke would reach. It was simply

89

just another bomb and more deaths. He had seen this many times before and it rarely took him by surprise anymore.

He inadvertently repeated his thought of earlier.

I hate war zones. I hate Middle East war zones. I hate that fucking smell.

Back in Geneva.

"James, we have reports coming from the teams from across the globe. A few threads that are interesting. Valeri gave a clean bill of health from Syria saying he talked to old colleagues regarding people movements and asked about the Latvian connection but got nothing useful."

Pierre was reading the reporting log file on his secure iPad.

Abernethy raised an eyebrow. Through a back channel to the UK's Government Communications Spy Headquarters, GCHQ, he had been given a partial transcript of the conversations Petrov had had with Rushkin a little earlier. A series of strategically positioned listeners with concealed receivers had been assigned to Petrov and had picked up the two friends' conversation as they talked and walked. The two men were right to be suspicious but had not been wise enough on this occasion to spot the listeners.

All members of The Committee team would submit reports or tippers as often as they could. This would complement the reporting coming out from those member nations who were party to the Tau community.

"A note from Koh about triad smuggling of Vietnamese nationals seeking to get into Europe, but no further detail and nothing yet to take away resource to check," Abernethy added.

"Valeri did say there were indications of Irish terrorists approaching Syrian government to open a source of weapons supply, that's one of your old stomping grounds is it not?" Melville added.

"Sorry, look at the news, Pierre, you mentioned Irish," snapped Abernethy.

He nodded towards his screen, the ticker tape from secure media links flashing across it as they spoke. He read it out loud.

"A 25-year-old from Lurgan in Northern Ireland has been arrested over the lorry deaths. It is believed he was the driver!"

The last time I was looking at Irish terrorist weapon procurement was in Croatia, Abernethy thought. *Were these smuggling animals responsible for her disappearance?* He could think of no other option. He could not stop thinking about her.

"James, this bit hasn't hit the headlines yet. I've just had a message from Miranda. Dutch police have intercepted three containers of counterfeit cigarettes and 200 kg of cocaine in lorries destined for Ireland. Melville was now more enthusiastic and bolder. "They had originated from Serbia and Interpol is conducting further enquiries with the Serbian Police," read Melville. "Miranda thinks it may have some connection to 'The Facility' but can't say how she has made that connection over this means," he added. "She will need to explain over more secure comms," he went on as he kept his gaze at the report coming across to him.

Ireland again and Serbia, thought Abernethy. *Is someone reading my thoughts?*

He went back to the whiteboard and jotted down more words; 'Ireland, Balkans, smuggling and weapons'. He drew lines connecting the new words with the Latvian but as quickly as he did he rubbed them out.

"OK, Pierre, here is what we need an analytics team to do but make sure it is only yours and my people. It will seem less suspicious if it comes from you. Let us do an AI enabled database search for the past thirty years on any and all reports with the following key words."

Then with that Abernethy sprung out a list of key words from which he hoped the powerful computers could find a link, 'Netherlands, Rotterdam, Tilbury, Latvian, people, Ireland, Balkans, Estonian, smuggling, migrants and weapons, drugs, cigarettes, blood groups'.

"Oh, and add in China, Russia, Organised Crime for good measure. I want full pattern and social network analysis linking reports and can I have them cross referenced with drug, weapon and people smuggling reports. That should keep out multimillion Euro servers humming for a while," exclaimed Abernethy.

"I'm on it," replied Pierre. He waited for a moment, as he saw Abernethy was in deep thought.

"James?" he called trying to bring him around and determine if he should stay to wait for further comment. There was no immediate response.

The bloody notebook, he thought now reaching for a drawer on his desk.

He pulled it but it was locked and for a moment Abernethy looked for a key then realised the lock was biometric. He depressed his thumb on the pad and a green light came on. Opening the drawer now he pulled out her notebook from Vukovar.

What is it about that bloody place and now, he thought as he flicked through the pages.

Melville sat back down and waited.

There. She was also on to this, years back. Christ it is so obvious now. Fleming you are a genius' he thought again. Then realising she was past tense his stomach churned.

Staring him in the face, as it had done many times before, were the words 'Latvian' connection to GRU – 'Irish?' 'Mass graves?' This was followed with 'Russia / GRU and people smuggling through V'? All scribbled but neatly on one page.

"Christ, she witnessed people smuggling through bloody Vukovar. She was onto them because she discovered that the mass graves were the dead from organised people smuggling and this Latvian was working with or for the Russians."

Abernethy then seemed to focus again and come back into the present.

"Pierre, I have just had a thought about the graves in Vukovar." But Melville cut him off.

"Yes, James, I heard, Fleming's notebook and the Latvian connection. All good. Got it," he replied. Then, standing again to leave the room for a second time Melville stopped. His hand on the door handle.

"She was good, James. Perhaps the best. And no doubt would have had this all solved by now if she were here."

Abernethy remained quiet as he watched his friend and colleague leave the room.

Chapter 8
America Calling

Autumn 2019

The tunnel was dark, hot and airless. It was not a nice place to be. The stream of people, desperate to get into the US by any means, had entered through the garage of a small house on the Mexican side of the Arizona border and through a specially hidden tunnel inside. They were being led under the wall and into the United States. But unlike some of their predecessors, transport would be waiting. They would not be left to their own devices. They were too valuable for that to happen. They had job offers, and the promised salaries were generous. The excitement amongst the silent group was palpable.

It was known as by both locals and those that worked there as 'The Ranch'. Only fifteen miles from Sierra Vista, in the Arizona foothills, its reputation as a rehabilitation centre for the rich and famous was well-known as was the extreme privacy and security surrounding it. One gate in, one road to the complex, one giant fence surrounding the property and guards and CCTV everywhere. It was more like a prison camp than a luxury respite centre for the now well-heeled sick and those who wanted the best in surgery to keep their youthful looks.

"Keep up, not far now." Came a cry in the dark from a deep Southern American drawl.

The tiny pinprick of light ahead of them was getting bigger. The smell of freshening air suggested they were nearly out. For forty minutes they had been in this dark hell hole.

"Right, stop." Came the cry. "Wait here and be quiet. I need to check all is OK," said the same voice, this time less friendly and more demanding.

The exit was from an old mine and the last twenty metres was through the blasted exit into the side of the hill.

The voice took a deep breath of the fresh air and shielded his eyes from the bright sun.

He knelt down by the entrance and watched and listened. After a couple of minutes, he pulled out his phone and typed into his Threema secure messaging app, 'Post ready for pickup.'

He then waited. Two minutes later he saw the reassuring cloud of dust coming down the track a short way off. He knew it was their transport.

Walking fast back into the tunnel he whispered, "Transport is coming. Let's move quickly and not fuck about. You don't follow on, you get left behind." With that, the ten people and their leading voice bunched up at the entrance to the mine.

Then, 'bang' a single shot rang out from a low calibre handgun. This was their sign.

"OK follow me," and they ran down the small track that once had the makings of a mine rail track towards the waiting minibus.

Inside, the nervous driver ran his fingers over his Glock pistol which was still drawn. He was looking around him but all was quiet. He could see nothing out of the ordinary that could prove to be a problem.

The side doors were open. Bottles of water waited on every seat. The 'goods' needed to be kept fresh.

"Welcome to the USA," barked the driver as the doors slid shut, once everyone was inside and putting their seatbelt on. He stifled a comment about the wave of body odour that hit him as he turned the ignition key.

"Mantén la conversación baja, it's a long journey, bit longer to go. So relax and stay quiet," he barked. Knowing he couldn't take a direct route to The Ranch he had to spend time making sure he wasn't tailed. It had to remain cleaner than clean to avoid being followed.

Not far away, Roz Cherrie looked at the feed coming into the screen in front of her. Beside this, was a second feed from a drone framing the minibus perfectly from 12,000 feet above it as it moved along the dirt track. The passengers inside had no idea they were being watched.

It was a routine training mission for the US Army Intel centre at Fort Huachuca. Nothing out of the ordinary, shadowing a moving vehicle with a drone so high in the sky it could not be seen by the human eye.

She was back on familiar ground. Just outside Sierra Vista you couldn't find such a secure base, and especially not one with all the toys she could ever need so close to the target. It was a mere thirty-minute drive from The Ranch. It was the perfect location for the operation.

"They all look knackered, poor buggers," she said out loud, looking at the being covertly beamed from the minibus to her screen. The drone had moved away to a high-altitude side angle and some of the new passengers could be made out.

You my people may be the lucky ones, she thought to herself. *You will avoid the fate that I fear befell many of your chosen predecessors.*

The FBI tech teams had spent the night before installing the latest tracking, video and listening devices in the vehicle before Chuck, the driver, collected it from the rental company. He would not be aware or suspect a thing. It gave Cherrie's team the perfect cross reference point with the drone imagery and a heads up if the driver or other employee suspected anything.

"He is doing his cleaning run, ma'am," Special Agent Bill Cortez said to Cherrie as he monitored the GPS tracker, showing the vehicle heading North on the 191 towards highway 10. "He is following the same route he did in his car yesterday, I expect, if so he should stop at a layby for a few minutes and flip the bonnet while looking around for a tail."

The overall surveillance operation on The Ranch and its employees had been going on for five weeks now and its end was very near.

After three years as a 35P, a cryptologic linguist in the special operations division of the Army, Roz Cherrie knew listening to comms was not for her. She preferred people and close quarter action and having been talent spotted by the CIA a while back, jumped at the chance to join them and get away from the constraints of the military approach. The CIA offered her the freedom to conduct her own operations in the manner she wanted without financial constraints. It also allowed for these same operations to fail if she had not planned things thoroughly.

This was her twenty-fifth year with the CIA and now the end of her first year assigned to The Committee.

She knew she was being side-lined when her boss suggested she should take a career break to finish her PhD in Terrorism, instead of her expected move to run agents into North Korea.

Throughout her career, her military training put her in a perfect operational position to support black op Seal Team across the globe. At 5' 5", petite and blonde, she looked out of place when with the brutal environment of America's killer elite. Most, however, that knew her, didn't realise the only thing that stopped her turning professional at either mixed martial arts or being a primary choice for the US Olympic team was her commitment to serve her country.

As a Russian and Serb linguist, she had seen her early days in the Balkans. Sent in initially to replace a young CIA officer, Richard Livingston, killed in a hit and run in Erdut in Croatia. No one had found the culprit or the motive and a while later his name forgotten by his colleagues, only remembered by a plaque on a wall at Langley.

She was part of Madeline Albright's negotiating team with Milosevic over the years and famously told by him what he had thought of her and her motives.

"If America was serious about negotiating, they wouldn't send a woman to do a man's job," he was famously quoted as saying. This hadn't put Albright in the frame of mind to compromise and in time she had got everything she wanted.

Cherrie getting politically visible scared her bosses and so her card was marked. So although a brilliant operator, her career would be limited and they thought the PhD, and then a move the international backwater, known as The Committee, would finish her off.

"Ma'am, you need to see this."

The comment jolted Cherrie from her thoughts.

"This is a picture from the side entrance to the Ranch, that man is John Magere..." Agent Cortez never got to finish his sentence.

"You have seen nothing," she interjected quickly and firmly. "Erase that footage after getting me a copy, remember, you have never seen it, it never existed, this is a compartmentalised agency issue, OK?" Cherrie surprised herself a little at her abruptness. She was anxious. She could not let on that the 'agency' was actually The Committee, and that the footage was now Tau classified.

What the fuck was Magere doing there at the Ranch? She thought. *A few hours later and he would have been caught up in the raid and we would have been shooting at the Secret Service without knowing it. Jesus that was close, lucky.*

She steadied herself, shaken at what could have happened, her mind racing. She needed to go over the INTEL again to be sure and to help her mind calm down.

Magere and Cherrie had been close. Fifteen years ago after hitting it off on an overseas diplomatic mission it seemed there were still some elements of sparks. She felt uncomfortable about how she still felt when he had popped back into her mind.

The blacked-out Cadillac left the gates of The Ranch at speed. Its passenger usually attracted a larger cavalcade of vehicles, including armoured back up vehicles and more Secret Service Agents. Today it was only Magere at the wheel. His passenger in the back was smiling. Today, this visit didn't happen. The number of people who knew where Magere and his passenger was and why they were where they were, was less than five. It had taken weeks of planning, but it had to be done now. Time was not open-ended anymore.

Opening up her secure case at the back of the ops room, the familiar screen with the Tau symbol greeted her on the modified MacBook Pro. It was as always, connected to a highly encrypted satellite phone so even if the signal were intercepted, which it was as all satellite comms was captured by various intelligence agencies around the world, nothing could break the encryption used. Not even the most powerful computers at Langley could decrypt Tau comms.

She sent her words out into the ether with utter confidence.

Abernethy had received a new message.

"James, op is a go in a few hours, but I need you to have a look at this as there seems to be a new player on the block or some dreadful coincidence that could bite us all," said Cherrie. "The picture is of John Magere, Secret Service, Presidential Protection detail. I knew him well a few years back. Please keep this FEO. Cheers R x," she wrote in a covering note to the encrypted file transfer programme. The upload took time as the encryption software got to work. FEO was Five Eyes only and that meant the message was intended for only between her and Abernethy as there were no other Five Eyes partners in The Committee.

As she sat back down, looking at the operation screens at the front of the room, watching the upload bar get closer to the hundred-percent line, her cell phone buzzed in her pocket. Swiping it open she saw the name Bruce Kutzer.

What the hell does that bastard want, she thought.

"Hello, Bruce, you stranger," she said. Not allowing him to intervene she spoke again. "Let me step out to take your call, hang on," and she closed her Tau case and walked out into the bright sun of the Arizona morning.

Kutzer was a Deputy Director in the CIA and on paper, Cherrie's boss. He had sent her to The Committee so he knew about Tau.

"I hear you have come home from your holiday in Geneva," he said. "I thought you were up to your neck in chasing those traffickers from Syria. Home for a family visit is it?" he enquired.

Cherrie knew the last report that would have crossed Kutzer's desk was The Committee assessment regarding human trafficking and links to European and Asian organised crime. What it didn't mention was links into Central and South America and specifically Mexico being the centre of activity.

"I'm well, Bruce, thank you for asking," she replied sarcastically. "Yup back to see family and check out a few things the team are working on, you know me. I don't like connections that fly off into the abyss, everything has to have an endpoint," she said, still wondering why he called and how he knew she was back in the USA.

"Well, anything I can help with, you know where I am," Kutzer replied. "Call in for a coffee if you are passing through this way."

With that the line went dead.

Hmmmm, what's he up to? She thought, as she headed back inside. *That was him just letting me know he is watching me, why now?*

She was quickly distracted.

"Ma'am, he is following the expected route on Highway 10 now. I estimate he will take a good forty minutes before heading for The Ranch. Then, perhaps allow two further hours for processing the new arrivals and we go in and hopefully catch them red-handed, so to speak," said a team member.

Cherrie nodded her acknowledgement.

"Three hours to the go. OK, is everything in place? I want to go in swift after the initial raid to inspect the place. Remember the order, self-defence only, non-lethal means first unless life is at risk, I can't explain a bloodbath. Pass the word. Nobody touches anything without my personal say so, get it?" she said to the room.

With that, a dozen men and women started to recheck tactical bags.

In their primary holsters for the assault, was the Byrna HD, compressed CO2 pistol firing an incapacitating .68 calibre round. The cover team all had the relatively new HK433 assault rifle, providing lethal over watch if necessary. They would then drift away and relax together awaiting the pending action and noise.

Meanwhile, inside The Ranch, Karen Martinez the Executive Director, picked up her desk phone.

"Dr Hofmann," she said, "so good of you to take my call. I hope you enjoyed your visit to us last year and the tour of our facilities. We have the same similar historical class and call as with Ireland but do prefer to be a little unique where able. I know most of our clients would find the trip to Europe too far and too cold.

"As I mentioned in my mail to you, we have a very special client who needs your help in the next couple of months at the latest. Due to who he is, we can't use any of our regular staff, but we need the best." She paused for a moment as she collected her thoughts before continuing. "We need utmost secrecy, like you have never had to guarantee before, and I trust you are fully comfortable with this request."

"Your fee is what you mentioned, fine with us, plus a bonus of half as much again. We have reactivated our supply chain and will be working to find suitable candidates," drawled on Martinez, in her south Arizona accent.

"Just let me know when," replied Hofmann, "it will only take me a week's notice to ensure I have everything covered at home and will then fly out from Shannon to you. Seems medical work still counts as essential during the pandemic so there shouldn't be any problems," he said with a smirk.

After enjoying his financial 'win', he decided to push a bit further. "First class tickets for myself, my assistant and my nurse, is the deal I believe."

"Of course, Doctor, and a week's notice or more it will be, thank you," whispered Martinez, wondering why she was whispering. "Speak soon," and with that the line was again dead.

Three million Euro for one minor operation, thought Hofmann.

Then he spoke out loud. "With that I may move from Ireland." He giggled to himself. "And if I take the doctor we repatriated from ISIS as my assistant, not only is she discrete and good, but she could be very pleasurable," he said, continuing with his words to be said out loud. He smiled.

Back in the operation room there was a quiet confidence and a buzz in the air.

"OK, they are turning into the access road, ma'am, roadside surveillance triggered. We have visual overhead." Came the call back in the ops room. "That means they are in situ in around twenty minutes and the clock starts to count down then."

"OK, right, move the ground teams into position," Cherrie instructed. "Fifteen minutes and we go. Let's head to the choppers, folks, and remember, non-lethal first please!"

Martinez returned from the toilet next to an open window in the corridor. Then, as she sat down stationary at her desk for a moment's reflection, she thought she heard something. Martinez was suddenly uncomfortable. She needed to know why she felt this way so left her office and went towards the main entrance.

Walking out the front doors she instinctively looked up at the clear blue sky but saw nothing. She breathed in the fresh warm air.

The slight dust cloud approaching made her smile again.

The first batch of candidates, she thought to herself. *I hope we find a suitable one or we will have to cycle them through quickly. Nowhere to keep them. Christ storage is always a premium.* She laughed slightly as she realised what she had just thought. *Storage of fucking people. Storage!*

She smiled at the approaching minibus and walked down the side of the building to what was used as the entrance to an underground carpark.

Moments later, the bus passed her. Its occupants now waking up as the sun stopped beating through the windows and the sound from the road changed. Shadows now filled the bus as it went underground. The minibus pulled up at an airport style entrance just inside and out of the sun.

Martinez stepped onto the ramp to face her recently arrived audience. She waited for the door to open and the occupants to exit.

"Welcome to the USA and thank you for asking to work at The Ranch," she yelled over the din from the air conditioning units and general hustle of fidgeting anxious new arrivals. "You will have the chance to shower and to change before processing for identity documents and medical checks, and then on to your accommodation," she added. "We will start you working in the next day or so, but in the meantime, relax and rest."

With that she turned and hurried up the passage back to the upper floors and her office. Welcome done.

An excited hum came from the party, realising they had come to the end of their journey and the thought of a shower after days on the road made everyone smile.

"OK folks, showers are ahead, get cleaned up," said their driver, pointing the wat. "There are leisure suits in various sizes on the racks inside, as well as sneakers. Help yourselves and then follow the signs to staff reception. I will see you all there in thirty minutes."

As they started to drift out of the showers, all in the same 'Ranch' branded purple leisure suits with 'Staff' emblazoned on the back, the group collected around a table laden with fruit, juice, and cakes. They waited for the driver, or someone, to come back.

Outside, and just out of earshot, the low rhythmic beat of helicopter rotor blades cut through the nearby sky. It grew louder.

The heavy dark blue armoured vehicle from the FBIs' Critical Incident Response team smashed through the front gates with ease. They raced for the front of The Ranch just as two Sikorsky UH-60 Black Hawk helicopters lowered rapidly and landed on either side of the building, with further assault and cover teams in a third just behind. Cherrie and her specialist team hovered a short distance away overhead, waiting for the 'All Clear' signal.

It was a perfectly orchestrated and timed movement and one that caused maximum confusion and paralysis for all inside the structure.

Martinez had heard the helicopters from her office, but her mind was still on the new arrivals. She also heard vehicles speeding down the long entrance track towards the building, but again, it didn't really register. It was only when the security team ran past her door moments later and she heard the first shot from her team, followed by the yell, "Fuck, it's the FBI," did she realise something bad was happening.

Going into auto mode, she closed and locked her office door and went up to the cupboard door on the wall behind her. She pulled on a large red semi-concealed handle before closing it again. There was movement revealing a seamless secondary wall covered by a hanging modern art statue centrally, filling the void. Next, she opened the control panel on the wall behind her desk that said 'Ranch Server Master' on its label and then turned a key in the red button before pushing it. *Set,* she thought.

Standing up, smoothing her dress, and checking her lipstick in the mirror, she opened her office door and sat back down behind her desk, calmly ignoring the commotion outside.

"No more shots," she heard over the staff radio, followed by cries, "Don't shoot, don't shoot, it's the Feds." Her security team knew not to resist.

The thudding of combat boots on oak flooring was everywhere and all of the phone line lights started to flash on her desk phone. The 'guests' were curious. They were scared.

Then, she heard the firm instruction.

"Your hands on the desk, ma'am," came from a deep, commanding voice. It was calm and measured but coming from someone in full tactical gear with a

Byrna HD handgun pointed at her forehead. Martinez wouldn't have known the difference between a Byrna HD and a Colt 45. Guns were not her thing, but she knew what they did.

"I have guests and patients to speak to, Officer. What is going on?" she said, trying to remain calm.

Cortez knew the charges they had already on her and the establishment and confirming who she was. She cuffed Martinez and she read her rights. Then, led her as gently as she could towards the foyer of the hotel.

The hovering Black Hawk had landed and Cherrie strolled through the front entrance as if she were arriving to check in.

"Main office is over there, Ma'am," Cortez said, nodding towards the direction from where he had just brought Martinez. "Building clear, we are assembling the guests in the dining room, and we have found the 'new staff arrivals' in the basement. They haven't got a clue."

Cherrie moved into the Martinez's office expecting to find nothing.

Simple enough, she thought, looking around. She saw a clean desk apart from one file and a computer. Cherrie moved over to the desk. Looking down, she moved the mouse almost instinctively and, as she did so, the screen came out of sleep mode.

'C://*' was all that was displayed. It was clear the system had been wiped.

Shit, she thought. It was already too late.

The smell was very faint. A smell of burning, but there was no sign of an actual fire in the office. The smell was there however, no mistaking. She looked up to the ceiling. There was an air con vent but nothing obvious came from it.

"Check for fire," she said into her tactical radio pinned to her left shoulder and immediately heard back.

"All clear," came from each of the initial six-man tactical team. But it was there, the smell, she knew it very well.

Cherrie turned her attention back to the desk.

Opening the file, she let out a low whistle. She continued to skim the initial page at speed.

There was no name, just a collection of numbers and characters. However, the description of 'the patient' was unmistakeable to her. There and around it, was a series of bar codes, QR codes, and what looked like deep web encryption symbols.

These number, character and letter codes must mean something to someone. The team will know, she thought.

Putting it into an evidence bag she shoved it into her tactical knapsack. Then she went back to looking for something out of the ordinary in the room. She was experienced in seeing what was not obvious. Criminals had developed ingenious methods of hiding drugs and counterfeit money and, in her long career, she had stayed one step ahead and beaten most at their own game.

"That smell," she said again to no one and anyone that could hear her.

Scanning the room, she saw the sculpture on the wall, "Seems expensive," she said out loud to herself. "Seems out of place," again out loud as if she were in a conversation with someone close by. Then, as she was turning away, to scan other items before reaching the sculpture, a wisp of smoke caught her eye coming from behind the images head.

Something behind there? A vent?

All her instincts told her not to touch it. She even caught herself thinking that exact same training scenario. *Leave alone, call the forensic team, get an explosive team in* but curiosity got the better of her.

Carefully looking around the sculpture, she began feeling over its smooth lines. The book being held in the hands of the abstract body looking to the skies looked awkwardly held. She found there was a bump. It seemed out of place. Very subtle, but unusual for such a perfectly manufactured piece. She pulled it a little. Nothing. Then applied downward pressure on it.

'Click.'

The front of the book moved slightly, and she could tell there was something on a type of hinge. She opened it slowly. There was a keypad behind it.

Christ, James fucking Bond stuff, she thought.

Glancing around the office for a clue, it took a minute or two to register. Then, in plain sight, taped to the underneath side she had flipped over was a type of code 25871349#. A second almost similar one was etched underneath the first. 25871350#.

Why two?

She did not give herself enough time to answer her own question.

The top code: Entering the numbers in order, her finger trembled over the # key.

Then, as she pressed it, she saw a flash and then nothing.

Cortez heard the bang. He was making his way to join her.

He saw Cherrie flying backwards out of Martinez office and violently hitting the wall in the corridor.

She was out for cold but a millisecond behind her, the fireball flashed through the room out into the corridor. He felt the pressure blast and was stopped in his forward motion.

Suddenly, a second blast, then a third. It was hard to know exactly what was happening and where was safe. At the main reception area, all the detainees had been burned or injured and were now lying around crying or begging for help to anyone that could hear their calls.

Most of the tactical teams had been saved from real damage by their fireproof gear but all had felt the blast wave thrown around.

The whole front of the building was now engulfed in flames.

"Fire, everyone out," yelled Cortez into his radio as he sprinted to grab Cherrie and drag her to safety. It was an instinctive call. The team knew the drill and were already shepherding the survivors out onto the grounds and relative safety.

Cortez had been in many war zones and in many blast sites. But this heat was like nothing he had felt before, well nothing in the US. He did, however, recognise the smell, 'Thermite'.

After the initial triggering device went off, further destruction had been followed by specifically located destruction grenades around the structure. They were designed to destroy top secret files and equipment, and any human evidence that could be compromising. Finding evidence of the Ranch's hidden function would be possible but difficult.

The incendiary grenades would burn through anything it came across and couldn't be put out easily, often reigniting time and time again, as was happening with two of the survivors on the lawn, despite the efforts of Cherrie's team to roll and dampen the flames.

Fuck someone had something to hide here if that shit was used, he thought to himself.

Moments later, one of the team reported back.

"We got everyone out that we know about. Mostly only minor burns." Cortez was told as he carried Cherrie out on to the front lawn. She was breathing but it didn't look good. Her stab vest had taken the brunt of the damage. It had certainly saved her life.

"Medic, immediate case vac to Huachuca for assessment. Go!" Cortez yelled.

Seconds later, and the well-trained machine of medical crew had Cherrie on a stretcher and lifting off. It was all very reminiscent of a military operation.

Cortez turned and saw the whole of The Ranch engulfed in flames. "Fuck."

John Magere was back leading his normal detail and had just come off shift for a break. He felt his cell phone vibrate quietly in his pocket. He was one of the few allowed to carry his personal cell at all times.

'Number Unknown'.

"Hello," he answered.

"I think we have a problem brewing," the voice said.

He recognised it immediately, it was Kutzner. He knew for him to call it was more than a little problem.

"OK, let me know the usual way when you can," Magere replied and disconnected the call.

"Only flash burns to my windpipe and a bit of concussion from hitting that wall," Cherrie whispered to Cortez lying in her hospital bed.

The beep, beep, beep of the heart monitor and the slight hiss of the oxygen from the feed to her nose was reassuring to both.

"Well, Ma'am, we got the Mexicans, twenty-five staff and guards, two doctors and four so-called nurses amongst them. Only ten migrants. Believe that is all that was present. All their backgrounds are in the file. Martinez was charged with tax evasion as discussed and we have now rearrested her and all of the guards for people smuggling and firing on federal agents."

"I think, Ma'am, the Ranch is no more. There was little left after the fire. But one curious thing from the initial forensic analysis. In the hospital, there was the usual cosmetic surgery stuff found, but in the basement, there was what looked like an ICU facility strangely well away from the main hospital bit, and with its own OR. Also, there were burned out remnants of a number of dialysis machines but not in the main hospital wing. Instead, in their own private area," Cortez said, with a puzzled look, "I doubt, unless the staff or 'guests' open up, we will ever know what was really going on."

"Right, good work anyway. We stopped those bastards. Oh, and Bill," she asked, using his first name to emphasise it as a personal favour, "in my tactical sack, you will find a file. It was all I got from Martinez' office before the blast.

Can you personally scan it onto a thumb drive for me and then destroy it? This is sensitive and you haven't seen it, no copies, no one else to know OK?"

"Yes, Ma'am, consider it done." Cortez liked Cherrie and smiled to himself when he thought of helping her. He was very curious as to why the secrecy.

I'll copy it at the FBI field station and then back to the hotel, he thought. *Will come back to see Roz in the morning.*

His smile grew as he walked down past the nurse's station.

The ward was quiet, a doctor and nurse were looking at a chart together as he walked towards the elevator.

There is more to this than I want to know, he thought. He couldn't shake off the feeling of unease, the feeling that something was about to happen. *That nurse, that doctor, there is something not right.*

Chapter 9
Geneva Analysis

"James, I have done some background work on those two names that came from Roz. Did she say why she wanted it?" asked Pierre.

"Nope, you know what she is like, some wild bloody goose chase. There will be some substance behind it somewhere," quipped James Abernethy casually.

But underneath, he was trying hard to hide the fact he knew more. The trouble with working in a den of spooks is that everyone can read when the whole truth isn't being shared. Like a professional sixth sense.

"Right, Let's hear what you have?"

"OK, James."

Pierre paused then took a deep breath.

"John Magere, US Secret Service. He joined the Service in 1993 after spending time in the military, where his infantry company was deployed to Croatia to protect a US Army MASH."

Pierre went on. Abernethy listened but was looking down at his notes.

"Apparently, he was being limited in his duties. Not sure why. But as a result, he became angry that he wasn't allowed to take troops out on the ground and would say to everyone who will listen that he quit because guarding medics wasn't what he signed up for. However, we have a classified personnel report that claims he was sanctioned after getting drunk with an Irish NGO team, so as a CIA officer, he was case vac into the MASH."

Pierre paused for a moment, Abernethy looked up from his notes, listening intently.

Pierre continued. "He was not squeaky clean. Magere had no direct role. Drinking was banned. The NGOs weren't aid workers and if you get my drift, it was used as an excuse to move him on. He had no choice. He was allowed to leave with full honours."

The two men thought for a second before Pierre continued.

"What was interesting was after his drinking session, apparently 'Brits Out' was pained on the side of the British Unit at the airport and it was thought that

Magere had done it. He is known to have close connections with different Irish Groups in the US, including some which raised money for the IRA and its offshoots."

"Magere joined the Secret Service and worked as part of the visiting diplomat team until Obama came in and he was allocated as some part of the protection detail for the VP, Joe Biden."

There was a pause. Both men considered the words being said. Their minds were busy with the current and the recent past.

Melville looked at his friend. Abernethy nodded slowly. Pierre knew he had the green light to go on.

"It was during that time with Biden that his career took off and he became a permanent member of the POTUS VP team. Apparently, Biden loved his Irish connections. We have a full brief in the folder," explained Pierre. "Now this will trigger an interest, James, for I know how you love your Irish connections," he said with a little smile.

"The second name Roz gave us was a Bruce Kutzer. He is one of the most unlikely Irishmen you will come across. A career CIA Officer where he was head of Balkans and Eastern Europe in the early 1990s and would have been briefed on the CIA Officer killed in Croatia. You remember the one?"

Abernethy nodded. He dropped his head slightly. He knew exactly the one and who he was linked with.

"He has been in a supervisory position for Roz for much of her career," continued Pierre.

"Kutzer was also loosely associated with the same Irish groups as Magere and it is believed he knew the same Irish NGO team that got sanctioned and could have been at the drinking party himself. What we don't know is if they knew each other at that time or was it coincidence. However, it is thought the two men struck up a friendship via different Irish groups. Kutzer's full bio is here, Mate, but he has been on a golfing holiday or perhaps gardening leave, difficult to say with Magere, and his wife, in Ireland in 2006.

"Kutzer has never been shy about his admiration for what he referred to as freedom fighters, the IRA, and this held his promotion back despite having impressive reports. Later, however, this 'block' seemed to disappear again through Obama's time as President and Biden as his Vice. Biden did seem to use Kutzer as a sounding board on various issues we believe."

Pierre stopped and drank from his glass. Thought for a moment and then started again.

"Of note, both Magere and Kutzer kept their positions when Trump came into office. Clearly, he saw something in both and he wasn't worried about their Obama and Biden connections. This strange 'loyalty' wasn't like Trump, but it seemed to work for both men," Pierre concluded.

"Shit, this could get messy Pierre," quipped Abernethy, "but what the hell is the connection with the Ranch in Arizona?"

Just then, the light indicating a call on his personal line started to flash.

"Abernethy," he answered.

"James, it's me," the soft American accent was unmistakeable.

"Hey, Roz, got those details you sent across, interesting. What's the real story?"

"I can't give you any details but there is another big file I will get a trusted friend to FTP to your personal account. I'll fill you in, once I get out of the hospital and get back to Europe."

"Wait, Roz, hospital, what happened?" exclaimed a shocked Abernethy.

"Oh, I just got a little banged up on the raid at the Ranch. A few bruises but nothing I haven't had before. You know what medics are like. They have to justify their huge bills to Medicare."

She laughed trying to sound upbeat, even though it hurt when she did so.

"I should be out in a couple of days after they remove the metal that shouldn't be in me."

"OK, but you look after yourself and be careful. Dinner is on me when you get back to the office."

"Yes, Dad," she quipped, "I'll hold…"

She never got to finish her sentence.

Abernethy recognised the sound instantly. The 'crack, crack' of a double tap, from a sub calibre pistol.

"Roz? Roz?" he yelled but her phone went dead.

Something was happening where she was in the hospital, and Abernethy felt instantly powerless. He couldn't help or do anything.

Cortez moved slowly but deliberately, reviewing the situation. The doctor and nurse that he had passed at the nurses' station, lay slumped in an expanding pool of blood, close to Roz's ward door.

Two head shots to each, no chance of survival. The HK MP3 9mm sub machine gun that he had glimpsed under the doctor's coat lay beside the bodies. The nurse had her hand frozen on the Glock pistol down the back of her trousers.

What the fuck have you got me into, Roz? Thought Cortez. *Who the fuck are these people I have just killed and why were they after you?* His mind was racing as he scanned the rest of the ward area and the corridor.

"Roz, you OK?" yelled Cortez, through the half-opened door now blocked by the bodies. Ducking through the door. "Roz?" he said again.

"I think so," came her muffled voice from under the bed.

Her reactions were swift and automatic. Standing with a wobble, she looked at the smashed phone on the floor and whispered, "What the fuck…"

"Pierre, I've just heard shots as I was talking to Roz. They sounded like they were in her room, in her hospital room. She was speaking with me and stopped halfway through a sentence. I can't get her to answer now. We have to assume she has been shot!" barked Abernethy. "Tau Alpha protocol now, Zap code RC0266 – everyone on this – team member down."

A chill seemed to pass across 'the pit'. Then, Geneva protocol kicked in. Like a wave crashing forward, everyone clicked the big red Alpha button on their screens and typed in 'RC0266', a code specific to Roz Cherrie. They all had been provided one. A number of things happened automatically.

Every electronic device Cherrie owned, that The Committee knew about, covertly 'lit up'. Tracking software hidden in the firmware source code started to execute. Giving every bit of data it could find about their surroundings and location whilst now deleting and overwriting confidential data held in the memory that was not unique to that device, but which had a secure copy somewhere else. Bluetooth devices, Wi-Fi, GPS coordinates were all sent to a hidden IP address buried in the servers of The Committee in Geneva.

"We have a location and number," one of the analysts yelled. "Canyon Vista Medical Centre, first floor, NE Wing, the GPS in her phone is pinging and stationary, along with her MacBook Air."

"On it," yelled Abernethy. "Pierre, can you call the hospital, standard protocol, I will call a favour in from Fort Huachuca military base."

Abernethy prepared to move off.

"Thanks, my friend. We need to tread very carefully. I can't help feeling this must be something to do with those two names she gave us."

As the local Sheriff's team arrived, Cortez had his badge around his neck, his FBI hat on and his pistol still drawn. He had already made a call, and MPs from Fort Huachuca were escorting a military ambulance to the hospital. Cherrie would now recuperate in base hospital, with a 24/7 guard. All were unsure if she was the intended target or not.

"First, the Ranch, and now, killing hospital staff," said sheriff not knowing if they were in fact hospital staff. "And there was me looking for a quiet weekend." He grunted as he took a preliminary statement from Cortez before letting him go with the military ambulance.

Cortex and Cherrie and the military team left the hospital with a small armed entourage and drove through the local streets towards the base and safety.

"Thanks, Sheriff," Abernethy said putting the phone down. Having had it confirmed Cherrie was OK and now in the Raymond W. Bliss Army Health Centre, on Fort Huachuca, he could relax and think a bit clearer. This was not the same for local sheriff, however.

He was perplexed, *the FBI, the Brits, the Military, the hospital,* he thought to himself. *What the fuck is going on here?*

Checking Roz was comfortable, and a guard was posted, Bill Cortez made his way back into town to the FBI field office. He had a task to do.

He finished scanning the file and put the encoded thumb drive into his pocket.

I'll give it to Roz in the morning, he thought, as the sound of the final page going through the shredder made him smile. *I'll never understand why shredding stuff has such a feel-good factor.*

Leaving the field office, Cortez jumped into his car for the short drive to his hotel and a well-deserved beer, steak and sleep.

What a day, he thought.

But he would not yet be allowed to relax fully just yet. His instincts drew his attention to a black SUV that had pulled into the carpark just outside the field office, as he turned left at the lights. *The boys working late again. Must be on the hospital job,* and he thought nothing else of it and drove on.

Instinct is something that keeps people working in the murkier side of life alive.

As Cortez walked to his hotel room, something felt out of place. He didn't know what as everything looked fine, but he had that feeling.

Drawing his weapon, he knelt down, so reducing the amount of himself as a target. He used the key card on the door and when he heard the mechanism open, pushed the handle down hard and the door forward. Weapon ready for anyone in the room. Nothing obvious straight away.

Slowly standing up and keeping close to the wall, he checked the bathroom, the cupboards, curtains and the balcony. His bed was made and his bag where he left it. Everything in its place. Everything too perfect.

He wandered over to the side desk. Lifting the pen from the holder beside the phone, he unscrewed the barrel. An old trick. His pen with a pinhole camera inside. Only $25 but a security trick many still missed. One that could provide vital evidence of what had gone on in his room as he inserted the mini-USB into his laptop, eighty-seven files showed up on the screen with forty timestamped late morning and fifty-seven late afternoon. Most had nothing of interest, the maid coming and making his bed and general cleaning. Nothing untoward as he flicked through the first few dozens. Then something. Showing as early afternoon when he was at the hospital. This time, it was the door opening again. Two figures dressed as janitors entered but with face masks. *Everyone has them with this damn COVID,* he thought.

Systematically, the two men went through his room. The way they did this with exact precision, told Cortez they had done something similar before. They were not janitors.

Professionals.

They photographed every area they moved to and things they touched on their smartphones first, then checking everything, and then very carefully ensuring it was left exactly as it had lay. Checking everything all against the photos taken before they left the area or item, to ensure nothing was out of place. Cortez now wondered about his bag which he had noticed on entering the room was as he left it.

Now that was a professional team, he thought. *The time stamp was when I was in the hospital with Roz...fuck Roz, what is going on here! Did they know I would not be around? Do they know I am FBI thus their method for searching the room?*

Instinctively and not knowing why, he lifted his pistol off the bed but didn't holster it. Its weight told him it was loaded. It made him feel safer simply holding it.

"I need to get this thumb drive to her this evening and find out what the fuck is going on," Cortez said to himself out loud, but as he did so, he looked around the room walls. He was planning and considering at the same time. It was not a strength of his.

Don't think I saw them plant any bugs. Will check later, he thought.

He was already out of the main hotel door walking briskly across the carpark, clicking the remote unlock lights on his car and was about to reach for the door handle when, "what the fuck?" 'Crack', then another.

He knew the sound of a bullet strike and the resultant damage of the smashed out, side window. Another two rounds struck. This time smashing the rear passenger window and drilling a neat hole in the door pillar just missing his head even although he was crouched and low.

Cortez went into auto.

In the car, engine started, and powering it hard as he could in his cramped position. It screeched across the grass but not before knocking over a 'No loitering' sign. Now, bumping down off the grass area, he was onto the main road just as his rear window shattered. Then, there was just the whistle of the wind through the shattered windows having sent its glass everywhere. He momentarily felt the scratches of glass shards cutting his neck and arms but kept driving. The sound of his heart pounding filled his ears more. Professional mode and evasion training kicked in, and he was out of range in seconds.

Driving past the hospital, he saw blue lights everywhere. He knew going there wouldn't help Roz or himself and a quick look at his wounds told him he was fine. He had been lucky and didn't need immediate attention. After a minute or two using the cars first aid box, the small lacerations were cleaned and dressed.

'Either she is Ok, or she *isn't,*' he thought as he pulled into a mall car park two blocks away from the local FBI field office.

Just then, he felt the gentle buzz of his cell phone in his pocket.

'Thank fuck' he thought, something good, until he saw the screen, 'Number Withheld'.

He took a gamble. "Roz is that you?" he yelled into the phone.

"Bill Cortez?" the distinctly British accent said down the line.

"Might be, whose calling," he replied, scanning the parking lot around him. In a second, Cortez had ruled out every car he could see and the taller vantage points around him. The caller was not close by. His heart slowed slightly.

"My name is James Abernethy. I am a friend of Roz Cherrie. We were chatting on the phone when the shooting happened. She told me to call you. She told me, I could trust you. I know you two were working together today and you are on her trust list for my agency," James spoke slowly and steadily. "I have just talked with her in the Raymond Bliss centre. Good move I might add, putting her there. The military will look after her until see's back fit."

How the fuck did he know about that, the Ranch, the operation and what fucking agency here has Brits? Cortez's mind was racing but he wanted to believe the words of the man on the line.

"Open Threema and download the link to the address I will secure transfer to you in a minute. Please don't question anything until we can talk on Threema. I think your life is at risk Agent Cortez and so does Roz."

"No shit, Sherlock," Cortez replied back. "I've just been shot at."

Abernethy wanted to give an air of superior rank knowing Cortez would be suspicious.

"Do as I say, Agent, and do it promptly. All will be made clear. Over." Abernethy ended the call and went about sending the link as promised.

Threema, thought Bill as he searched the app store and hit download, *in the absence of anything else I will run with this for a bit and see where it goes.*

He took position in an alley where he could see the carpark of the FBI Field station, then called the Raymond Bliss Medical Centre. He now wanted to know for sure if she was safe.

"Sorry, sir, she has gone to surgery to get a small piece of shrapnel from the explosion removed. She did leave a message for you, Mr Cortez," the nurse said, "it was simply to trust James, that's it, Sir. I hope, it means something to you."

"Yes…Thanks," replied Cortez, and ending the call, he focused back on the Threema app.

Cortez went straight to the app and opening it he stared at it waiting for something to happen. Then it connected.

A code popped up on its secure message screen. He then pressed the telephone symbol.

"Bill, good, that was quick. Thank you for calling back. I wasn't fully sure you would. Right, simple intro. I'm James Abernethy, former Intelligence and more and on the same team. Roz and I are also in a sort of international team. It's a deniable team which you won't find on any law enforcement system. Hell, you won't even find it on Google."

Abernethy was now trying to make Cortez relax and listen.

"She often mentions you. She has a lot of time for you clearly. Tell me what you know of Tau. Anything?" Abernethy asked, knowing if he were right, that Roz will have mentioned it to him but in a context that would show Abernethy was home team, and the group as totally clandestine, and not to be talked of by Cortez.

"Tau, yes, Roz did mention the word on a few occasions but said it was a special, private type team. I am assuming you knew what we did today, James. If it had a Tau element to it?" said Cortez as he relaxed but remained very curious. "Roz had emphasised that that word was only known by a very small number of people."

"Yes, today was part of an international ring of people smugglers, hence the connection, but Roz sent me a couple of names just before we talked, and before she was shot. You saw one of them today." Abernethy paused. "John Magere. I think there is a connection. Did Roz say anything to you?"

Cortez then explained what had happened on the operation and about the file Roz had told him to copy to her and then destroy. The one she had found on the desk at the Facility. He explained that, from what he saw of it as it was scanning, it appeared to be just some medical file but no personally identifiable data. References, if that is what they were, seemed only to be a mix of numbers, letters, and more characters, perhaps doctor references. The only full copy was now on an encrypted USB stick.

"That file, we believe, shows a political link from the highest levels to a people smuggling racket that Roz and the rest of the Tau team are investigating. We believe some will stop at nothing to ensure Roz and you are silenced and that file is destroyed. Do you know the name Bruce Kutzer? He's CIA, I believe he could be behind what is happening around you now, be careful."

Just then, Cortez heard the sound of glass smash in what felt like an upper window of the building across the street from him.

Flames flickered from another window in the same building. The FBI Field Office in Sierra Vista was on fire.

"I have to go. There's a fire now, think it's FBI quarters." The call was ended but not before Abernethy heard Cortez speak out loud in apparent frustration "What the fuck next, this day…" and the connection was gone.

Both men, many miles apart, only connected by a phone call, had similar thoughts.

Is this day ever going to end?

Cortez called back a short while later. He had not been granted access to the building and the fire unit seemed to now be controlling the scene and the fire.

Abernethy was glad that some trust had been established and that Cortez had called back so soon.

"Can I send you the file over this Threema thing?"

He was sounding nervous.

"Yes, and Cortez, stay safe. Trust no one. I will send you my personal number. Call if you can't use Threema but do so only once you are safe. I will message when we have the file," said Abernethy, "and avoid Kutzer or anyone who says they are CIA, if you can," he added.

Forty-five percent battery, good connection, should have enough juice and time, thought Cortez as he fiddled with the attaching a document from the phone files app allowing him to connect to the USB thumb drive via a special connector. He always carried every tool for the job. He hit send and without waiting to see it go, went back to the police cordon and the flames of The Fort.

"Pierre, I have just copied a folder into the database. Can you personally cross reference anything tangible in it with what else we have already and see if we can break the patients' and doctors' codes? Cheers, Mate."

Abernethy was being overly familiar with his equal to try and dispel any air of tasking and to suggest the need for privacy.

He then placed his phone into his jacket pocket and waited for Pierre to call back. Abernethy had not properly viewed the file Cortez had sent, merely glimpsed at it instead choosing Geneva's powerful computer to do the work.

"James, this is big," was Pierre's opening line when he called back. "There are similarities between the dates in this medical document and travel dates from a doctor in the Irish Manor, you know the hotel. We have cross referenced the codes on many of the medical scans and blood tests and they come from a so-called John Hopkins in Washington. But looking at the age, and medical description, it can only be one person. It would explain Megere's presence, but not what is going on, and at what cost to Roz?" he said.

"So, I have been doing some digging also," replied Abernethy. "It seems 'The Ranch' was bought by an anonymous corporation three years ago according to the local land registry. No easily identifiable owners' address. Seems the ties to the owners are weak, likely deliberate. Also, this corporation has close links to various property firms in New York and elsewhere including Scotland and of course, Ireland.

"The interesting thing is their Chief Operating Officer, a Connor Turner, visited an Irish Manor hotel several times over the past year. And there was suggestion in the local papers that The Manor was to be sold off to a US consortium who wanted to develop the facilities, including the local golf course. It ran in the recent editions but nothing on their website."

Pierre nodded in agreement. "That Irish Manor is at the centre of something and lots of it link to all of the investigations we are involved in. We need to get greater visibility."

"Irish connection, organised crime and a luxury manor. Then add a US connection, people trafficking, medical records and Roz attacked." He paused for a moment.

The Estonian? An all-too-easy operations at the Ranch. One where they were happy to destroy everything. Every path seems to lead to or have some fall back to Croatia years ago. *It makes no sense,* thought Abernethy as he headed for the exit.

He needed fresh air. He needed a walk. He needed thinking time and he needed a beer.

Chapter 10
Ghost

The present day.

She sat and reflected for a moment. A faint smile appeared on her face as the good memories pushed their way to the front of her mind.

She saw her two brothers again. Her two younger brothers refusing to come inside for their one hot meal of the day. She remembered how this day they smiled and laughed and ran as her mother chased them around the street outside.

Everyone was laughing and smiling.

This day was a good day. She watched her brothers evade their mother, wishing to play longer in the sunshine. Going inside for the daily meal meant the end of play, it meant the end of the sunshine and it meant soon to sleep. As much sleep as the noise would allow.

Going inside meant it was nearing the time when the sniper came out. The darkening sky was his playground and his rules. Everyone was a player in his game of life and death. A game with no rules. A game where a child was as big a target as a man.

She sat back and focused on the sunshine and her brothers laughing and running around their small house. It was her memory, and she knew this, but did not want it to stop. This moment was her own good place to be.

2018.

The mosque was now blocking the street to anything but heavy government armoured vehicles. Built on the side of the square four hundred yards from their house, it was now rubble with only the Midrib in one piece but instead of towering above the worshippers' homes, it lay pitifully on the road separated from the rest of the broken structure.

By day, the children played among and around the broken playground that was this town's main mosque. By night, it became a more sinister place to exist. It would become the temporary home of the 'sniper of Aleppo'.

He would chamber his rifle and focus his skill on the target of whoever paid him the most. No one had ever seen this ghost killer. Most believed the ghost to be a man for no woman could do what he did. His actions were against all that was womanhood, all that was being a mother and all that was being a loving human being.

The sniper of Aleppo targeted anyone of any age without mercy. The cross hairs allowed him the freedom from direct sight of his actions. The accuracy of his weapon meant he was too far away to see the damage his released 'ball' 7.62mm (short) would do to a child's still developing skull or the frail and arthritic bones of an elder moments too late in reaching the sanctity of home.

They knew spring had arrived. The sun came up a little earlier and the birds sang their happy songs but what day it was, they didn't know. Each day was the same as the last. There was no school. Destroyed by government barrel bombs. There was no family gathering at mealtime.

They were either dead, hiding or had escaped the hell that was Aleppo.

Either way, the wider family were all in effect, dead to the two younger boys. They did not comprehend that they would never see their cousins or grandparents ever again so it was not worth asking anymore. Nobody knew when this would be over.

It didn't matter to anyone but today was Tuesday. It was also to be the end day.

She helped her mother in the kitchen prepare the bread and cook the beans. They had a few small bottles of herbs and one of paste so getting the right mix into the beans made her younger brothers believe they were getting something different each day.

Her mother hummed her a song passed down from grandparents and soon the kitchen sounded out the sound of harmony. For a short moment in time, it was a happy place. Living as they did in Aleppo, they had only moments of happiness but never complained. They would exploit these moments fully, not knowing if another would follow.

She stopped for just a moment and looked out the small window above the sink. The window next to a circular hole in the wall where a bullet had once ricocheted and penetrated the wall, luckily not hitting anyone inside. The hole served a reminder of the constant danger they faced.

The sun was getting low but it was not yet nearing the danger hour. That period of transition between relative safety in the streets and the anxiety everyone felt about whether the sniper had arrived yet.

"We need to get the boys in soon," she said to her mother.

Her words were received with a nod. Both women then went back to their task at hand and the preparation of that day's one hot meal.

The two boys were special. With the loss of their father on an unknown battlefield, they alone had the future task of providing for their mother in her later years. It was the traditional way and without this option, there was little hope for the elderly living alone in Aleppo.

The bread was readied and placed into the small cave-like oven while the dried beans were taken out of the soaking water and placed now into a pan of hot salted water. They would eat soon.

Both women would hear the sound of the 'crack'. Both women would momentarily stop what they were doing to help them focus on what it could have been, but it would take the screams of her middle child before the mother realised something very bad had happened just outside.

The chair fell to the floor as she quickly rose and, pushing past her daughter, moved as quickly as she could towards the street door.

She was met at the door by the screaming and crying and utterly confused youngest son. His face and upper clothing was covered in blood and more. He could not find the words. His mother would not listen anyway. He tried to drag her towards the mess a few yards away that was once his smiling elder brother.

She tried to push him inside but did not do a good enough job.

A second pop. Then a third.

There were screams coming from nearby windows and her neighbours pleaded with her to leave her dead child and get the youngest inside.

The young girl rushed to the door in time to see her mother fall to her knees, grasping the limp bloodied body of her brother. She froze. She did not feel the warm liquid trickle down her legs as she lost control of her bladder. She just saw something so horrible, it could never be unseen. The sight of a child, a family member, a loved one, with pieces of skull and face missing, replaced now with the dirt and mud and rubble which he would not know.

He had died without awareness.

The action of an accurate sniper.

She collapsed just inside the door.

It was to save her life.

She would not see what happened next.

A door flew open across the street and a neighbour rushed out towards the tormented mother quivering over the pieces of her son's body. He held a makeshift shield of corrugated iron in his hand covering himself and reaching the mother and did the same with her. He grabbed at her long hair and forcibly dragged her back up to her feet. In that moment, he knew persuasion and kindness would not save her or him. Time was not on their side.

In a state of near delirium, she stumbled her way towards the rescuer's doorway and pushing her inside first, he followed quickly behind.

He looked at the mother and let out a breath of sheer relief.

Then panic.

The other boy.

Turning to look back out of the door towards the youngest child, his face fell.

He would have to go back out. He was ready to do so.

Pop.

Why it had happened now and not when he was dragging the mother he could analyse later. For now, he saw his reason not to return back out into the firing line.

The young child's head exploded.

Smaller than his elder brother's, the ball round cut his head in half and parts fell away quicker than the small body could fall to the ground taken by gravity.

It was too late.

The 'ghost' had struck again with no conscience and with no regard to age. It was the world they lived in. Where life was fucked up at the best of times. A good day was one in which your heart was still beating when you slept that night. It was truly a fucked-up part of the world.

The present day.

She smiled as she remembered her two brothers playing and the sounds of young mischievous kids being naughty. This was a good memory. It was what she wanted to remember.

For now, as she opened her eyes and took in the sights and sounds of her environment, she came back to her reality. It was a type of freedom from her village, but she needed more. She needed to have a life and live it fully as if her whole family were with her. To do this, she needed to get to the promised lands of Europe.

She was alone with no friends in a refugee camp, having fled war. Now waiting on the promise of transport out of this different hell, on a bus to Europe and the chance of a new start and new hope.

Almeda had heard many good things about the tall Estonian, and word was that he was coming to the camp that day and would be taking some of them to a new start in lorries with water and food.

Almeda was determined to be noticed.

She would make him see her and want to take her.

She would not know that this was the worst route she could possibly take, but she would not stop this day until she was on the lorry out of the camp.

Chapter 11
A Manor of Reporting

Present day.

He walked the main street. The same street he had walked many times as a boy, but it was much different now. Sure, retail chains had taken the space where previously stand-alone locally owned shops once stood, but it was now much different.

Today, because of the economic downturn caused by the virus pandemic a few months earlier, this same high street was void of people, shoppers, and open doors. Charity shops and some off-licences struggled to fill the gaps, but the reality was that the virus had killed more than just the ill and elderly inhabitants. It had stolen the 'life' of the whole community.

Still, this was no moment to dwell. Instead, it was possibly a moment of hope. Hope that perhaps this day, and, if his energy banks allowed, this night, he would get 'that' shot. That click of the camera that would prove his theory and would make the national press sit up and take notice of him. It would also make him rich if he got it right. Yes, hope existed in him, even it did not any longer on this high street or the wider community.

When Davison reached the perimeter wall, they already knew he was at the wall. When he scaled it and dropped over into the grounds, they knew already he was on their property. When he sneaked to the same clump of overgrown bushes and hedges and settled in for the long haul, they also knew where he was, what he was doing and when he would likely leave to return home.

They also knew where 'home' was.

Every square inch of the manor grounds was covered by both sophisticated CCTV, and hidden portable devices. Pressure pads lay strategically around key locations just out of sight under the surface. No one was getting in or out unless the authorities sanctioned it.

This manor house hotel was not your normal hotel. It was why Davison suspected something was not right and why he would do his pilgrimage each day to try to capture the evidence, without knowing he was also risking his life each time in doing so.

He would sit and periodically move position to avoid cramps but try hard to stay within his chosen two square metre domain where he assumed he was invisible to the occasional sharply dressed man that would walk the lawns and stop, light a cigarette, and then move on. Clearly, Davison was spotted each and every time the patrol went for a moment's relaxation, but they had decided it best to know where he was and control what he saw than, at this time anyway, expose him and drive him into a possible more secretive location unknown to any in the hotel or have to deal with him and worry about the consequences.

It had been a quiet, windless day until it approached.

Right, game on, he thought, as Davison first heard the sound of the helicopter, and then caught sight of it, coming over the Irish hillside towards him and he hoped, to this hotel like many others had done so before.

Camera check time.

Then full sight of it.

It looked like the same blue and gold Sikosky S76 helicopter he had seen before but could not be certain. It had no tail markings, as if it were unregistered to anyone or any company.

He hunkered down knowing that the down draft from the helicopter's blades would move the tree branches and bushes and had the potential to expose him. In this position, he could not see the signaller look over to his position. A gesture was made to the pilot to hover a bit longer. Had he seen this, perhaps Davison would have known that they were playing with him and that his cover was blown. But he didn't notice anything amiss.

He remained in a crouched position and waited close enough to see people numbers and movement, too far for detail, and even with a camera zoom, in a situation where the glint of glass or push of the draft may make the click of the photograph worthless.

The downdraft eased somewhat and the trees returned mostly to the full upright position despite the blades continuing to whizz dangerously fast.

As he was now, once again, more safely concealed, he decided to risk the long lens camera. The helicopter door was open and stairs were down but he was sure no one of interest had yet exited.

The security personnel continued their usual routine. This was an anxious time for all, an exposed time for security and patient, and, while they knew

Davison was around and controlled and not an issue, they feared more lethal interference at any moment. Perhaps from an enemy of the newly arrived guest, or worse, a forceful movement of British special forces disguised as local Garda.

Then, a tall man emerged from the helicopter, walking backwards down the three steps and onto the pristine grass lawn. He reached into the open door of the helicopter and lifted two handles of a stretcher, walking slowly backwards, he was followed seconds later by a second man holding the other end.

Davison reached for his camera and raised it without thought for the sun's location in the sky and any reflection the lens may reveal and pointed it towards the elderly man on the stretcher.

The camera self-focused and all he had to do was aim and press, right? He had no idea if he was getting face or body or even if the self-focusing lens was in fact focusing through the wind of the blades and his body movement.

His camera clicked and whizzed into action. Picture after picture taken and stored on the digital memory. He had brought a cloth which was supposed to dampen down the already quiet noise of the camera but in his rush he had forgotten to wrap it around the cameras operating mechanism.

When he realised this, he shrugged it off. He was busy.

I am too far away anyway, and the helicopters blades are still making a noise as they wait, he thought.

The recent admission to the Manor House Hotel was taken inside, and the pilot was instructed to power up and leave the area. This he would do while Davison quickly scanned the digital images to ensure quality and to see if any head shots could be used with his home face recognition software. It was difficult to determine quality. It would have to wait until he got back.

Who are you, my elderly friend? He thought. *Am I to be lucky this time and hit the jackpot? Why, when everything else is closed or struggling because of the ongoing effects of the Corona Virus, does this place prosper? Why do privately chartered helicopters with foreign looking admissions come here on an almost weekly basis?* He thought, as he tidied his camera away and prepared to attempt to return his hiding place to its previous condition. No twigs broken, the mud and dust smoothed over, no boot prints left. Once he happy with his efforts, off he left out into the early evening sunshine and the shadows across the lawn made by the very old and established oak trees. Back towards his usual perimeter wall locations and back to his flat to review this day's work, off sight from the CCTV.

Fingers crossed, he would think.

Fredrick Hofmann was coming to the end of a full 'shift' in theatre and he was already visualising that cold alcoholic drink and the spa pool in the hotel as he injected a mild sedative and pain killer into the woman lying in a small pool of blood in front of him.

"Fucking knackered, fucking knackered I am," he said out loud to anyone who was in earshot of his improving English, but still with a slight German twang.

He looked down at her on the surgical table.

"So, my pretty young lady friend, I am sure you will be fine, for a while at least. You need to be. You're young enough to get by on one kidney so let's hope it takes in the Russian's wife for, if not my dear, I come back for the other to try again. Then, it may be trickier for you to see the light of another day again anytime soon."

He wasn't really talking to her as much as semi-hallucinating out of fatigue and weariness. She could not hear him. She would not have wanted to hear his voice anyway. She had fled Syria weeks earlier, spending time in a refugee camp before her natural beauty caught the eye of the Estonian and was 'luckily' added to his list last minute. Now, Almeda was in a deep state of induced sleep but not in a place of safety.

Leaving the operating theatre to clean up, he acknowledged his assistant and implied that she was to clear up the mess by gesturing to the sleeping victim and then back to the nurse. She would duly have obliged as she had done way too many times now to remember.

Hofmann patted the large and slightly overweight guard on the shoulder as he left the scrubs area and walked the short distance to the elevator. When it came, he entered and pressed floor two and on exiting, walked the slightly longer route to the annex. From there, he climbed the few stairs and entered one of only two rooms on the large and recently modernised extension to the Manor Hotel property.

"Fuck, phew. Really need to stop saying fuck when no one's around," he said again out loud. He was tired.

He used his left foot to push off his shoe and reversed the manoeuvre for the remaining one. Walking over to the sofa, he collapsed onto it.

"Fuck, drink first," he said again but this time to himself.

His tired muscles lifted his body upwards as instructed and over to the well-stocked bar by the kitchen island.

He lifted the bottle of German gin that he regularly had shipped in and poured a larger than normal measure.

Ah, my lovely friend, Duke Gin, how we have enjoyed our chats over the last few weeks, he thought as a couple of ice cubes and slim line tonic entered the large measure with a splash. He insisted on a large supply of the hotel's slim line tonic despite the weight piling on him. He would not use the very well-equipped gym instead believing that an active mind was exercise enough.

Falling back down onto the large and accommodating sofa, TV remote and room telephone nearby, Fredrick Hofmann was settled for the night. Soon enough, he would pour his second, then his third and fourth large gin. He would order quick snack food to be delivered to his very grand room and then start flicking through the channels until he found the adult channel that would entertain him long enough until he fell asleep where he lay. For, soon enough, he would yet again spend most of his next day in blood, in organ removal and organ replacement. He would only know which it was to be when he made his early morning rounds of the clients, the rich and the influential together with the pitiful and enforced body part donors.

Now, he would fall into a different world of sleep and dream and visualise the money raining down on him as it had done for many years now.

He was a very wealthy man, and it was this money that allowed him to keep an element of sanity.

What Aston Martin to buy next? What high end escort to fly over from Poland to entertain him, and what luxury yacht to charter next when he was allowed that magical three-week break? Yes, he thought, *a three week break soon and where to go?*

Hofmann slept well that evening.

His nursing team cleaned up his mess and treated the latest victim as best they could. Like Hofmann, they had been turned by McCann's money. His money, and the threat that they did as was asked or their families would suffer. They chose to focus on the money and do as they were asked. All sense of right and medical integrity had long gone.

When he would arrive early next morning, the theatre would again be spotless clean and awaiting his next insertion and his next rather clumsy cut and downing of the patients' blood onto the white tiled floor.

When this was done, when the walls and floor shone white and dazzled, they would take turn to sit with her. To sit with she who struggled for life minus one

127

kidney, doing what needed to be done so she stayed alive until the next day. It was always about 'the next day' and 'the next procedure'. Would it be kidney two and game over or would she have the luxury of a form of existence for a while longer being drip fed life through a number of tubes and runners entering orifices and exiting pre-arranged wounds.

Existence of a sort it was.

None of those in the holding room would voluntarily choose this. All would choose the mercies of death. Hofmann, but mostly, McCann took that choice from them.

The 'holding room' was behind closed doors, only a few key staff were allowed in, but it was staffed 24/7 by medical staff brought as refugees, smuggled through the same networks as those lying there, partially dissected, waiting to lose that final organ that would finish them off.

Until then, they were wired up to a variety of the latest machines; dialysis, heart/lung, and monitors for everything, all in a form of suspended animation. It was a cold room, and not just because the temperature was kept cold, but because of the horrors that it contained. One doctor and two nurses at all times, keeping the machines working, the bodies sedated, the wounds clean. Hofmann called it his special 'kuhlschrank'. The sign on the door said 'Ward seven' but Hofmann had written on the whiteboard under it 'Ersatzteillager' (Parts Store); it was his little joke.

It was Tuesday, and the sun struggled to shine across the Irish hillside this time of year but try it did all the same. The birds sang and occasionally there would be the sound of tractors or similar farmyard machinery.

Tuesdays were important in the Manor House Hotel. Hofmann looked forward to Tuesdays and would often have that extra gin or that extra attempt with the prostitute the night before. He knew it was the planning meeting and he knew McCann started these later than he started his 'surgeries'.

It had been many years since Brendan McCann had visited his 'friend' Drako in Serbia, and sometimes he wondered what happened to him. Sometimes, he wondered who the 'sad fuck' was that died so he, McCann, could live. He held his side and felt the wound.

Mostly, however, McCann just didn't care.

It was Tuesday, and it was planning day. In the hotel's conference room were his closest security guards, his full-time nurse Sarah, and of course, his reassurance package Fredrick Hofmann.

Further around the long oval oak table was a collection of shady characters. McCann himself called them the shadow mob.

There was a problem.

A number of 'contracts' had been signed and yet no match had been found, never mind prepared. Worse still, money had exchanged hands and some of the backup donors had inconveniently died of respiratory issues. Worse was to come.

"Right, listen up. We have lost two fucks to some bloody coughing bug and now two others are coming down with this fucking cold or flu thing. This is a bloody hospital, isn't it? They should not be dying here unless I wish it. Right?" Demanded McCann. "So, what's going on?"

He looked slowly around the room. The shadow mob heads lowered slightly. None wanted to speak first, unsure of what type of response would come back their way.

Most remembered the time when a small communication slipup three years back had brought the worst out in McCann. The Royal Ulster Constabulary, also known on this occasion, to actually be the British Special Air Service, had pounced upon an intercept and after killing three carriers recovered a lorry load of munitions and explosives. The next day at the next team meeting, 'Irish Scottie' was shot dead right in front of some of them.

McCann liked his big gestures. He liked that they remember the failure and his anger.

He had once stabbed his then-closest associate in the eye in front of others, after he had admitted a minor security slipup and McCann then boasted proudly that if this is what he could do to his friends, imagine what he can do to his enemies.

He stopped his glare at Hofmann. It was obvious that the doctor takes the initial rap but he was not fazed. Hofmann knew he was invincible.

"Look boss, ask the others. I have no idea. I deal with what's put in front of me, on the table not what happens before or after," he said in a slightly arrogant manner. He knew there would be no gun raised on him from under the table. He was far too profitable a commodity.

"Boss," said his number two, Paddy Richards, "we need to be considered here."

Richards was a beast of a man. Once an all-Irish power lifter, he still commanded an audience despite being well into his sixties.

"Boss, it's the virus thing, must be. Some fuckers brought it in and now those weak lot in the basement are catching it. There was something on the news about a Chinese virus. Likely, they all have it and we're fucked for a quick fix," he concluded.

"Right, Paddy, and?" Came back his way from a slightly more calm McCann.

Richards and McCann shared everything. Their bond was too strong. Their joint pasts cemented this bond of 'brothers' and only he could openly challenge Brendon McCann without his metabolism sparking up a faster heartbeat or an adrenalin rush pending the worst.

"Well, Brendon, we need to consider those fucks still alive down there in Ward seven as now dead. We can't risk putting some infected shit into one of the guests. We can't risk a failure other than the surgical route not some outside crap."

"So..." interrupted McCann.

"So, Brendon," as he looked back towards the others across the table, "so, we get more fucking replacements and do it fast!" Richards barked out.

McCann stood and as he did so, his chair fell backward with the violent motion. As he walked to the door he turned to his friend.

"Contact the Estonian," and with that he left the room.

When the door closed, there was a moment's silence and reflection.

No one actually knew the 'Estonian's name or perhaps McCann did, but in his line of work, it was perhaps best not to say too much about him.

Now, it was Richard's turn to stand and prepare to leave the meeting.

"Fredrick, get on with your day. There remains one task to finish that we know isn't infected, and you lot, we still have one new task. Get this place sorted, get it cleaned and ready," as he pointed to O'Connell.

He went on addressing the others but still directing O'Connell.

"Get the boys ready. Don't mess this up and be ready to move quickly when he delivers. I will call the Estonian now."

Silence once more descended over the remaining members of the meeting as the door closed behind him.

Hofmann stood up and grabbing his now cold coffee, summoned the two nurses, and headed out to prepare for the only surgical procedure of the day.

The room would be empty a few minutes later as each would go about their tasking. None would leave any stone unturned. If they feared McCann, they also feared the Estonian and rumours were abounding of his weapon of choice being a meat cleaver. They could not expect protection from McCann, if the Estonian had reason to use it against them.

The shadow mob would be ready for his arrival. He always delivered despite being on the radar of Europol, the Five Eyes community, and worse for him still, The Committee. That aside, he always seemed to deliver and then disappear into thin air.

Thirty minutes had passed since Richards had left the room. McCann had already been informed about the conversation he had had.

Richards went into the hotel kitchen where he knew most of his team would be, likely pilfering the fridges of finest Scottish salmon or expensive Russian caviar destined for the hotel's demanding guests.

"Right, he's on. Arrival in twelve hours so listen no sleep tonight. None until after delivery. Do we understand?"

The now less hungry members nodded, and Richards left.

It was a hot and windy day in the Turkish migrant camp. Even the wind threw up hot dust and sand into the makeshift tents that thousands called home. Thousands of fleeing refugees from all over Asia and Africa who had descended upon this holy grail, this gateway to a new life. More and more piled into the cramped and guarded enclosures every hour. There was very little running water and what was available was both shared amongst hundreds and at best caused only mild illness in children and the weak.

The volunteer charity doctors and nurses tried as well as was humanly possible to care for the sick and the elderly but with the world turning a blind eye on their plight; equipment and supplies were scarce. However, there was always hope when a truck arrived. Often a truck with the blue insignia of the United Nations across it but mostly the camp came alive when the Estonian turned up, with his many trucks full of rations and bottled water, sometimes medicines, sometimes surgical gowns. The migrants and the doctors would feel a small sense of relief.

The doctors would get equipment with which to use on the ill and the migrants would hope that he chose them to be transported to the new life somewhere in Europe. This leader of men came at will and chose whom he wanted to go with him towards the hope and promise of a better existence. That none ever returned to the camp was evidence enough to others that he was indeed a saviour.

The charity workers knew he trafficked people across international boundaries did not bother anyone. He was providing them hope and a new beginning. Something they themselves tried but rarely achieved. They did not suspect that these movements of people were for a far more sinister reason.

"There, there and you, over there," he bellowed. The other drivers followed his direction instantly and after parking up where they were told, started immediately to unload supplies from the back of the lorries.

"We must be efficient. After all, our friends in London have helped us to get here by granting us transportation contracts. Now we must honour this and move our precious cargo as quickly as we can," he said with a smile that oozed illegality and sarcasm.

The camp became alive with movement and noise.

Young children ran all around the lorries and his off-road vehicle, shouting and clapping and some laughing. This was a treat. This was their week's highlight and it might just get better if he had chocolate for them. He would often have chocolate for the younger ones.

He would not let them down this visit.

Reaching into the glove compartment of his vehicle, he took out several very large bars of chocolate and shouting for them to share, threw them away from where he stood so the children would leave him and allow him to start the purpose of his visit.

He walked towards the camp's command centre. He knew exactly where it was and who he wanted to speak with.

Some strangers may fear walking alone without a weapon, through the tents and dusty establishments. These were desperate people, in desperate times. But not him. Not the Estonian. He was the 'bringer of life' or, so they were told. Rumours were abounding within the camp that he and only he could get the eldest son or daughter into safe haven in Europe where they could then work and send money back to their family. He had 'connections' and he was both trusted and given safe passage wherever he walked in the camp.

Walking up to the main building, he brushed the dust curtain aside and as if he owned the place, he strode briskly inside.

"Where is my French friend?" he said calmly to the nurses and administration staff inside. "I wish to meet with her right away."

Despite the smile on his face, everyone knew that they had been given a firm instruction. He was not smiling inside. The instruction was one that must be actioned and resolved promptly before the smile changed to something other than friendly in appearance.

He walked through and into the back of the building as if he owned the place.

"French lady, where is my beautiful French lady friend? I wish to speak with her now. I am busy and will wish to leave here very soon," said the large Estonian man, now dominating the environment.

When he walked back to the front again, he looked at those at tables and desks for an answer to his question.

"Someone has gone to find her, Sir," came from one of the nurses. She didn't know what to call him. None did. No one actually knew his name just that he was the 'kind Estonian' but all still feared him at the same time.

He walked over to her and placed his large hand on her head as she sat.

"That's good. And how long do you think it will take to find her?"

He would not wait long.

"Bonjour, bonjour, sorry I was with an ill man but have left him for you, my friend," she said slightly out of breath from her fifty-yard sprint to the main office building.

"Ah ha, my pretty French lady is here. Good for you. Good for me, in fact good for everyone this day. Come, let's go somewhere private. I have a new list and you will find me these people now."

Without waiting for any acceptance, he firmly led her back to the rear of the building where from memory, he thought she kept records of all the migrants age, place of origin and basic medical records.

The others watched until they disappeared out of sight and then, now anxious, returned to their duties and actions.

She was indeed very beautiful. He had not lied about that part. Natalie Delphine had been chief medical administrator at the camp for over a year now, and, at times had to support the doctors when more than usual ill migrants came to their attention.

"So, my Natalie, what have you done since my last visit?"

It was a very strange question to ask someone stuck inside the wire of a guarded migrant camp, but she answered all the same.

"Well, I have treated patients, conducted medicals and of course, wondered what lovely lives those who left with you last time are now having in Europe."

She chose her words carefully but really wanted to ask him the detail.

Where were they? Did they actually have jobs? Were they in fact alive and OK? But that stayed in her mind never reaching her mouth.

"Yes, enough already. Thank you, my little French friend. Business, for I am busy. Let's please now look at the registers. I have many jobs waiting for the right people. Helping many people now it's a busy time, French," he said now getting a little irritated at the possibility of not having the right candidates available. The waiting to find out was less than comfortable for either of them.

He reached into his jacket pockets and pulled out a neatly folded piece of paper.

Delphine stared at him. There was a look of shock or surprise on her face at this 'shopping list' of people, but if he noticed it, he ignored it.

She lowered her head and waited on him to speak.

Does he think this to be a supermarket? But her thoughts were interrupted abruptly when he placed a second firm hand on her small frame and encouraged her to sit straight in front of the only computer in the back-office room.

"OK, I need eight people. Eight specific people, two women and six men. I have places and roles ready for them, but they have to be in good shape and all under thirty years old. The work can be a little tiring you see," and so the Estonian started his demands and she typed and searched as he did so.

It was unnerving work for her and yet she felt obliged to continue. She had to believe he was giving these helpless migrants a second chance at life.

Nearly an hour passed and all this time, the Estonian stood over her watching her keystrokes and looking up to the monitor. He had what he needed.

It would take only one further hour before they were rounded up and secured in the now empty and prepared lorries. Most of the eight were orphaned at an early age so had no family to say goodbye to. They had very little in way of possessions to gather up either.

The Estonian sat in his car with the engine running and sent a message. He let McCann know he was en route with gifts.

The sun was at its highest and hottest when both trucks were ready to set out with their new cargo.

There was no celebratory cheering now. The children were back inside their makeshift accommodation waiting on the next day and something to happen, anything.

Satellites from the National Geographic Intelligence Centre (NGIC) feeding into the CIA, MI6 and GCHQ were ready and waiting to track the Estonian and the two large trucks. They had followed the vehicles move into the camp and seen the hustle and bustle of the children surrounding the target. They had also seen the rushed movement of a small group into the lorries.

Europol was readied to act on human intelligence of HUMINT from one of their agencies who reported first and intercepted the target.

The Estonian stepped behind the wheel of his SUV and set off. He knew that people wanted to find him. He even knew that they were very likely watching him from many miles up in space, however, in a relaxed and uncaring mood, he started the ignition and set off.

When to let Irish know what we have, he wondered.

Back at the Manor Hotel, plans were likewise beginning. Just under eleven hours until the Estonian would rescue the paid contracts and their credibility with the new arriving paid 'guests'.

Inside a secure bunker-like complex, hidden in plain sight from prying eyes behind a graffiti wall and rusted metal door, Abernethy stood and watched the many monitors around the room. The Geneva complex was well-hidden. Their activities were also well-hidden.

He knew that the Estonian had his new cargo and that the world's two greatest secret services were monitoring the shipment. Despite this, he still felt very uneasy. He was too far away this time to help directly. He did not know the shipments' final destination yet nor its likely route to get there. Neither did he know what the Estonian had ready this time, to get past Europol, but he did know the Estonian had something and was not simply moving his live cargo direct. Abernethy felt very uneasy, and he didn't like it. Not one bit.

Thirty minutes into the journey, he picked up his secure Encrochat phone and moments later the triple encoded message was being read by McCann.

He then sent a second and third and separate fourth message one after the other two sources in his contact list named simply Q7-1, Q7-2 and Q5.

When the read receipts were returned to the Estonian's phone, he put it away and continued on towards the first rendezvous spot.

Hofmann slept. He slept lots for he knew he would be busy soon enough. No expensive prostitutes or fancy red wine or gin. He knew he had his make-or-break moment hours away, so he had decided to sleep and recover fully from his fatigue.

During this nervous time, McCann and Richards spoke often. They spoke with the guests and the guest's representatives many times, reassuring and promising and appeasing. It was a tricky time for them but not for Drako. He was aware of the issues, but he had no anxiety. He had his anonymity assured should things go wrong and, more importantly, he had his money already.

Davison had tried to return to the Manor Hotel but changed his mind and left his investigation temporarily when he saw the increased presence of men in dark suits with sunglasses on. This was Ireland, late Autumn. It was rarely sunny enough for glasses, certainly not this day, so he knew they were not guests or staff and but instead types he should mix with.

A short while and a couple of bribes at check points later, one black SUV, shadowed closely by two old trucks were seen from high in the sky crossing into Bulgaria. It would not be too long before they would reach North Macedonia and then into Albania where the next phase of the journey would start.

Tracking became a little harder in Macedonia.

A number of black SUVs appeared on the motorway at what the analysts thought was the same junction at the same time. Abernethy picked up on this immediately.

"Here we go, people. This is his move. He has thrown in decoys. Eyes wide. Do not lose him or the trucks," he shouted.

A moment later and his attention now drawn to the trucks, he continued, "and those bloody trucks." He paused. "Don't let them disappear into thin air, people. He is one of the hardest men you have ever tracked, and he already has two hours' head start on us. He will play every trick so be better than him!"

The game of cat and mouse went on for a while.

All through North Macedonia, the trucks would dance between a different black Toyota SUV all of which were driving at the same speed switching lanes periodically.

Reaching the border with Kosovo, too quickly for authorities to put a legitimate blockade up, they started the game all over again into Kosovo and driving along the southern route towards Albania. The routes were so small, too many tunnels, it would be impossible to keep track of them and it was likely they had paid off helpers along the route. His euros were valued highly here.

Abernethy was worried. *They must know, they must,* he thought.

He was referring to the CIA and MI6 and the Estonian's direction of travel. Once they crossed the border near Kukes, it was only two hours to Tirana where they could get lost easily in the criminal underground. *Hell, we could lose them in the tunnels in Kosovo long before we even get to Albania,* he thought, remembering the route he had driven many times before.

The Estonian also knew this. He had planned it to be this way.

He loved this phone, it was a special device from a firm called Encrochat, it looked like any other phone but was totally secure. Looking in his rear-view mirror, he was pleased to see the two lorries still close by. A glance at the three other black SUVs close around him, he made the call.

The call was answered by a woman with a strong Northern Albanian Gheg accent to her softer feminine tone.

There was a short conversation and without any pleasantries, it was ended.

The tunnels were close.

The Estonian gave a hand signal to the closest SUV and almost immediately the car moved off in an opposing direction. Simultaneously, upon sight of the first movement, the second, third, then the rest of the black SUVs slowed, sped up or changed direction in a pre-arranged dance-like formation.

The road tunnels just across the Kosovan border were much closer now.

Into them went the Estonian, and, seconds later one decoy black SUV. Two further SUVs followed a little behind. Seconds after that, the two trucks entered. Two further black SUVs then slowed the following traffic a little until they blocked the whole dual carriageway. None of the affected cars would sound their horn or driver exit their vehicles. This was Kosovo and despite the NATO and EU presence, criminal gangs ran the country in any way they pleased.

When it happened, it was with military precision.

He had done this before in cities all around the Balkans and it just happened to be Tirana's turn this time.

Just inside the tunnel, he stopped his black SUV and stepped into the waiting blue Audi Q5.

Within thirty seconds, he was on the move again, slightly faster than before to make some time up for the tunnel exit and the likely waiting eyes in the sky. They would have monitored the speed of the vehicles and know the length of the tunnel. They would also know when vehicles were due to exit the other side.

His black SUV started up and its new driver went off at a leisurely pace soon after.

The trucks would prove a little harder to coordinate, however. They also stopped inside the tunnel at the designated spot and the drivers hurried their cargo out at speed and in around sixty seconds, both trucks were empty and new vehicles were on the move once more. Now, however, the migrant cargo was traveling in two Audi Q7 vehicles. One white and one dark blue and which had stopped minutes earlier untracked, inside the tunnel to wait. Both would exit the tunnel and go down different roads to avoid suspicion. In time, they would meet up once again at the next agreed location.

The trucks would leave the tunnel and together go a third route taking them nowhere in particular and in doing so, simply drive until stopped by Europol officers.

The SUVs at the tunnel entrance moved off. Their engines suddenly fixed and the flow of traffic into the tunnel resumed as normal once again.

Abernethy suspected something was going very wrong with their operation. There was nothing specific that told him this but all the same, instinct had kicked in very hard. He wanted to take the monitoring off the trucks. He felt they were a decoy. He felt that they had taken too long getting through the tunnel, but he had no idea what to switch the watching to and he knew that the command wouldn't agree to his hunch.

For now, the three vehicles went their separate way. The migrant cargo would sit patiently and quietly. They did not know where they were destined for but as long as it was not a sandy and dusty hot camp with little food and water, they were happy to wait.

The Estonian made a call from the bluetooth in the car. It rang out for a few seconds.

"Yes?"

"It is me," he said.

"Who?" came back over the car's speaker system.

He would change his mobile phone every operation so was not surprised that his contact was a little reluctant to open up just yet.

"I have the cargo en route and arrival of the shipment to you is in three hours. Will you be ready?"

He did not want to be too specific either. Neither the Estonian or his contact suspected that their calls were or could be intercepted but both men knew that it was best to be nonspecific all the same.

"They are expecting the plane to arrive in five. We will be perhaps six more hours to you. Will you be ready?" he said once again. This time giving just a little more information to reinforce his legitimacy.

The contact knew the flight to Ireland would be around four hours from take-off, so he felt a little more at ease now with this additional confirmation.

"We will be ready, my friend. Call when you are closer, almost to us," and with that, the car fell silent. The Estonian looked down at his phone then back at the road ahead. A smile came across his face.

He wanted to call McCann but decided it was safer to wait until they reached the plane at Tirana Airport, the cargo terminal. He knew no questions would be asked.

His phone received a second text. This one was via the encrypted app Telegram. The Estonian needed to slow and apply the two-factor authentication to get access to the message. He knew it was from his source in Whitehall. He only used the app for his communications.

It read; 'Suspect heightened awareness from watchers. Still to receive benefit. Timescale for receipt?'

It was not signed and the number, once stored in his phone, did not show on the screen either but he knew it was from his London source all the same.

Getting greedy, my friend? Impatient? He thought to himself.

Back in Ireland

Davison sat in his flat and wondered why there had been no new arrivals at the Manor House Hotel recently. He had biked up to the entrance a few times and walked the public paths close to its grounds, but no helicopters flew in and no escorted large cars drove up the drive. It was almost like it was closed.

Why so many men in suits wandering around if the place has no or few guests at the moment? He thought. *What am I missing,* and with this moment of reflection he sprang up and went into his office to review the dozens and dozens of photographs he had taken over the last few days.

"So, matey boy, what have you missed? There must be something," he said out loud. As he retrieved the carefully catalogued digital photographs from his PC to review, he looked around.

"Alexa, play RTE Two."

"Here's RTE Two," came back in a feminine voice.

The music started in the background.

He spent the next hour scrolling through the pictures of private helicopters on the lawn, the many faces that came and went, trying to concentrate on those faces that appeared in pain or weak and ill. This was the missing piece to his puzzle and as of yet he had not found any clues to who they were and why they came to this specific hotel.

As Alexa played music and radio chat in the background, Davison stopped only to get a second or third coffee from his small kitchen.

Approaching lunchtime, Davison's stomach rumbled, and it talked to him requesting his fullest attention.

Lunch, have I got anything in?

Reviewing the contents of his fridge, he decided a short walk to the local coffee shop was in order. Picking up his wallet and keys he closed the door behind him and bounced the few steps down to the street.

"Hey Steve," said the lady behind the counter as he walked into the shop.

"Hi Petra, brilliant day for it, isn't it?" he replied.

She never knew what 'it' was but also never asked.

"Your usual?" she said.

"Yup, and this please," as he placed a large sandwich on the glass counter.

"Right," came across the counter as she turned to start to make his latte.

Davison stood by the counter and looked around. The shop had a selection of pastries and cakes behind the glass counter and up on the wall was coffee in tins on shelves from what looked like every continent of the world.

The walls were also adorned with colourful images of food and drink products. He skimmed the surroundings while he waited. He liked Petra but had nothing other than his coffee order to say to break the ice, so instead, he idly looked around the shop.

Something happened this day that had never happened before.

His eyes had seen it many times before but perhaps not straight after spending a while looking through photographs of people he had snapped arriving at the hotel. This time, he saw something else in one of the images.

Franzese was shown in the image as a luxury hot chocolate make. There and then, Davison knew it as something else. Indeed, someone else.

"Franzese!" he exclaimed. "That's it, I have seen Franzese!"

Petra turned around a little puzzled. *Why is he claiming to have seen hot chocolate,* she thought as she smiled at him. *Bit daft, but hey its hot outside,* as she turned back to finish the coffee.

"John Franzese Senior."

There was a pause. A second customer had walked into the shop and she was also puzzling over why this man had said his full name out loud.

"Sonny Franzese!" exclaimed Davison. "The man in the wheelchair. The one on my office table, the one I saw, of course," he went on.

None of this made sense to the two others but neither spoke.

"Going now, Petra, em, coffee later." And with this he left the shop in a hurry and rushed back to his flat.

"Bugger, come on," he yelled as he stood at his front door. His excitement stopped him from coordinating his hand and eyes with the key and the lock.

Once inside, he went straight into the office.

"There, fucking, there," he said to himself, the words had come out and were audible to anyone close.

As Davison picked up the two images of Irish American mobster John Franzese, he heard his front door close. He had left it open in a hurry and his neighbour, hearing him swear loudly, thought it best to close the door for him.

Davison went onto his computer.

"Come on, load up, hurry…" He was impatient. He knew it was him but wanted Google to confirm it.

John Franzese Senior, he thought internally as his fingers tapped the keyboard.

'Images' – click.

Then it all appeared.

'John "Sonny" Franzese – an Italian-American mobster who was a long-time member and underboss of the Colombo crime gang. His crime career started in the 1930s and extended eight decades…' the text went on, but Davison only saw the face on the screen. Raising his images to the screen his eyes flipped between them.

Sure, the Google image was a younger man but there was no doubt in his mind that this was the same person, now elderly and frail, and it seemed a recent visitor to a luxury five-star hotel not two miles from Davison's flat.

What to do? What the fuck to do? There is a story here but what?
He took his eyes off the images in front of him and turned towards the window. No inspiration was forthcoming.

Right settle, what is the next move? Lots of thoughts whizzed around his mind. He was awash with irrational thoughts.

Going to march right up there and demand to know why a former mobster and crime lord is in my tow. Perhaps get some security, Garda, and then march up there.

This initial idea was very quickly quashed.

He is now a free man and can go anywhere he wants. Why would he not come to Ireland. He has the roots, and it is lovely here… So, do nothing I suppose.

Finally, he decided to put it on the back burner and use his presence as a 'celeb' spot if nothing else came up soon.

Davison stewed for a while. Should he just let this man be or take and make a story from it. Around an hour later, he made the decision.

Off to the Garda and let them know he's in town. Get a guarantee from them that if there is a scoop to be had they call me, job done! It felt so obvious now and logical.

So, for a second time that afternoon, Davison grabbed his keys and phone and rushed out bouncing down the stairs of his flat and out onto the street.

Walking swiftly past the coffee shop, he looked over and raised a hand to Sarah behind the counter as if nothing had happened. She stared back until he had passed.

Soon enough, he reached the police station and once seen clearly in the door security camera, was buzzed inside to a sealed off reception area. The heavy metal door slammed hard behind him.

Moments later, a rather overweight constable appeared through a second door behind protective glass. He acknowledged Davison.

"Afternoon. How can we help today, Sir?"

"Hi officer. I came straight away when I saw him, well not straight away I guess. First I rechecked photographs of him and then when I went for a coffee, I realised…"

Davison was abruptly interrupted.

"Hold, Sir," said the officer. "Sir, hello, wait…please."

"You saw someone. Then you took their photograph, and, then you went for coffee? Did I miss anything, Sir?" he said a little bemused and with a hint of sarcasm.

It was a slow day for news or crime reporting in the station and, suspecting he may have a weird one the other side of the glass the officer wondered about prolonging it a bit, for amusement.

The officer waited until Davison was about to speak.

Just as he was, he said, "Take your time, Sir. Nice and slowly. Perhaps a big breath first."

Davison missed the joke being too occupied with the images of Franzese and his potential scoop.

"Yes right, OK. So, I was monitoring the Manor House hotel, there has been an awful lot of strange unmarked private helicopters coming in and out of the place. You see, I'm a journalist you see and it's my job to watch stuff." Davison gulped then carried on.

"So the other day, I saw this guy and he was ill and so I took pictures of him and it was when I was reviewing them bang, I recognised him," he said. The officers tone changed from jovial to slightly more serious. He became a little edgy.

"Where does the coffee come into it, no wait? Forget the coffee. Why were you taking pictures of an ill man? That, my journalist friend, does not quite seem right to me."

The police officer moved closer to the glass. It was interpreted by Davison as a suggestion to keep quiet a bit longer.

"Tell me, Sir, you said you saw 'him' or was it 'someone' I believe. Who did you see…this ill man, who was it?"

"Sonny Franzese Senior, you know, John Franzese. I saw him being pushed in a wheelchair into the hotel after being lifted off the helicopter by stretcher. He's a former New York crime gang war lord, some underworld mobster and he's here, at the hotel!"

The officer stayed quiet for a moment.

When he did speak it was not friendly and not what Davison would have expected the words to be.

"Bad, Sir. Bad news I'm afraid. Wait a moment," and he then turned around and went back through the door he had appeared from.

Davison looked up to the clock on the wall. The minute hand was passing the 'four' and would do so three more times before the internal door opened.

Two men came through. The original overweight officer was not one of them.

"Sir, these photographs you have taken. Of the mobster chap…"

"Yes, Franzese," came quickly from Davison's lips.

"Yes, that will be him. Where are they now and do you have others, other people of possible interest who have come and gone from the hotel?" said one tall senior looking man not in police uniform.

"Yes, em, Sir, I have lots and of others but when you investigate, I do want to be the Journo that exposes this. Can we agree?"

"Expose, yes. Am sure we can sort you, Sir. I will send an officer around later tonight to review your evidence. Now if you could provide details to my colleague, we can sort this mess." And with that the tall smart man left through the internal door and the second man picked up a pen and some paper close by.

It was now only a few short hours until the arrival and the 'guests' of the hotel had had their final chat for the day. It would take between twenty-four and thirty-six hours after arrival before any procedure could even be considered and so the task was to maintain comfort and acceptance within the paid-up and waiting guests.

Hofmann had extra duties and would oversee the administration of a very small sedative into the intravenous drips, keeping the guest comfortable. Their minders would not be told and the guests would simply fall into a calming sleep.

McCann's phone had received a message notification.

He read it and then turned the screen to allow Richards to see the message.

It read, 'On plan. We be skyward very soon then to you in two thereafter. Be ready, E.'

Richards stood. He was anxious although he did not know why exactly.

Everything was ready. The pending arrivals temporary quarters. The welcoming committee and the paperwork that would convince them that they were indeed coming to Ireland for a new start. They would be treated to proper food and drink and be allowed to wander the grounds under close supervision for a short period the next day. Then, into their separate quarters where guards would be posted by their doors to ensure their 'safety'.

Despite the plan and having done this all before, Richards was anxious.

Again, when he received a return notification that McCann had received and opened his message, the Estonian recorded a voice note in reply.

"Send location and estimated arrival time. Send confirmation that all is well, and we remain good to go onwards."

He would, in the next few minutes receive a text from Q7-1 and Q7-2 that all was well, and they were closing in on the plane with their cargo.

Getting 'the cargo' on board was the only tricky bit but plans had been rehearsed many times and diversions were in place to distract any unwanted watching eyes, people had been well paid to see nothing.

He smiled again. All is well. For now, he did one final bluetooth call to the cargo terminal informing his contact there that the cargo was less than thirty minutes away.

Abernethy knew he had lost them when the two trucks were stopped in Kosovo. Their paperwork was all in order and clearly there was no migrant cargo on-board or any sign there even had been some or other illegal goods being transported. Nothing.

The CIA and MI6 agreed to stand down for now but continue to monitor the airwaves and known accomplices of the Estonian in a hope they could again pick up his trail.

Brendan McCann took a short walk to his temporary hotel accommodation. Poured himself a Scotch, which he had often been called out for preferring over the Irish version and sat down in a large comfortable chair to rest and await the arrivals.

Chapter 12
Fresh Blood

Davison woke a little later than was usual for him.

It had just gone six thirty and he still lay, now wide awake, in his bed. Wearily, he climbed out of bed and wandered into the kitchen. Passing the window, he noticed that the sun was already out. It looked like it was going to be a nice day.

He switched the kettle on and as he reached up for the coffee and a mug, he changed his mind and switched it off again.

Petra's latte, went through his mind and he returned to his bedroom. As he did, a stale smell entered his nostrils.

Hmmm, perhaps it is to be a cleaning day today, he thought to himself as he opened the small window to let the air and the street noise in.

Still in yesterday's boxer shorts, he put on a pair of trousers and a t-shirt in great need of an iron and prepared to leave to get his favourite coffee from his favourite barista.

Again, the little coffee shop was empty when he went in. It had not long opened and sure enough she was there.

Petra was standing around waiting on customers and had seen him as he crossed the street towards her shop.

"Morning, Steve," she said.

"Petra," he replied. "Em, sorry about yesterday. I just had a moment and needed to dash off. I will pay for yesterday's coffee and a second latte for now please."

"No need. I drank it myself when you left," she said. "So, one latte no sugar coming up," and with a hint of a smirk she added, "and I will lock the door before I start this time." She turned to wipe the coffee machine down prior to use.

Davison smiled. *Is she flirting with me?* He thought. *Quick say something. Ahhhh say something back quick.* But he couldn't think of anything quickly enough.

He was not shy it was just that she grabbed his attention, and he really did not know why. It was a pleasant annoyance, and one he accepted, but one that made him act out of character.

Instead, he looked back at the framed print of the Franzese hot chocolate on the wall. Instinctively, he took a photo of it on his phone.

It was so bloody obvious. How did I not see it earlier? He thought to himself.

I need to go on the dark web to see what I can find. Bet, I can find out more than the police. As he thought, he had to stop himself getting so determined that he would again depart the coffee shop at speed.

Petra turned around while the milk was foaming.

"Someone came in looking for you yesterday. Not seen him before and it was late. Just as I was closing up. He seemed keen to get to you. I thought it must be some lead you're looking for or needing so I told him that you're often in here first thing and that you're a local," she said. "Hope I've helped, Steve."

"Cool, yes," he started. "I have lots on, very busy and got something big, very big waiting to come out. You'll know when I break it. Thanks. Did he leave a number or anything?"

"No but he did promise to come back real soon," she replied, now facing away, and pouring the coffee.

Garda? Do they have something for me after all, he briefly wondered. He had no irons in any fires and was waiting on no one with crucial information, so he was a little puzzled as he reached for his wallet to pay.

"So, I am getting money this time?" Petra said, poking fun at him again as she took the ten Euros offered to her.

Think, think, something funny, he thought again. However, for a second time nothing came to mind.

"Yes Petra, you are, keep the change please and thank you again. See you soon," he said and reluctantly turned to head back to his flat now wondering who was looking for him.

He would not have to wait very long to find out.

As he exited the coffee shop, Petra had retrieved the change that she was now allowed to keep. She looked down at the two small denomination silver coins and smiled.

He's funny, quite like him, she thought to herself.

Davison crossed the street and drank from the cup as he searched his pocket for his flat keys. Reaching the communal entrance door, he noticed a small scruffy man speaking into the security speaker. Davison stopped and pretended to admire the sun's rays while he wondered who this man was. He had not seen him before and did not feel like he could be a family member of one of the other five households in the small block.

A few seconds later the door was buzzed, and this stranger was allowed passage into the block.

Guess it's nothing then, he thought and walked the few yards towards the very same door now closed and locked again.

He took another sip of coffee then like a contortionist with keys, coffee and phone in hand opened the door and slipped inside as he had done hundreds of times before.

The door slammed behind him as it always did. While Davison didn't think anything of this, someone else inside did.

Davison started up the stairs and almost immediately as he did so, he caught sight of him. The small scruffy man from moments earlier coming half hunched, out from underneath the stairs. This same man then straightened and walked to the corner of the stairs.

Davison felt scared.

This is weird, bloody weird, he thought as he walked slowly up the stairs.

What to do. Challenge him or be pleasant and ask if he needs help? However, Davison already suspected this man needed no help.

He avoided eye contact and simply mimicked the movements of Davison. Stopping when he did and continuing when he moved up the stairs.

Don't want to show this guy which door I live at but also, don't want to just stay here and get thumped if he's after money or something.

Davison took a deep breath as he reached the landing at the top of the first floor and turned to face this small but bulky and intimidating man now a few steps below him.

"So, em, can I help you with something?" Finally, came out from his slightly quivering lips.

No answer.

"Look I don't think you live here or know anyone and it's like very quiet here," he forced out next.

Nothing, but now this stocky silent man was right next to him. Davison stepped back and tried to shout out. He thought he had done but nothing came out his mouth. His ears heard nothing but this strange man's breathing.

The man looked up and at Davison. Eye contact for the first time. As he did so he brushed past him and behind him.

Davison reached for the stair banister as he expected to feel two firm hands on his shoulders. He was at the top of the stairs but felt compelled to hold his ground.

Fearing what he might see, Davison turned around and there he was smiling. Perhaps five or six inches smaller, red hair all over his unshaven face and head. He could see the start of a tattoo on his neck disappearing down under his clothing.

Then he spoke. His tone was firm.

"You see, my nosey friend, my boss has a problem with you sneaking around the gardens, and, if he has a problem with it, I have a problem with it," he said.

He then reached into his jacket pocket.

Fuck how does he know this? How does he know I live here? Fuck! Thought Davison.

"The guests that come and go are none of your business. You see, 'WE' see everything," and pulling his hand from his jacket he revealed a 9MM Sig Sauer pistol. Davison only saw 'gun' and that was good enough.

Davison instantly felt the release of urine onto his boxer shorts and tried to speak. Again, only unidentifiable noises grunted from his mouth.

Patting Davison on the chest with the gun, he smiled at him. Then using the gun for leverage pushed Davison to the side with the barrel and walked down past him and toward the stairs.

The man descended a couple of steps and stopped. Without turning his head, he spoke.

"I only give one warning," and then moved off again, down, and out the building.

Davison stood eyes fixed on the street door as the man disappeared onto the street.

What the fuck just happened. How the fuck did he see me at the hotel. Thoughts whizzed and rushed around his consciousness. *Who was he and did he mean I was dead if I go back?*

Several seconds later but what felt like minutes, Davison gathered his thoughts and picked up his flat keys. He must have dropped them but did not remember doing so or hearing them fall to the concrete floor.

He unlocked the door then glancing over to the door of his only neighbour on the first floor, and seeing no one, he went inside.

He touched his groin and felt the dampness.

Shower and clean boxers after all, he thought as he entered his bedroom and started to undress.

Should I let the chaps at the paper know?

As he was undressing, he contemplated the pros and cons of widening his findings to his employer the Irish Times newspaper. Before stepping into the shower, he went to the front door and dragged a heavy chair across it so stopping any forced entry. He felt better after doing so.

McCann was restless.

His trusted friend and right-hand man Richardson was in control and had taken delivery of similar cargo as that was pending but all the same he remained restless. Something this time felt different, and he could not put his finger on what this was.

"Right, lads, the three cars are likely to arrive separately but within the same hour. We need the passengers out quick, out of sight and separated into the holding rooms as quick as," said Richardson, looking at his team and waited to see them acknowledge.

"I am going around the building one more time and then we are eyes and ears till the third car, and all are out of sight. Don't wander off for a fag, and don't sneak into the fucking kitchen for food. Stay put," he ordered sharply before heading off to check that the grounds had more than usual designated 'walkers in suits'.

Neither the security walkers nor the reception crew would have to wait too long. Within fifteen minutes of Richardson returning to the front of the hotel near the reception, his phone vibrated. He answered… It was the gate keeper, and he was asking if he could let in a dark coloured Audi Q7 car enter the grounds.

As it approached the hotel entrance, the sound of tyre on gravel could be heard becoming louder and louder. There would be no valet parking for these new arrivals to one of Ireland's most glamourous and expensive hotels. Instead, the passengers would be off-loaded and firmly but not aggressively moved inside and separated into their temporary quarters. The driver would be taken for refreshments and a debrief by one of the now many guards lining up to assist the operation.

"Gate to house, we now have a black Audi single occupant. Opening the gate now," was his next conversation.

The first car pulled up in front of the oval concrete entrance stairs, and the driver opened his door and exited. He turned to the occupants in the rear and said something to them through the window. The rear doors stayed closed.

He walked up to the closest man, and they spoke. Seconds later, both men went up the same oval stairs and disappeared out of sight inside.

They waited for the second car to stop. The occupants in the back of the larger Audi and the gathering hanging around the hotel entrance waited for something to happen.

McCann waited but now he knew the Estonian had arrived, and his supply of fresh blood had, likewise, started to gather below his room at the front and centre of the hotel. He felt a little easier now knowing that his own 'waiting ill guests' may have to not wait too much longer. He did, however, just want it done and over, and for the Estonian to leave the grounds as quickly as possible.

McCann feared the British spies and while he had temporarily ignored the amateur reporter, he knew he could not do the same with the professional spooks that could be following the Estonian. He had seen first-hand what they could do during his time in the 'RA', the IRA and when he dallied with joining the follow-on Real IRA.

Closing the window of his hotel room, he looked skyward. He would not see a drone even if there was one, but he looked upwards all the same. Then he heard another car pull up on the gravel outside and the sounds of people speaking but not in English. Then it went quiet.

All arrived then. Just get them out and done and away, he thought.

Abernethy had been frustrated at the 'loss' of his targets in the tunnels of and had taken it out on those around him.

The Americans had backed off and seemed to be becoming more isolationist, choosing instead to go about the business in their own private manner, while the Committee seemed to be focusing more on the Chinese angle and the Myanmar human rights abuses.

Abernethy knew that similar atrocities were happening right here in Western Europe, and he could not get his French counterpart to agree and commit resources and time to it. Instead, he just got more and more frustrated. He remained angry that his one big break was lost in the tunnels, and he would not let it go.

Things were happening. Illicit drug and migrant trafficking gangs were on the march and only he seemed to see this.

Davison left his flat later that day and decided to walk the local street and visit the shops. He needed time to reflect on his earlier visit and thought the fresh air would help.

He called his mother which was routine every two days or so. Losing his father to a terrorist bomb during the 'Troubles', she was his only remaining direct family member and his sounding board when anxious.

"Hey Ma, how's about ye?" he said as she answered the call.

The two chatted about the weather and a few known friends before touching on the Corona Virus situation and if she fine stuck at home and did she need anything. Then five or six minutes later, they ended the call with a promise to speak again soon.

He wandered the streets in and out of shops trying to be interested but all the time wondering if he should return to the Manor House hotel. He was both scared for himself and now, more than ever, convinced something illegal was going on there. It was his job as an investigative journalist to take calculated risk to expose wrongdoing, however, he was a little more afraid and alone than others in his trade.

Why would they threaten me to stay away from a public hotel if it were all legit?

It was late afternoon now, and the sun was trying to break free of the clouds in the sky.

Beer. Let the beer decide, he thought with a smile. *I wonder if Petra ever goes to the pub,* he thought always hopeful of accidently/deliberately bumping into her.

Entering a nearby pub, he reviewed the beer choices and after a few seconds was approached by the barman.

Davison chose and paid and took his drink over to a corner table and sat down to decide about the hotel.

He watched the barman cleaning, then the few other customers sitting chatting and glanced up periodically at the to monitor and the breaking news streams running along the bottom of the Sky News banner. There were crowds of football supporters breaking social distancing rules outside a football stadium in Glasgow. The local protestant team had won the league again after a spell in the doldrums. It seemed to be the main topic that day.

Slow news day, he thought.

After finishing his beer and acknowledging the barman on exit ,he walked towards a taxi rank.

It was not the beer talking, for Davison was a seasoned drinker, and one solitary beer would not be sufficient to blur his thinking. It was his journalistic integrity. It was his drive for the 'story' and 'truth' that obliged him to reach for a taxi.

He would go to the hotel and walk the grounds. No camera, no pictures, just a walk through the garden and the flowers and show whoever was watching that he was both not a threat and that he was not scared of what had come his way earlier that day. It was his 'free press' moment, and he was going to take it.

He walked up to the taxi first in line but was called back.

"Son, I'm free. He's not working today," said the driver of the second in line now half exiting his vehicle to show his determination.

"Not working? He's first in line, Mate," Davison said back.

"Yes, he's gone ill suddenly so not working, as I said, Son. Here jump in," the driver replied.

Davison looked at the driver in the first cab who refused to speak or turn his face away from the straight-ahead stare.

Weird but whatever, thought Davison.

"Where to Son, the hotel?"

"Emm the hotel…" he had repeated the word.

"Manor House, Son, yes, good choice, Son?"

"Yes, the Manor please," said Davison assuming that this was a popular fare and that all the drivers took a stab at the hotel's location first.

Perhaps, he should have thought this rather strange but he didn't.

He was dropped off a short way from the main stairs where earlier a group of migrants had been delivered. It was ironic that the very thing he searched for had been so close in his grasp.

He paid the driver and with a look up to the hotel entrance turned and began to look for a route around the perfectly kept gardens. This was a common occurrence not just with guests but the locals would often be seen walking harmlessly through the plants and trees on a pre-determined route.

As he walked and tried to look as inconspicuous as possible, inside the hotel the new arrivals were being prepared. Most had been given fresh clothes and food and reading materials but had been instructed not to leave their rooms. In fact, guards had been placed around the corridors to ensure that they did not leave to look around.

Fredrick Hofmann was also preparing. His two nurses were with him in the spotlessly clean operating theatre in the basement of the hotel. They would be there for a while preparing for the next day when they would be busy for most of that time in surgery.

The sun was failing to win its battle against the clouds when Davison decided to leave the hotel grounds and wander the mile or so downhill back to the main streets.

Stopping in the shop closest to his flat, he stocked up for the rest of the day with food and beers and strolled back home.

As the hours passed, at several places throughout Europe simultaneously, people and events were slowly unfolding.

Some had heavy hearts while others had a faster beating heart. Some could sleep and some were unable to sleep, being too excited about their new country and opportunity. However, for one, in a first floor flat not far from the Manor House hotel, the beating of this heart was about to stop for good.

Davison answered the door, expecting to see a uniformed member of the local Garda as had been suggested to him earlier in the day. He had expected a call prior to be informed of their visit and statement taking but this had not happened. He still believed it was the local police, and putting down his beer and plate of food, he went over to answer the knock.

When the door opened, revealing the person on the other side of it he saw a red-haired small man. He was a little bit scruffy in clothing. Surprise turned to horror. Then he saw two other disturbing things. First, his elderly neighbour lying just outside their flat door in a dark red pool of liquid and second, a black metallic object in the red-haired man's left hand.

Then the flash. It was the last thing Davison was ever to see.

Chapter 13
Guest Operation

The next day, McCann woke early. He wanted to see off the Estonian and get out of the hotel before the doctor started his work. He would often leave the grounds of the hotel having arranged to visit old friends from the days of the 'troubles'. He knew that in doing so he would be watched by local law enforcement. However, he also thought it would give him some form of immunity from the work the doctor was carrying out. He was also awaiting news from Rotterdam about an intercepted smuggling cargo and knew his past friend Drako would come looking.

If he wasn't present, he didn't know and so was not responsible. That was how he thought. Also, however, in his twilight years and a little frail himself, he had lost the stomach for all the screams and smells that slowly rose from the theatre room below in the basement. He was happy to accept the money his 'clients' would bring him but just not the gruesome actions required to fulfil the contract.

When it was time, the two men met at reception. The Estonian having had an enormous breakfast was his usual arrogant self.

"Irish, thank you Irish. I always enjoy so much our transactions but today I enjoyed the breakfast more. Perhaps, I will come stay with my mistress for fun not business next time," he said with a wry smile across his face. He knew that McCann was not his friend and he knew that they always wanted to see him turn and leave after the handover was complete. This time, he had insisted on staying the night.

"Yes, my friend. As always you never fail me. Spend the money wisely and stay safe," came the reply from McCann. It was short, insincere, and deliberately direct.

They shook hands and both men turned and walked in opposite directions.

Looking back over his shoulder, the Estonian added, "I have task now with our friend Drako, he sends his best wishes, Irish," and with this he was gone again from the hotel and for now, the equation.

"Tell me when he leaves the grounds and close the gate behind him," McCann said to the man in the CCTV room as he passed by it.

"Yes, sir."

McCann continued on walking back to his room to ready himself for his short stay away from his hotel and to the secluded farm and his friends from his past.

Soon enough, the gate closed behind the Estonian and McCann seemed to breathe much easier.

"Paddy," said McCann calling down from his room telephone, "get the car ready. We should go in ten. We are off to the hills and the farm."

"Yes Brendon, will do. Front of house in ten, right. I will just round up the men first and remind them to be vigilant with our new guests," Richards replied. "When the fun starts, we don't want any issues."

"Right, yes, issues. OK will be down in ten." And with that McCann put the telephone receiver down and went to retrieve his pre-prepared overnight bag. He always had a bag packed and ready just in case he had to leave in a hurry.

The two men duly met around ten minutes later at the main front door of the hotel. Neither spoke but simply entered the waiting car which would take them to a small farm near the town of Limavady, just across the border in the North, where they would sit out and wait for the next few days.

Hofmann had woken a little late this morning. He knew he had a busy day ahead and nonetheless stayed up late the night before and drank himself asleep. Now, he had to schedule the day's theatre work and so got himself readied for the morning briefing with his small team of two nurses and a guard. It was strange to have an armed thug in the briefing, but Hofmann always felt a little more comfortable when there was one in the theatre room with him.

He exited his luxury room and went down to the breakfast area where he sat by the large bay window overlooking the grounds. He hated to be kept waiting and banged a glass on the table. It caught everyone's attention.

When asked, he ordered a large jug of coffee, a large portion of potato farl, mushrooms, beans and four eggs. He suspected he would not get another chance to eat that day until late into the night, so he needed to fill his stomach.

Looking out over the grounds, he saw his future patients walking and laughing in two separate groups. This was normal for new arrivals as it made them less anxious and more sure that their dream of a new life was coming. What was less normal was the number of armed guards that tried and failed to pretend that they were just there for hotel security and not to ensure none of the new guests wandered off.

Hofmann stared at the closest group. *He's not in the first group,* he thought to himself, looking for the tall Syrian man who had been paired with the wealthy Russian waiting for a new liver downstairs in the treatment room. He did see his second 'job' of the day.

There, such a pretty young girl. How old are you, my dear, I wonder? Went through his mind, *Nineteen or have you reached twenty yet. Alas for you, money is much more pretty than you so I suspect you won't reach much older,* and he lost himself for a moment wondering what she may have become if she had not entered his uncaring and sinister world.

A few minutes later, his breakfast arrived at the table.

While eating, he was interrupted.

"Mr Hofmann, we are waiting on you in the preparation room. You said ten fifteen and it is now past. What do you wish us to do, Sir?" asked Angelle, his main surgery nurse.

"I wish you to leave me to eat my breakfast," barked Hofmann, and, with that she returned to the room and would sit with the other two in silence and just wait.

Filling his face with fried food, now a little faster, Hofmann reverted to the local paper from the nearby rack and skimmed the first few pages not really caring about the stories or topics but just to distract himself for a small moment from the day ahead.

While pretending to read the paper, Hofmann did not see the guards shuffle the other group of migrant guests back into the hotel through a side fire door. They too were on a schedule and for one tall Syrian man, it would likely be the last ever time he would see the sun or walk on the green grass.

Hofmann stood, poured himself yet another coffee and took the cup with him. He walked the short distance down one set of stairs and along a windowless corridor, to the preparation side room where the other three were patiently waiting on him.

There was no acknowledgement or apology for his lateness. Hofmann simply took charge of the situation as usual.

"Tell me what we have starting, please," he said.

Then standing up to speak, Nurse Angelle spoke.

"His name is Abud El-Kater and he is…"

Hofmann screamed loudly.

"I do not care about his bloody name, I want to know what we have, Christ!" he yelled. "We do not personalise these things, these people. They are merely money to us, do you understand, do you all understand?" he said, looking at the small group in front of him.

The nurse tried again, now a little nervous.

"We have a very healthy 31-year-old Syrian man. The others have spoken of him being a strong runner in his country. The medical came back as a positive blood group match as his records indicated." Then pausing, she wondered whether to tell him which group, but in a second, decided not to, *a positive blood group match is enough,* she thought.

She carried on.

"No signs of infection, tests for all hepatitis and related viruses all negative. No obvious internal bleeding, no cancers detected, and liver function is perfect." Then again, the doctor interrupted but this time constructively.

"Yes, liver perfect. It is why we go to Syria for livers. No temptation to drink alcohol and ruin themselves that way," *and no fun either,* he thought. He looked at the nurse and she knew to continue. The list seemed endless, but all sat and listened as they always did. Even the guard seemed fully immersed in the medical aspects.

"Urine normal, bowel movements normal, no history of migraines or nausea. No pain, swellings or lumps of any kind, no abdominal pains, no breathing disorders or any history of fevers or night sweats. We are working on what I am confident is a simple, healthy, 31-year-old male and a solid candidate for the client," she concluded.

There was a short pause before Hofmann, now satisfied with the choice of candidate, spoke again.

"Covid?"

"Swabs came back negative. He neither has it, nor has he had it. No antibodies detected. In fact, all the new guests came back the same way," she replied.

"All of them? Neither have, nor had?" he gently challenged. "You know they can have no symptoms and feel fine," he continued.

"Yes Mr Hofmann, none, nurse Ruth tested them all on arrival."

Hofmann looked around at Nurse Ruth, and she confirmed with a nod.

"Good, are we all ready to go? Room ready, instruments cleaned, oxygen and injections primed and all," he asked full well, knowing the answer already.

"Yes, Mr Hofmann," said Nurse Angelle.

"OK, we just need our two guests to get to pre op readiness. Let's go, do this now," he said.

The guard was first to rise and acknowledge, "Yes, sir, I will separate the Syrian guest and ensure he goes under with the help of my colleague and Nurse Ruth," and with this he left the room.

"Yes, Mr Hofmann, I will ensure that our primary guest is comfortable and mentally ready and will wait for you to switch the room to 'green light'," she replied, and she also left the small preparation room.

Hofmann drained the last of his coffee and also left the room to look for more.

It would be an hour later before things started to move at pace.

Abud El-Kater was sitting on his bed reading. He had taken the chance to grab leaflets and newspapers to assist with his English and today he was trying to figure out from the sports pages.

The door to his small private room was unlocked from the outside and in came Nurse Angelle. He had seen her several times throughout his stay and had even smiled at close quarters towards her, but she had either not seen this or had chosen to ignore it.

He looked at her and waited to be instructed. He then saw movement behind her in the corridor. It was one of the many guards seen walking around the hotel and in the grounds. *I wonder why the hotel needs to have so much security,* he thought.

"Abud, you are needed right away. We need to do checks on you because we may have a job for you and the employers want to make sure you are healthy," said Nurse Angelle.

A beaming smile appeared on his face.

"A job, a real job, with money I can send home to my family?" he replied. "What is it, please?"

"Erm, well, I am not sure. I think it is working on a farm with the animals," she replied hurriedly, not believing it herself or caring about sounding sincere.

"Please now, let's go. David will show you where to go," and so off the three went. Abud still smiling and very happy that his dream of a new start in life could be beginning at last.

It was a short walk to the pre operation area, down two short flights of stairs and along a short corridor. The three went inside and the door was closed firmly behind them by a second man who had stared at Abud the whole way along the short corridor.

"Sit here please, Abud. I will be with you shortly. I need you to roll up your sleeve so I can take blood," the nurse said. He duly obliged with all instructions.

The nurse then knocked on the entry door and the man from the corridor opened it. She exited the room leaving only the first guard and Abud sitting waiting.

He didn't know how long he was waiting exactly but he was a little taken back when the door opened again, this time fully, and a bed with a man on it was wheeled in.

The brake was applied to the bed wheel and the patient on the bed tried but failed to sit up.

"Please Mr Sukinov, stay still. I don't want you to rip any stitches. We are going in soon and the anaesthetist will make you comfortable very quickly," said nurse Angelle.

However, in a frail voice the patient spoke.

"I want to see him, the other man. I want to see his face."

"No, sir, he is not ready for you to see him," she replied now a little worried what might happen.

"I insist I see him," and Sukinov somehow managed to push himself up into a near sitting position. He looked around then saw Abud.

"You," he said. "It must be you. Thank you so very much. What you do is a good thing for an old dying man."

The nurse quickly moved to shield Abud from the patient and helped him, now a little firmly, back down to the lying position.

Abud was confused. *Why did that old man thank me?* He thought. He looked to the nurse for an answer.

She smiled back to Abud.

"Old," she said, as if to say, 'He doesn't know what he is doing or saying.'

Abud smiled back but he was not reassured. Something just felt strange. The hairs on the back of his neck rose as his hand went to scratch them.

Something's not right, he thought to himself.

"David get Tommy in here to join us," she said to the guard who was well aware of what had just happened. She had experience of the moment when the donor realised, they were to become a donor against their will. It had often turned violent with panic and fear. She wanted to be in control if Abud El-Kater was to become the next such patient.

With both guards now in the small room, she felt confident to move Sukinov through the internal door and into the theatre for real. The light inside was bright. It illuminated the faces of all three men still in the small preparation room. It illuminated the slowly changing facial expression of Abud from curiosity towards anxiety.

He wanted to stand. It would help alleviate some of the growing uncertainty and the adrenalin now starting to whizz around his body.

"Sit. Sit, please," said one of the guards but now with a firm hand on Abud's shoulder. This was clearly not a polite request.

The hospital bed had disappeared from sight but with the door still open, Abud could hear the sounds of voices inside and smell the scent of cleanliness. What little he could see inside showed him what appeared to be a room with specialised equipment.

He tried to listen to the voices. He thought he heard a second female voice not just nurse Angelle and a man who had an unusual English accent. He could not properly hear what they were saying. Then, when the conversation inside the room stopped, nurse Angelle came out and closed the door behind her.

"Right Abud, let's worry about you now. I am going to take some blood from your arm but first I have to inject you with an anticoagulant to make sure that we get a safe flow of blood to test, right?" But she was not asking, and what she was preparing was no anticoagulant.

When she withdrew the needle from the small bottle of liquid in her other hand, Abud flinched.

He tried to speak but now of all time was the worst time to panic and forget the meaningful words of his newly learned second language.

"Nurse, I, eh, nurse, I no need anticoagulant, I no need this needle. Happy to blood without this needle nurse," he forced out, but it was too late.

The guards had grabbed either shoulder and closest arm and Abud was now totally incapacitated.

She tried to reassure him.

"Listen Abud, we do things differently in this country. We have lots of good medicine and this one will help you." But it fell on deaf ears.

The needle was pushed into a large vein in his arm. There was no need for a rubber strap around the arm to raise further the protruding veins for he was having his arms held so tightly the veins were all up and ready for the needle, which ever vein she chose.

He screamed in his native tongue, and, in the few seconds he had left of consciousness, appeared to mumble words to his God, asking for his help. His eyelids becoming smaller and heavier from an extreme wide to a forced calm and eventually, a reluctant sleep.

Abud's former life was now gone for good.

Inside the theatre, there was much space. Around the walls were rows of different machines, all serving a purpose but none of this was relevant to either man, patient, or reluctant donor. Both slept under the influence of drugs.

Sukinov had tubes and wires going in and out of him with some leading to a bedside machine whose display flashed, with changing numbers, and in different colours. He looked peaceful. He was, perhaps, the most peaceful he had been in weeks. His failed liver had taken a real strain on his face as well as his body and mind, yet while it was being propped up with tubes and drugs, and it was working again, his face looked calm and relaxed.

Hofmann spoke.

"I do not want that noise again, please. If we need to tie them and tape their mouth so be it. That was loud and I could not concentrate on the guest. If we make a mistake with him then we will all pay one way or another," he said, looking at the guards while standing over a drugged sleeping Abud.

"He," he continued, looking at the currently healthy patient below his glare, "is a commodity and like all commodities, we can get another off the shelf if we need to. We just don't want to wait. Do we understand?"

Both guards nodded.

"Right, Tommy, I do not need you in here. I need the space to work. You can leave but stay close in shouting distance. You," as he looked to the other guard, "you can entertain yourself over in the corner chair. If I need anything, I will call you," and with orders given both men moved away accordingly.

The theatre was one person less busy but still had two sleeping patients, two nurses, a guard and of course, Hofmann. It looked like a busy room and was to look more so when the surgical procedure and cutting began.

Both patients lay patiently.

Both seemed to be waiting for a destiny moment. A moment in time which for one, could extend life, and for the other, would surely severely limit any future chance of life.

It began.

The lights flickered on the machines nearby. Often green, sometimes amber, occasionally red, but Hofmann did not care for their colour. He would not see the traffic lights dance across the equipment's display screen.

He cut and deeper and faster. He wiped the blood away that they two nurses missed, and then he carried on.

The Syrian was a product. He was a prize from which further wealth and women would come. Hofmann was ruthless and as such he blatantly and consistently contravened the Hippocratic oath that he once gave and once abided by a long time ago when his modus operandi was saving not ending life.

Hofmann did not need to go into his chest cavity but he was a driven man, breaking the lower two ribs of the Syrian 'product' that lay motionless and vulnerable in front of him, not for his convenience or any surgical need, but because he could. He smiled. His thinking was clear. His thinking was focused.

Do not want any shit to stall me from getting the liver out, don't want any shit from stopping me from doing the other organ operations quickly if need be, he thought as he sawed, as he pushed and pulled, like a chicken wishbone on a family Sunday lunch.

On this day, both nurses saw a side of their doctor they had not seen before. They had been by his side many times and mostly took the necessary precautions. This was not evident today, mind you it didn't need to be, this was a one-time donor, unlike most.

He was taking risks, big risks and not the risks that his patient may perish. That was a given, but that he would sacrifice further healthy organs that could have been used for follow-on financial reward, for this one prize, this one healthy, blood-filled, valuable, beautiful liver organ from a stranger, a stranger whose only desire had been to start a fresh new life.

Instead Abud El-Kater would never see daylight again, he would be gone, unlike the majority who fell under Hoffmann's knife, donating, they would be kept alive for hours or perhaps days, depending on whether their body parts had further value and use in the short period of time they could be kept healthy. The guard that had been instructed by Hofmann to exit the sterile room now returned. He handed the nurse a tray of energy drinks. She smiled and took the tray allowing him to once again exit the sterile room, and the weird tranquillity to return to the morbid shiny room with small flashing lights and a quiet hum of machines keeping patients and now victims alive as needed. The living needed refreshment.

The two nurses and the doctor opened their small energy drinks. The guard had done so first and had sat back down quickly which was a little ironically as he had done the least physically.

Hofmann stood erect over the Syrian and gulped down the sugary liquid. He stared down into the body of the exposed patient and its moving parts. Both nurse Angelle and nurse Ruth soon followed his gaze.

Over the stench of an exposed human body, still alive but soon fighting death and decay as environmental bacteria would attack, these three health professionals appeared to look a little perplexed.

All confused looking, as if trying to figure out where the next piece of their jigsaw was to go. Is it a sky or sea or land piece, for they held an imaginary piece with few obvious and distinguished markings to make the location more obvious.

Hofmann seemed strangely to be in no hurry this day despite earlier actions and a ruthless proficiency with the surgical knife.

A second 'task' was being identified and prepared for her pending trauma not far above his head in a comfortable room in the hotel, while a second suffering guest, the wife of a Russian politician undergoing life extending surgery, waiting, and wondered. Yet Hofmann was strangely slow, strangely enjoying his small can of energy drink and for a perverse moment, he smiled at his two female colleagues and laughed out loud. Both, after a small lapse, did likewise back to him. The adrenaline and the acceptance of gore and blood had taken a toll on their mental health. This was no funny moment.

The empty cans were placed in the refuge where used saline bags and cheap medical instruments were placed and the three moved on towards the target organ.

Clamps were put in place.

Nurses with tight rubber gloves placed carefully controlled hands in and out of the chest cavity in a choreographed ballet-like motion. All had done this before. Many times before and it was almost mundane. However, the extraction of a human being's organs while the heart still beat should never have been this mundane, but it was. One would hold the stomach to one side while the other held the bowels of the young man in both her hands outside the cavity space freeing up space for Hofmann to do his deed.

The macabre performance went off for a while longer.

Two more nurses were now in the room and over the Syrian. They were tasked with the care of the soon to be freed liver organ. To keep it hydrated and keep it fresh for the Russian.

When the final scalpel incision was complete, the organ was lifted out of the cavity in a speedy careless manner. Then, the blood lines were secured with clamps, not to reduce the risk of the Syrian bleeding to death, but to save on mess and cleaning up time. He wouldn't be needed again. His death would be a major inconvenience, with still health organs that could turn a tidy profit. No longer was there relaxed mundane activity. In its place, there was a flurry of voices and movement.

A new stench moved through the room, but no one seemed to care. Everyone was too busy.

"Move, move," barked out Hofmann as he lifted the organ out towards the ice box. His hands were red with blood and soon droplets were falling onto the theatre floor. It was placed into a breathable bubble and then moved towards the iced and gaseous box.

"That lives or you don't," came next from the anxious doctors' mouth and once he saw the organ secured and stored, he took off his bloodied rubber gloves and threw them into a nearby sink.

A moment later, he left the room and went to the scrubs area to change into fresh whites before then moving into the restroom and what he believed was a deserved coffee and a short break.

Inside the theatre room there remained much activity.

The nurses were securing their Syrian patient in a temporary and rushed manner. They had positioned the organs back into his cavity and were now sewing up the chest area while spraying a sterile disinfectant spray around the wound. She smiled, not knowing why she did it, knowing her patient had such little time to live.

Another was replacing the saline drip with new, while a fourth prepared more painkiller and anaesthetic to be injected into him to keep him from waking, and ease his passing. Soon, he would be wheeled away into a recovery room and left for a while, alone in the dark. His role was complete.

The solitary guard also had a role.

He started the cleaning down which the others would soon follow with. All surfaces needed to be spotless and disinfected for the important patients. The floor would need to be mopped of the blood and sweat, and a whole new array of instruments and tools would be required all to ensure no cross contamination or infection risk to their key participant, the paying guest, the Russian.

The same Russian was next in line for Hofmann.

The nurses would finish up and take a short break themselves, while two new guards would enter the room in one-piece whites so as not to bring in any germs. They would relieve the first guard of watching duties and sit with the Russian and wait. What he needed guarding from in his current drugged state was uncertain, but it was their role to do so anyway.

A few hundred yards away, outside in the warming sun, three of the newest arrivals sat on the grass and chatted. Each knew enough English to be able to hold a conversation. All three were watched by a man in the CCTV room, and a further man nearby sitting on a bench facing where they were gathered talking.

She had only recently turned nineteen, but Almeda Irfan had been away from her family for almost a year. There had been no birthday party or celebration. It had been just another day.

She had witnessed her younger brothers die in a government led airstrike on her town Sinjar in the North of Iraq, and this was followed, a few days later, by her father being forcibly taken from their home one night. She knew he was now likely dead after a time of pain and torture.

She feared for her mother even pleading with her to come away with her on the lorries out of the town, but her mother insisted on staying and waiting for the return of her father. She had not seen family or friendly faces in so long, but it had not changed her from the positive happy young lady that she was. The others in the group delivered by the Estonian days earlier, liked Almeda for she never appeared fearful of her future. She would speak to them of a new start and how they must remain strong and look to the future. She was only nineteen, however, the others, mostly older, looked up to her and saw her strength when she spoke of her troubled recent past.

This day, Almeda sat on the grass with two others, and they chatted about what dream job they would wish for and what sort of family or employer they would prefer, all the while being watched and listened to by the guard sitting a few yards away. He also noticed Almeda but for different reasons to the others.

She was a very attractive woman whose face would light up any darkened room and whose athletic physique would be admired by all who would glance upon it.

She laughed and joked with her new friends as if she did not have a care in the world. But this would all change soon enough.

For the rest of the afternoon, a carefully planned sequence of events would be followed. This much practiced chain of preparation had always worked so smoothly. Everyone involved scurried and scampered along corridors and in and out of rooms, carrying and moving both people and equipment.

While Hofmann rested and tried to grab some sleep, many others would prepare the Russian for his moment.

Now in position in the theatre, he was once again wired up to the many machines and life preserving liquids hanging above his head. He would not be brought to consciousness for many hours yet but reassuringly for the watching staff, he would moan and grunt to himself, moving his eyes and fingers whilst in deep induced sleep. He remained alive and the likelihood of the contract being fulfilled remained high.

The Syrian man slept alone in the dark. He too was dreaming and trying to wake; however, his sleep was not as restful and his mind was not always a pleasant place to be. At times, it was a tormented place, a dark place and the more the hours passed, the more he returned to the here and the now. Slowly, he was coming back to life but one that was so different from the existence he had before he received that injection.

His body swollen, his face blue and sagging with the trauma, an irregular pulse and then bit by bit, the pain. He would feel the pain build, but he would be unable to stop it, incapable of reaching out for help. No one would come anyway.

Hofmann returned to the theatre momentarily.

"Get the girl ready. Get her isolated from the others. I will be ready in one hour to start on the Russian, but we need now to get her ready for tomorrow's job," he said.

The nurse acknowledged.

"Remember, she cannot know what is happening. It is about her new life and job. You choose where and what I don't care, but she cannot suspect."

Then he left the room.

There was an obvious tension growing.

McCann could feel it, and he was many miles away relaxing on a friend's farm. He knew the schedule of events and had asked to be called if the timings slipped. He had not been called by anyone from the hotel but that brought no comfort.

He knew it was very soon to be the Russian.

He returned to his malt whiskey and looking out over the peaceful glen and waited.

Almeda had been asked to go to and stay in her room. She was informed that there may be some good news pending and now she stared out of the small window and waited. There was no view of the gardens from her window, but it was the best she could do at this time.

When the knock on the door came, her heartbeat became noticeably faster. The guards had keys to all their rooms and did not have to wait, however, this time she got to answer the door herself rather than it be opened.

"Please, Miss, follow me. It's your turn," said the guard in a calm manner. She remembered him from earlier when she had sat and chatted to her new friends outside on the grass.

"Yes, of course, a minute please while I get my jumper," she replied turning towards the small clothing unit and her jersey.

He stared her up and down as he had done earlier. He liked what he saw. *Pity,* he thought to himself.

"I have not seen Abud today," she started, "do you know where he is?"

"Gone from the hotel. He has a job on a farm," came the unconvincing reply.

"So is it my turn. Does someone have a job or something for me now?"

She had many questions as her excitement grew.

"Something like that," he said.

"What is it, please? Am I to also be on a farm? I have seen pictures of the farms here and the animals. I hope it's a farm for I have never seen a cow or a pig before. Just in pictures. I do hope it is a farm for me."

He decided not to reply but let her imagination wander as did his own as he watched her walk along the corridor and down the stairs in front of him.

"Here, Miss," he said suggesting she stop.

He brushed past her and knocking on a door opened it wide. The light from inside further illuminated the hall and as she was gestured in as her face glinted off the light. She truly was a beautiful young woman and in any other circumstance would have much to look forward to in life.

She was greeted inside by a woman she had not seen before. This woman looked official and was wearing a smart black uniform.

"Right, my dear, I am a nurse here and before we go on, we have to check your health. I will be conducting a simple medical and taking blood and urine samples. OK?" said the woman.

Almeda nodded but did not really understand what was going to happen and why she was in this room.

"Good, right clothes," said the woman in a firm tone.

Almeda stood and waited. She had not understood that this had been an instruction she was to follow.

Again, "Clothes, off, leave your underwear on, now please," said the woman this time pointing to her garments.

She turned to the guard.

"I do not need you in here please stand by the door outside."

The guard walked over to the only chair in the room and sat down.

The woman sighed but carried on with Almeda.

"I need to weigh you and get your height you see. Need to establish how healthy you are, my dear. All simple things so hurry now, I have not got all day," now in a slightly frustrated voice after the guard had refused to leave the room.

Almeda looked at the woman and then around at the guard. She became very self-conscious very quickly.

"All clothes?"

"No this and this please," she replied pointing to her blouse and trousers.

As she unbuttoned her top, the woman was looking at a chart before picking up what would soon be seen as needles and a syringe. Small bottles of clear liquid were positioned next to each other on a table next to the bench. Almeda started to look around the room as she stood now almost naked in front of these two strangers. She did not look at them, instead she surveyed the room for clues, for anything that may help her understand better what she was doing in this place.

Whether it was out of confusion or anxiety she did not know but her questions started again, this time to the unfamiliar woman.

"So please do you know about my friend, Abud? Am I going to the same farm as he is on? Is it close and please, does it have pigs and cows for I have only seen these animals in pictures? I am so excited if I am to work on a farm. In my country, we do not have farms like here."

The small room fell silent. No reply was forthcoming.

Her embarrassing predicament would soon be over, and she would be allowed to cover up again. Her body mass and fat levels were calculated, lung capacity checked, nails and hair were checked for signs of any pending health issues, a strong beam of light from an ophthalmoscope looked deep into her eyes looking again for any signs that there could be an issue with an organ or two but soon enough this was given the all clear.

Now blood.

A fresh new white hospital gown was handed to her, but she had to figure out herself how to put it on. She failed the first time much to the amusement of the preying eyes of the watching guard. He found her bending and tying of the flimsy product much to his liking.

"Wrong dear," said the woman, "other way around," as she pointed to the tied strings being at her rear. Again, there was an uncomfortable moment for Almeda.

She was then instructed to sit on the side of the wheeled table. As she did, it moved slightly, and this surprised everyone a little.

"Stop the wheels please," she said facing the guard.

He stood and walked close to Almeda who felt quite vulnerable in her almost transparent white gown. He pressed the brake on two wheels of the portable table and went back to the chair to watch again.

Her arm was positioned to allow the woman to find a suitable vein. A pressure wrap was applied to the upper arm and the veins rose to the surface of the skin.

Almeda could not look when the needle came close. She did not like the thought of needles puncturing her skin, but she also wanted to hide from what was happening. She did not really know what was happening to her in this room but watching would not be helpful, she thought.

The guard stood just in case he was needed.

In it went. Deep into her vein.

She flinched a little as it pierced her skin, but she did not look. The syringe withdrew slightly from its tube and was then followed by red blood up and along a tiny tube. A few seconds later, the woman withdrew the needle and offered Almeda cotton wool to place over the tiny wound.

"Here, take this to the test room," the woman commanded. "Do it now, please."

This time the guard obeyed her and reached for the small sample bottle of Almeda's blood and left the room.

"Right my dear, please sit here and wait for my return. There is water over there if you need it, otherwise, stay put." And as she walked to the door, she spoke again, "oh and I will lock the door just to be sure. Keep you safe."

Keep me safe? Safe from what? Is that what she said, and she meant? thought Almeda.

The door closed and Almeda heard the sound of the door being locked.

She did not know how long she sat there, motionless, alone, almost naked, wondering what was happening to her, but she came around to the present when she heard a key in the lock.

"Right, hello again, my dear. I am happy to tell you; you are a healthy young lady. Nothing indicated in the blood sample, but I guess you knew that being so young and all," said the woman.

The words went over the head of the recipient, but Almeda smiled all the same.

The nurse had kept the door open this time and soon enough Almeda knew why.

The guard appeared a few seconds later and closing the door, he sat back down on the seat near the corner. This time he pulled out his phone and started to scroll through some favoured app on the home screen.

"Just one last thing to do, young lady," said the woman not looking at Almeda but instead reaching for one of the small bottles on the shelf. It was a clear liquid and as she reached for a second new syringe Almeda knew that this time nothing was going out her body this time, instead, something was 'going in'. This alarmed her.

"Madam, please, what is now happening? I see the needle, but the blood was good, you said it was good healthy," quizzed Almeda.

She did not respond again.

The guard looked up from his phone and watched, ready.

The liquid from the tiny bottle was partly transferred into the new syringe and tested to confirm its release when pushed back into the tube. A small amount of the liquid came out of the end and ran down the steel length.

She stepped towards Almeda who withdrew her arms.

"Please madam, what is this now, please?" she said fearfully.

"Arm please, my dear, there is nothing to worry about, just something to help us test your heart rate," said the nurse. It was the first thing that had popped into her head.

171

Almeda did not know what to do. She suspected resisting would be futile with the guard in the room. She just wanted a reassuring answer, and none was forthcoming from this woman in front of her.

What to do, what to do? She panicked.

The woman held her arm but did not force it into a more useful position. She just held her arm and looked Almeda in the face.

She released her arm. Almeda sunk into herself. She conceded.

For a second time a needle punctured the vein, the same vein, but this time the woman pushed the end not pulling and the transparent liquid went into Almeda's arm.

Her head went fuzzy almost immediately. She tried to move her lips to speak but she did not hear any words for she could not say anything. Her lips, her face could not move. She felt heavy, very heavy, and unstable.

"Quick, hold her," she heard but did not know who had said this.

Almeda was asleep.

Whether she would ever wake again was in the hands of a German doctor now residing in a five-star hotel in the beautiful Irish countryside. One thing was certain, however, if she were to wake again and see the daylight, she would be forever incomplete, without an organ she had been born with.

Neither forced patients would ever know, but Almeda now slept only several yards away, on the opposite side of a wall from her friend Abud. Both in a suspended state awaiting someone else's decisions that would determine their fate.

The woman would disappear from Almeda's life and in her place would appear a more sinister but unknown German doctor. She would neither see him nor would she speak with him but for the next few days he would dictate her life.

Occasionally, she would be visited however not by any of the nurses, nor the doctor himself who was too busy working on the replacement of the old man's liver, but by the guard. The one who had watched her, who had enjoyed her body visually and while she slept and vulnerable, was now doing so physically. She would never know this either.

For now, Hofmann worked solidly on his Russian oligarch well into the evening.

The nurses performed his every command and as the lights of the machines flickered and changed from green to red to green, no one spoke. The air condition struggled to rid the room of the stench of the next opened chest and the next paying, but sleeping, 'customer' receiving a new lease of life, courtesy of an unwilling and unsuspecting donor.

Hofmann would spend the next three hours putting a thirty something healthy Syrian liver into an 83-year-old very wealthy retired Russian gang leader and friend of the Russian President, so that he may, once again, travel extensively upon recovery and visit his close family living a luxurious exile because of his former actions.

McCann slept comfortably. He had no immediate worries. No one had called him from the hotel. He had been informed that the doctor was progressing well with his paid-up Russian guest suggesting no pending issues with his men and that of the guests.

The doctor would finish in due course and leave the five others to finish up with the follow up after care support for the Russian. He would have himself a quick shower before moving to his room balcony with his favourite whiskey and once again, end his growing torment of illegality and unhuman actions, with excessive drinking and speeches to himself out loud when drunk. Each time, his inner morality fought a little harder to get out and spoil his party.

He had worked this way for almost four years now and conducted many unethical surgeries on innocent kidnapped migrants and the whiskey kept it right for him. It kept him going on to the next and many more after that, however, it was building. His guilt was building, and he would have to drink more and more to defeat it.

He slept well that night. The alcohol helped. It always did.

Check your tenses here again, you've slipped into 'would.'

The next day would become much like the others. New patient, new victim, new paid-up recipient. More paid for sex and more imported German whiskey. It was his life now and he had chosen it to be this way.

In London, a weary and frustrated Abernethy stared at a PC screen. He had three surrounding his eye line, but he stared at just one. It showed the picture of an Irish journalist assassinated by a hired gun whom he knew, whom he had tried and failed to reach before. *Who was the employer?* he thought. *Why the journalist and is the timing significant?*

For now, Abernethy just stared at this one still image. Not much else went through his mind for he was tired and needed to switch off and rest.

The next morning, the doctor surprised himself and woke early. Demanding his full fried breakfast before eight, surprised the hotel staff. He followed this up with a quick check on the Russian now back in his luxury room surrounded by both nurses and armed guards.

Then Hofmann started his routine and mundane day but not before kicking his latest prostitute out of his room and his life.

Almeda did not move nor cry out when his scalpel went deep and firm into her stomach. Almeda would never know and, for now, she would not care. The drugs made sure of that.

Chapter 14
Almeda's Awakening

Like always, he operated at a fast pace.

His patients were less human more product.

Almeda was no different to him.

His ethos was more haste more money and, the others around him and supporting his work, could see his lack of care and at times lack of accuracy. They too did not care. They were sanitised against all ethical and moral feelings of guilt and wellbeing as well as the often violent and gruesome imagery in front of them.

For now, she slept peacefully. The drugs had brought on her sleep. It had also brought on an out-of-place and inappropriate smile across her face.

"How long do we have, nurse?" he said.

When in his theatre, on his turf, he kept all contact formal. It was his way to show his authority.

"How long, nurse, until we need to anesthetise her more. I don't want to stay here a minute longer than I have to. I am tired and I want a drink and some sleep," he repeated, but this time stopping his attention from the growing cavity in her abdomen and turning to look at the nurse direct.

She was the main supporting nurse and the anaesthetist. She was his right hand 'man' and also his point of attack whenever he chose, yet she always stayed with him. Perhaps, because of some inner twisted loyalty or perhaps because these two had to stay together. One could bring the other down with a slip of the tongue and a lifetime in jail.

"I can put a second dose in, doctor, if this would help you not to worry," she said in a calm supportive manner.

"This stuff costs money. I don't want a second dose in unless we have to. I want to know when she may wake so I know how long I have!" he barked back at the nurse.

"It will be fine, doctor, please, carry on, it will be fine," she repeated.

She was puzzled as to why this day he asked. He had done so before but this day he really did seem to be in a rush.

Hofmann paused for a moment to take in what he had heard. He stood motionless for a moment. Scalpel in one hand covered red and dripping with blood, while the other hand remained firm on her abdomen holding open the wound where he had cut like a butcher carving up a pig's carcass.

Then, head down he carried on.

It was a strange moment inside the theatre, but most had experienced strange moments many times.

When his phone rang, McCann was startled.

He had been out late the night before and now, safe on a trusted friend's farm, away from the madness of the Manor House Hotel, he had relaxed to the point of not expecting any interruptions.

He immediately thought, *shit, what's happened at the hotel.* It was as if he had advance notice of ill doings.

"Irish. Hope you're doing well, Irish," the voice on the line said.

The voice puzzled McCann but clearly it was someone who knew him.

"So, who is this?" McCann replied.

The accent was not British or Irish, so the withheld number was not likely law enforcement. This thought by itself seemed to relax McCann a little.

There was a small pause. Clearly, the caller was enjoying his moment of advantage.

"Irish, I am a friend of a friend and have been asked to remind you about the money. My friend doesn't seem to have his full payment yet for the recent delivery to your hotel," the voice came back.

The penny dropped. It was to do with the Estonian.

McCann had to be careful how he reacted.

"So, who am I talking to. Do you have a name and I assume you mean my friend from Estonian?" he said in a firm tone.

A second pause followed.

"Yes, I am a friend of his and I am after the full payment. It is late, Irish, and I do not want to have to visit your nice hotel, though I am told that it is," he said.

So, it was clear that names were not being mentioned. No doubt both men were using some form of encrypted device and not likely being listened to by the police. It was obvious that the subject matter was to remain vague.

"Tell my friend the second payment will be with him very soon. I am awaiting confirmation on the quality of the delivery before he gets full payment. He should know this."

McCann stood firm but with an anxious expression across his face. This could easily blow up in his face and bring in law enforcement if he were not careful. He had never chased McCann before for money. He had never had to chase.

"And when shall I say to him this confirmation is to be had. You see my friend is very keen to get his money soon and I am likewise very keen to get back to my country. I like Ireland but the beer is better back in my country," the voice said.

McCann looked out over the flowing hills in front of him.

The Estonian had left a hitman on site just in case.

"And are you here in Ireland then?" McCann said already knowing the answer but allowing himself a few more seconds' thinking time. McCann skimmed the horizon for a glint of glass in the sunlight. The sign that he was under the cross hairs of a snipper's rifle.

Nothing obvious, he thought to himself.

"Irish, when shall I tell him? I want a date." This time the voice was sounding impatient.

"He will have his money the usual method and it will take forty-eight hours. That, my new Estonian friend, is what you can tell him."

Yet another pause.

Have I pushed him too hard, thought McCann.

"I can stay two more days, Irish. I enjoy sitting and watching your staff tend to the hotel grounds," and as the last word came across to McCann the phone line went dead.

McCann continued to stare over the hillside thinking. He had the money and payment was not a problem. The problem was that leaving a man behind had never been a tactic of the Estonian before.

What's changed this time? He thought, as his stare moved to his inactive phone and then to the farmhouse door. *Whiskey,* he thought to himself as he began to move inside.

Hofmann worked furiously on her. It looked to the nurses that there was much less care than usual. It was as if she were only valuable for the one kidney and there was no need to protect her on going health and future organ extractions. The reality of the situation was different, however.

Hofmann had one further task that day and no doubt into the night. He had to put the organ into the paying guest, the Russian and so seemed to be in a hurry on a task where hurrying was the enemy. It was his second procedure of the day. The Syrian man had 'donated' earlier so a second wealthy Russian could live better.

A third hour would pass and together the doctor's team inside the morbid theatre worked away inside and around the bloodied cavity of a once beautiful young innocent teenage girl. Her guts had been moved and bruised and to free up space, her intestines and much of her stomach were awkwardly and ruthlessly clamped outside the cavity to her side and the table.

She now no longer had the strange, relaxed smile across her face. Instead of drug induced calm.

When the third hour on the operating table became the fourth, Hofmann decided even he needed a break.

A short discussion followed, and he and the two nurses left the theatre and went to clean up and rest. The guard who had shown an unhealthy interest in the once sleeping Almeda was left alone with the macabre breathing vessel on the table. His interest in her long gone.

There would be no rest for anyone, however.

There were stirrings in the dark.

Not far from the exposed chest and abdomen cavity of the innocent teenager, whose only crime was to wish for a chance of a new life away from fear and war, was her former friend and earlier victim Abud El-Kater. Less than a day earlier his dreams were also shattered, and he was now stirring from an induced sleep, in a dark recovery room, next door to the theatre where she now lay.

The drugs were wearing thin, and pain was returning to what was left of his body. This pain would grow and grow as his conscious mind likewise came around to the here and the now, and once started, not much could take the waking pain away again.

At first, there were grumblings. They would grow louder and louder and then the grumblings became words. Confused and mixed-up at first but as his mind started to focus and thoughts reappeared into his brain, the realisation and fear of what had happened to him, of what was still happening to him, took control in the only way his mind knew how to.

At first, he screamed. Trying to move his limbs and sit up but this did not work. He remained strapped to the bed. Yet to him, this did not register. Only that he could not sit up. This brought even more confusion and terror, and even more anguish and screams of pain.

Now the guard in the room next door could hear Abud. The guard could hear the violent cries of pain and terror and what he interpreted as the banging of metal as he believed the earlier patient to be fighting against his shackles and moving the wheeled bed around.

At first, he was unsure what to do. This had never happened before. *Leave the girl and investigate or to sit it out and wait for others to arrive?*

Instinctively, he stood and went outside to the alarm.

Fisting the small square piece of glass, he pressed the inner button.

Instantly, the noise intensified ten times as the hospital alarm system kicked in. The sound proofing would keep most of the noise away from the guests further up and away across the hotel, but they would hear something and have to be told in time that what they heard was a fire drill.

For now, the nurses and the doctor ran quickly to the area.

Two further guards joined the growing number of confused hotel 'staff' and for a short moment none knew what to do first.

"It's the first one. The Syrian, he's screaming, he's awake," said Almeda's guard.

Nurse Angelle pushed one of the new arriving guards out of the way and ran to the side corridor which gave access to where Abud had been left. The guard followed right behind her. Hofmann had arrived in the corridor. He suspected his late night working on the paid-up Russian might now be an extremely late night and he was angry.

Almeda's guard was encouraged to go back into the theatre room by the second nurse who came in with him.

The door swung open, but it would not swing close easily for both the guard and the nurse froze in the entrance when they saw Almeda. The swing door landed on the leg of the nurse, but she did not notice this. Instead, she saw a moving, flinching, cut in half and exposed teenage girl whose face stared back at them both. She was upright and organs moved now exposed the air. She was holding her intestines in her hands and as the blood poured from many parts of the wound she stared and screamed and stared again, not quite sure how this horror was happening and even if was real and not a nightmare.

179

The horror in her eyes worsened only by the lack of noise coming from her open mouth. There were no screams. She had forgotten how to scream amongst the grotesque imagery of what she saw inches below her chin.

She saw the workings of her own body. She saw her heartbeat and part of her lungs move upward and downwards. She saw blood and after she saw enough, her brain would then tell her about the pain.

The Manor House hotel secret hospital had not experienced this before. Hofmann had not experienced this before and no one inside, down below ground in an illegal hospital, knew what to do first.

Hofmann was stuck between the sights of a rapidly stitched up man held down by straps fighting his binds so hard that the stitches were bursting open in front of his eyes. Blood was beginning to pour out of the unwilling patient and as he was rapidly going into hypovolemic shock. His blood pressure was crashing, and he would die in seconds if nothing were done.

The nurse tried to search around for something. Hofmann assumed a syringe and drugs, but he really did not care.

"Gag him he is making too much noise," shouted Hofmann who was a bit dazed himself at the sight but quickly decided that Almeda was the prize. She would save the Russian and his fee.

The Syrian had done his bit and whatever happened would happen. He left the area and walked rapidly back into the theatre area.

The hospital alarm was silenced and now there was just the noise of the two tortured patients and the bloodied mess all around.

There was no sanctuary for Hofmann in this room.

Instead, he saw the guard try and partly fail to hold Almeda's upper body down. She had been loosely tied as they had been working on her, but now she had broken free somehow and was beginning to find her screams. The guard struggled. She seemed to have superhuman strength having adrenalin and who knows what else being generated and moved around her body by her brain now in survival mode itself.

"Fuck, fuck," shouted the guard whose hand on her shoulder seemed to slip and move and land inside the open cavity of her body. Retrieving it again, he saw his left hand covered in blood. He had pulled up flesh and guts from inside and as he looked down at his hand he threw up in his mouth turning away only to release the vomit onto the floor and his trousers.

The nurse shouted to Hofmann.

"She's bursting up inside, help, man."

Hofmann reached over, moving the guard away who was now in shock himself and happy to leave the immediate area.

Hofmann reached for the metal box nearby. His emergency box of drugs and tricks and opened it.

Almeda kept screaming now. She had found full volume and each and every time she did so, blood squirted upwards and out of the cavity and from her mouth and nostrils.

Her blood was covering the theatre floor, making it slippery and handling Almeda more difficult. It got worse. Fighting back against the nurse trying to restrain her so the doctor could inject a tranquilizer into her, forced a movement that spilled her stomach partly out of the open cavity. The nurse went into a moment of shock before, then grabbing the organ and forcing it back into her body as best as the screaming woman would allow.

Hofmann found what he thought he needed and pulling the safety cap off with his teeth, plunged the needle deep into Almeda's upper torso. The liquid went in and throwing the needle away he went for a second.

In it went. Out into her remaining body went the contents.

"Not bloody sure what one I got in first so tried a second," he said to the nurse in some form of weird apologetic tone.

Both the nurse and Hofmann relaxed their grip on her ruined body and watched and waited.

The guard holding his left wrist with his right hand just stared at the three in front of him. His hand still fully red with her blood and puss.

No one was sure how long the drugs took to work but when she fell back down onto the bed and her tormented screams stopped, becoming more unconscious mumbling, there was a noticeable physical exhalation of stress and relief from the nurse and her doctor.

A strange silence fell across the room.

Hofmann looked over to the wall behind which the Syrian was being held. He listened. Nothing. Both rooms had fallen silent but that would not necessarily be a good thing.

Sure enough, his wondering of events next door became factual.

Nurse Angelle entered the theatre and Hofmann knew straight away that Abud El-Kater was dead. Also, straight away, the tiny twinge of guilt left Hofmann.

I can give McCann a good excuse, he needs me, he thought to himself.

"Right, so we have lost one. No matter we have what we need. You," he said looking at the guard, "get others and dispose of the body properly. Leave nothing behind and if I am up late, so are you. I want that room spotless."

The guard, happy to leave the theatre, and, more comfortable and used with the dead rather than the dying, went off as instructed.

Even when the lifesaving machine alarms went off yet again and the theatre became awash with red flickering lights, did the guard feel any need to return.

Hofmann, however, panicked. Not for the wellbeing of the girl but for the wellbeing of her kidney. It was possible to extract it from a corpse. He had published papers on this very subject in a different life, but it was just healthier if it was from the living.

Almeda had given up.

She had died on the table.

The sights and the pain were too much and with her passing had gone her dreams of a free and fulfilling life.

"Shite, we have to go now," said Hofmann. *McCann won't take the loss of two,* he thought.

Nurse Angelle would join her two colleagues for the next ninety minutes. It would not take as long ripping and tearing the organ out of a dead body that could never again feel pain or have secondary complications.

The prize would be taken and after a short break and some food, all three would begin the reversing process and the operation to implant the organ of a dead teenager into the very elderly body of a very wealthy Russian man.

Chapter 15
The Hotel Visit

He would be almost invisible.

Through the VPN he was in Austria, whereas he was actually many miles further East close to the Turkey-Bulgaria border. Using the TOR search function, he would be further made untraceable to most. This specialist, originally military-only, search engine went deep down into the dark web. Using one of his many legend fake accounts, he felt confident that he could post on forums and not be found out.

He would post on many dark web forums. All riddled with illegal activity or at best want to be criminals, but it was on 'Endchan' forum that he usually had his success.

Under the username Blooddrop4, he posted again.

Delivery successful. As always. More parcels required quickly. Prefer newer reliable products targeted for the female market.

Then he would set up a response notification and sign out. He would wait for any notification to bring his encrypted phone to life.

A slightly run-down area of a sleepy Irish town had woken up to the additional interest placed upon it. Even during the 'troubles' of an earlier Irish historical period, reporters were given of a type of immunity from intimidation and victimisation. Here, however, a journalist was assassinated. A journalist, Steven Davison, known to everyone in the area, was killed in broad daylight and the killer simply vanished. It had come to the attention of more than just the local constabulary. Details of the journalist had landed on Abernethy's desk.

"Right, get this name over to the OSINT lot and see what we can find," said Abernethy. "There is some connection between this man and the foreign traffickers, and the fact he lived in that town with the hotel and is now dead suggests he was onto something of interest to us."

"Sir, yes, right away," said Hanson, one of the team as he left the room to deliver the file to the investigators on the lower floor.

The central control room whizzed and buzzed with activity for the next few hours. Abernethy and his team referenced and cross referenced each miniscule piece of evidence. They were searching for the break that would take them closer to solving the puzzle that was the disappearing migrants and the identity of the people traffickers.

Hanson returned.

"Sir, we may have a break. I mean the OSINT lot found his nearest and dearest and all his social media, but they also found images and notes of the hotel, the Manor House Hotel Just North of Letterkenny, a little town South East of Derry, on the Republic side of the border," he said, handing back the file to Abernethy leaving it open at the first new added page from the investigators. "I told the team to keep at the social media and search for connections and groups that may give up further clues I have also authorised one of the guys to visit the family."

Hanson moved away and waited a response. He scoured the rapidly put together dossier on Davison, but his eyes were repeatedly drawn to two photographs of the hotel. They were from different angles, but this was not really what grabbed his attention.

"Look here," he said as he summoned his team closer. "What do you see? In fact, wait let's put them up," he added, as the two photographs were scanned and instantly appeared on the top of Abernethy's viewing desk. With his fingers, he pushed the electronic photographs away and they instantly appeared enlarged on the screens pinned to the wall in front of him.

"Right, what do you see?" he repeated.

The team simultaneously lifted their heads up to view the images and consider the question.

Then words flew around.

"Could be a concealed door on the East side."

"Modern triple glazing on a nineteenth-century manor house."

"Guard, possibly carrying."

"Nope that's the easy part," said Abernethy.

"The branches of that tree seem to be bending in an unusual manner."

"No, wait, yes, but not what I am asking for. So, the branches, why would they do that and yet the thorn bushes remain upright?"

184

"Helicopter," said one from the back.

"Exactly. Downdraft enough to shift the smaller branches but not the firmer thorn bushes. What distance do we think?" said Abernethy.

"Sir, the grounds could land a chinook, but I would suggest even the thorns would feel it if it were one of these. I suggest something smaller, single fixed wing, perhaps the AW trekker class as it shifts the wealthy around the world and looking at this grounds map, and the photo, I suggest it could be landing around 40 yards from that corner over towards the tennis courts."

"Good, Jones, off you go and search landing rights for helicopters in Letterkenny over the last month and I want origin points and owner details."

"OK, apart from that, what else do you see?" Abernethy asked a third time.

This time, no one answered...

"Nothing?" said Abernethy while waiting for a reply. When none was forthcoming he spoke again, "I see Griselinia."

"Griselinia is the darling of the Irish hedge family. Its maximum growth height is two feet. Now what do you see?" He was enjoying the moment. It had been a slow and dull day but at last Abernethy was enjoying this part.

Then came a female voice.

"If it grows to two feet tops and both photographs have a slight upward taken trajectory..." said the transfer member from Scottish Department, Pauline Fraser. "The taker was under two feet or, more correctly, was lying down on the ground taking these pictures."

"Precisely. And why would someone be lying down..." Pauline Fraser butted in, "to not be seen from either the hotel or the helicopter." There was a pause. "Or both," she added.

Abernethy smiled and nodded slowly.

"OK, we need to get inside this hotel and fast, and find out why this journalist did not want to be seen," he suggested, as he contemplated the best method to do so.

"A team, sir, one that can conceal hidden cams and mics?" said Hanson.

"Too risky. We need someone who can hide in plain sight. Someone who looks like they might actually be a guest of this five-star mysterious spa hotel." Again, there was a pause. The others could see Abernethy was in thought.

"OK, I know the person. I will contact him. In the meantime, focus attention on this hotel and get a two-man team into the journalist's house. The constabulary will have missed something, and we need to find that thing. Go!"

he shouted, and the room once again whizzed and buzzed with activity. Then, without turning, he stopped and again shouted to his team.

"And get in touch with that Bellingcat lot. See if they can dig up what you lot have missed."

Abernethy wandered out the control room while scrolling through his phone contacts.

"*Roy McCabe, Roy McCabe where are you?*" he said in a sort of, 'long time no see', manner as the contact list reached 'M'.

"Right, old chum, let's see what you have to say for yourself," he said out loud as he found the entry and pressed the call button.

The phone rang out and after a few rings went to answer phone.

Yup, just as I would have thought. Left the NCA now living it up somewhere exotic. No time for the hard work, he thought with a smile as he wandered down the stairs heading to the lower ground cafeteria and a short rest.

Before Abernethy had reached the bottom stair, his phone rang. It was McCabe.

"Now then, Roy, how the hell are you?"

"Growing suspicious as to why you of all people are calling me, and why now. Other than that me and the missus are fine and enjoying life at last," came McCabe's reply.

Unseeingly over the phone, both men smiled. Both men smiled but the other would not see this.

"I have a wee job for you, my friend. It involves you and your better half taking a weekend break in a five-star spa hotel, with magnificent coastal views and a golf course that challenges the best I hear, courtesy of my employers. It could be tasking and tiresome in the Jacuzzi and posh restaurant. Are you game?"

Abernethy knew his friend. He already knew the answer.

"Yup, I am in but better check with the boss back home first," he replied.

"Tell her the wine's on me also, that used to swing it in our favour in the past," said Abernethy.

"Will do, mate, will get back asap." And with that the line went dead.

Abernethy would spend the next few hours going over then back over the file given to him in Amsterdam a short while earlier, and the new leads which had come from it.

Roy McCabe would spend similar time packing a bag for a stay at a five-star hotel with his wife.

McCabe switched his house alarm on and exited locking the door behind him. His wife Nicola was already in the car, a tidy almost-new Mercedes, and was busy on her smart phone messaging her two closest friends about the pending free adventure to the five-star luxury hotel.

The car sprung to life and soon, both had exited their drive and were racing towards the retreat only forty miles away. When they entered the hotel grounds an hour later, in a small town, where once an Irish Times journalist was the talk of the town, two men were entering the police restricted apartment of the dead man. Both had broken into many properties before. They had been trained to do so without leaving evidence of their presence.

"They are in, sir," commented one man to Abernethy.

Abernethy turned to face him, and they turned back to the file and his screen. Acknowledgement done.

The two men moved around the small flat in total silence. They never spoke to each other nor made any sound which could be heard from the flat below or neighbours, always aware of their shadows and how they could be seen from the street outside if they let their guard slip for just one second.

Both men knew exactly what to look for.

The obvious.

The authorities were trained to be suspicious and to expect the hidden or the secret and often as a result, they would miss evidence that looked them square in the face. Abernethy's two men were trained differently.

Their rubber gloves left no marks on items searched or touched and their masks ensured that their warm breath left no residue on glass or shiny surfaces. Even the soles of their shoes were made from a fabric that was designed to leave much less of an imprint of the ground than normal footwear. Ghosts they may not have been but almost invisible they were.

"Good afternoon, sir, are you checking in?" said the lady at reception in a soft Irish accent.

"Yes, we are, in the name of McCabe," came the reply as both guests waited.

McCabe knew that his good friend would have crossed every 'T' and dotted every 'I' but as he himself had not arranged the stay there was a tiny moment of anxiety.

The receptionist lowered her head and tapped on her computer.

"Mr and Mrs McCabe, let's see," she said and a very short moment later, she faced the couple again. "Yes here we are, the master suite, no less," then, seeing the smile on her guests' faces and within the relaxed atmosphere she laughed. "What have you done wrong Mr McCabe to be treating your wife to this luxurious stay?"

Turning to retrieve the key from its pigeonhole she gestured towards Nicola McCabe, "Best you take this Mrs McCabe," as she handed the key over.

Roy McCabe tried to come up with some funny reply but could not.

"Please leave your bags and go into the bar where glasses of bubbles will be waiting. I will get your bags taken to your room," said the receptionist, and almost immediately a second lady appeared and encouraged the two new guests to follow her into the bar.

Both would sit and enjoy the view and the drink in silence. One would smile as she watched the clouds move slowly across the blue sky. The other, more reflective and pondering if he was going to be able to assist his good friend Abernethy.

Roy McCabe entered the room and immediately went over the large wall-high window to look out. His wife wandered the extensive room looking in cupboards and drawers with a large grin across her face.

Right, now I get it, he thought to himself. *Master suite my arse. I can see the main entrance and the staff entrance from this room.* He was right. Abernethy was business as usual and had specifically chosen that room as a vantage point.

As the day started to darken, McCabe would be in the dining room enjoying a meal when the wrapped body of a young dead teenager would be taken from the side entrance where staff would often smoke, and hurriedly dumped into a branded trade van 'Glencore Specialty Meats'.

The flat was very quiet.

Little noise from the street one floor below even when the many buses and lorries went past. It was a small flat but well insulated against the Irish winter and coming and goings of the people and traffic outside. It was this lack of noise that caught his attention.

Killick looked at the window closest to him. Then, the other in the room. Wandering over to the second window but remaining out of direct line of the light streaming in through it, he stared at the design.

Killick took hold of the handle and opened the window. Then, immediately closed it again. Curiosity satisfied. His colleague stopped what he was doing and watched. Again, he opened the window a little and again closed it. The noise of the street filled then left the room as he did so.

He looked up towards the trickle vent. It was closed. Designed to limit the cold air inwards but to allow a 'trickle' of fresh air into the room. But this vent was closed. His colleague read his mind and was already walking over to the second window on the same wall.

"Open, this one's open," he said.

Both men wondered if this was significant. Likely, it was just a 'nothing' both men looked at the windows closest and wondered.

A second or two passed.

"It's bloody open," said Killick. "Look, it's actually open but covered," he went on. Would he be speaking out load if they wanted to be completely quiet?

He reached up and tried to get his fingers into the vent but was unable. Pulling out a small screwdriver he prised off the front cover and took out the neatly folded piece of paper. Replacing the cover, the vent was now clearly open and allowing a tiny flow of fresh air into the room again.

Killick unfolded the paper and read out loud.

"Blue L 36 1618."

"Locker," said his colleague. "Likely the bus station, can't think where else in this town would have lockers." But after a few seconds, he added, "Except perhaps the police station."

"Hmmm, let's hope it's the railway station. The police option could be tricky," replied Killick. "Right, let's finish up here first," and immediately both men went straight back to work searching the flat in silence.

"Another glass of wine, sir?" said the restaurant manager.

McCabe nodded.

"And for, madam, shall I refill your glass?" he added.

Again, there was a nod of acceptance.

"So, darling, why are we really here?" she asked her husband. "I mean its lovely and all, but I know you. Who have you spoken with recently to inspire this treat?"

He paused for a moment. *Should I just say because we deserve it?* He thought.

Then he spoke. "James called me."

"James? After all this time he called you?" she said. Her voice turning a little angry. "He doesn't want you..." but she was interrupted.

"No, he doesn't. He just wants me to help just this time, and, here in this place. To look and to listen, that's all. Nothing more."

She looked down at her plate then back to her husband picking up her glass as she did.

"Right, call the waiter please, Husband. I feel I am going to have more of this rather nice champagne." And with that she took a sip.

McCabe was a little relieved. He summoned the waiter as instructed.

The two shadows left the dead journalist's flat and, unseen and separately, exited the building out onto the street. Both waiting for the right moment and a passing bus or lorry to assist with being unseen before merging into the natural public flow.

Killick made his way towards the small local bus station. His colleague headed back to the team van and onto the surveillance equipment to wait for his return.

The bus station was unmanned.

A small commuter type hub, however, Killick was wary of the multiple CCTV units around the building. He was easily able to avoid the focus of most but inevitably would be picked up on a couple. He stood and reviewed the best route in and out while pretending to be reading a message of his smart phone a few steps outside the entrance.

Looking at the timetable on the monitor, he made his move. He had ninety seconds until the next arrival, which would be useful.

He walked briskly but not unnaturally into the station. There were no barriers so his passage towards the lockers was unhindered.

"Blue L 36 1618," he said to himself.

Locating the specific door, he entered the code and opening the door, he reached inside and took out the A4 brown envelope. Trying to look like he knew it was in there he locked up again and made his way the short distance outside to the bus bays just as the 1435 to Donegal Town was pulling up.

Three passengers got out beside him. Turning his back to the CCTV, he invaded the space of the elderly stranger and walked with him into the building. His new best friend did not fully realise Killick was literally on his shoulder. Then, once the two men were outside, he left the stranger to his own devices and set off to the van and his colleague to review the contents of the envelope. Job done.

Son meeting Dad off the bus, he thought. *Nothing obvious or suspicious with that,* and soon he was approaching the van.

He stood across the road from the team van and waited. He knew that his colleague was watching. Then, the right indicator came on for one show and stopped. The signal.

Killick crossed the road and went straight to the driver's seat door, pulling it open he quickly climbed in… Starting the engine, he belted up and drove off to their secure location.

The sun was now setting across the Irish countryside and as the two diners finished their meal, Roy McCabe's thoughts were buzzing. His numerous drinks did not help but the buzzing was triggered by his need to do something real. To do something constructive, and, to give something back to the community around him. Retirement was fine but he had one further chance to help his old friend, Abernethy and the project that he must be working on.

"I am not close to being ready to retire to the room, love. Can we sit and have a gin in the lounge bar after?" he said. He knew it was on the same West facing side as the entrance and their own room windows, so his motive was not fully honourable.

"Hell, yes dear. Retired not dead, remember?" his wife replied.

He smiled back.

Soon enough, the two had said their thanks to their waiter and were entering the lounge bar.

"Mr and Mrs McCabe, welcome," said the lounge waitress. "Please, let me show you to the booth, our best area."

"Em, well can my wife and I have that smaller table over by the window? We want to see the last of the sun. Is that OK?" he replied.

"Yes sir, of course sir, please follow me," she said.

Reaching the table his wife spoke.

"Roy, which chair do you prefer?" She knew he needed to have the viewing and strategic advantage. It had been his way for years.

He pulled back the curtain a little and looked out and down.

"This one, my dear," came the reply as he gestured to the waitress that his wife should take the other.

Drinks would soon follow as did the conversation, and she knew not to stop but to carry on chatting when her husband looked away from the table and out and down through the window. It was just easier that way.

The night would be uneventful, and the lounge bar would quietly empty and fall quiet as the staff switched the lights off.

In Geneva, in an underground car park, in a subterranean secret location, Abernethy received Killick's transmission. There were eleven photographs and a few scribbles written on most.

There would be no sleep for anyone in this room.

Next morning, McCabe was woken by a call on his phone. It was an unregistered number, and it soon rang off. Moments later a second unknown number rang his mobile and stopped abruptly. He made no attempt to answer either.

"Right, dear, I'm just going to get dressed quickly and wander the garden. I have a call to make." It had been Abernethy and it was standard procedure. *Oh, how I miss the old days,* he thought to himself.

The series of photographs had been analysed time and time again by the AI software. Metadata extracted and a situation map drawn up. The computers were still running face recognition software but there was already a growing list of suspects when Abernethy's mobile vibrated with the name of McCabe flashing up on the screen.

"Hey fella, how is the hotel?" Abernethy said as he accepted the call. "You and the misses blowing my entire accommodation budget?"

"Huh, not yet but that seems to be authorisation to do so."

Abernethy and his good friend McCabe just chatted. Both men enjoyed talking about things other than the task at hand. It had occupied both minds too much for too long and they simply enjoyed their catch up. It couldn't last, however.

"So, Roy," then a pause.

"So, I can provide you a little more detail, but not the full story you understand," said Abernethy.

"Yup, shoot mate, tell me what you are able and how I can help you with this?" came the reply.

"The Manor House Hotel appears to be a front for something much more sinister, Roy. You can't tell Nicola for she won't be able to sleep at night. OK?"

"Yup, understood."

"Somewhere inside, we believe there to be an unauthorised hospital. We believe the owners are in league with a Latvian people-smuggling gang and that it is facilitated by someone only known as 'The Estonian'. We believe that migrants, mostly North African and Middle Eastern, are promised a new life and a new start and are brought to the hotel secretly where they undergo mutilation and organ extraction to further the lives of the rich and the very wealthy. We believe some very senior and very recognisable people have passed through this place and…" he paused, took stock for a moment and then spoke again.

"We believe your old mate Brendan McCann to be heavily involved." Abernethy waited for his friend to digest his words.

"McCann. McCann and I have some unfinished business, James. Did you know it was him before you asked me to this place?" asked McCabe.

"No, mate, I did not. Recent intel from a local journo was run through the system here and we have a few positive confirmations. It's McCann and he is living in the hotel. Records and sightings go months back. That said, he left a few days back and a hack into the CCTV has shown he has not yet returned. We don't know where he is currently."

McCabe thought for a moment.

Knowing the answer already he spoke again, "OK, James, so knowing this, what do you want me to do for you?"

"Roy, I want you to enjoy your stay. I want you and Nicola to have a couple more late nights in the lounge bar by the window perhaps. I want you to, perhaps, wander the gardens and perhaps look into the windows to admire the architecture, and if you're up for it mate, I would love you to get lost looking for your room one time. Just you and be bloody careful."

"Of course, I can do that. I sense I have the easy part, James. How are you coping, mate? Tough times for you and losing her without knowing must still be taking its toll."

"I am fine, Roy. She wasn't important. Job first, remember. As always. So, you are clear? Will you call me tomorrow when it is safe to do so?" asked Abernethy.

"Will do. Oh, and if you get wind of that bastard McCann returning, you let me know, yes?"

"Have a good day, Roy. Say high to Nicola." And with that the line went dead.

Chapter 16
McCann's Return

Abernethy was astonished at the list. The software had identified a mass of high wealth individuals who had visited the Manor House Hotel. None were admitted as regular guests, of which there were many, but entered on either a wheelchair or supported by helpers. All looked very ill.

Russian oligarch, former British Ambassador to China, that chat show host from CBS, hell a player from the National Basketball Association, he thought to himself. One less famous, but much more intriguing face popped up in the report.

Jack Geddes, what the fuck is Jack Geddes doing here? Abernethy had met Geddes once at a dinner party in Washington, and now he had been photographed in Southern Ireland.

He needed a moment to think. Then he picked up him phone and called Roz Cherrie.

"Hey, James, what's wrong?" she answered.

"Why does there have to be something wrong?"

"Because we spoke yesterday and now you're calling back, so soon. What you got?" She was right. They would never talk on consecutive days. Too much to do.

"Em, well its Jack Geddes."

"Secret Service Jack Geddes. The President's detail?" Now she was fully attentive.

"Yes. That Jack Geddes. He's been to the target building and not as a guest I believe." He waited. Nothing was forthcoming so he spoke again.

"Roz, Geddes has scoped out the hotel. Why would he do that?" Abernethy's voice slightly raised now. "We knew about John Magere and we were comfortable with him but Geddes is different. We need to know why the security detail has changed." There was a new urgency in Abernethy's voice.

"James, I don't know. Do we know when?"

"We believe it to be two weeks ago. I have this photograph and the metadata was still present."

There was a second short silence.

"Right, leave this with me. I will ask around." And she hung up.

Abernethy looked at his phone for a moment longer deep in thought.

"OK, folks, listen up," he shouted, refocusing. Those in the room turned towards him.

"We have a list of highly recognisable people who have attended the target, and none appear on the hotel system or guest register. I want to know where they are right now," he said as he moved towards the exit…"Big world out there so get going now."

Coffee I think. Christ, no wonder the journo hid the photos. He must have suspected something big and now the sad fuck's paid for it with his life, Abernethy thought as he closed the door behind him.

"I will have the traditional Irish please," said McCabe to the waiter. It was breakfast time back in Southern Ireland and McCabe was feeling buoyant.

Funny, I feel like getting my money's worth but I'm not paying, he thought as he chuckled a little to himself.

"Add coffee strong and white toast please."

"Are you ready to order, Mrs McCabe?" said the waitress with a smile.

"Eh, yes please. May I have the eggs benedict with a pot of tea, and I will also have white toast," she replied.

"Good choice, I will get onto that straight away." And off she went into the kitchen to place the order.

"You should have also ordered the full Irish and I would have eaten anything you couldn't manage," McCabe said to his wife.

She smiled and turned to look out the window and the clouds as they rolled across the hillside.

"Right, we'll get going very soon, my friend," said McCann. "Thanks again for your hospitality Peter and that of your lovely family." He began to walk to the waiting car where his closest friend and confident Paddy Richards was waiting, bags already loaded.

Strangely for McCann, he stopped and turned around. The farm was quiet.

He did not know why he spoke but something inside him felt he must.

"Peter, my friend, it may be a long time before I visit your wonderful farm again. I fear the law is getting closer and smarter. I wish you all the very best and remember, stay away from the past and out of trouble." And with a small wave of the hand he turned back towards the car and off the two men went, back to the Manor House Hotel.

McCabe wouldn't know it yet, but he would be revisiting his past whether he wanted to or not.

Very soon after the dust from the wheels of McCann's car had fallen back down to earth and settled, a second vehicle drove the dirt track towards the farm he had just left. This time this visitor would be much less friendly.

An associate of McCann's, Drako, who had provided him sanctuary in one of his illicit hospitals in Belgrade a while back, was now en route to establish exactly what the Irishman was up to while hiding up at the farm. Drako had not received an order for migrants in a while and had employed two local thugs to put pressure on McCann as to why. Just a quick note about inverted commas – you use them quite frequently in places they don't need to be used.

He had long suspected that McCann had interfered with his movement of migrants through the Port of Rotterdam and onwards to Britain and Ireland ever since two of McCann's foot soldiers were seen taking photographs of the lorry driver and stowaways. Shortly after which the lorry was held up at gunpoint and the cargo taken.

Now Drako's thugs, not yet aware that they had missed McCann himself by minutes, drove on up to the farm. His close friend Peter would suffice for their information gathering. Drako would not be disappointed. By the time the two thugs had finished with the farm owner, he had told them enough to believe McCann was indeed double crossing him.

The farm owner and McCann's friend would be found bloodied and battered, hanging upside down by a rope around his ankles from a barn rafter. His family would likewise be found tied, gagged and hungry two days later inside the farmhouse.

Unaware that this was going on, Abernethy got a small break. His phone vibrated and the LED light signalled he had received a message.

A long unused number and contact reappeared on his screen.

Wow, had almost forgotten about you, my sneaky friend, he thought to himself.

It was Drako and the message simply read: 'The Guinness was a fantastic pint that isn't supposed to travel.'

Abernethy had received these same words a while back when McCann was in Belgrade working up an arms deal together with some form of illness recovery, as yet unknown to him.

McCann's on the move then, he thought. *Likely back to the hotel now the migrants are settled and out of sight.*

"Fuck," he said out loud before calling his colleague, "Roy."

"Listen up, McCann's on the move. I believe he's going back to the hotel. I want three teams on him pronto and listen, no fuck ups. He cannot get to know we are onto him." And with that he reached for his phone.

His long-time friend needed to know.

"Done!" he exclaimed and for a few seconds he was slightly relieved.

Abernethy wasn't finished.

"Sarah, I need a flight quick. I am going to the hotel. Not sure the closest airport. Check Derry and the surrounds, and I will need a car the other side. If nothing there, we will go to Belfast airport and see if there are other options via London airports if there is nothing direct. Quick please!"

"On it sir," replied a female voice.

Abernethy went back onto his phone still warm from his holding of it retrieving Drako's message.

Pierre, Pierre, where... he thought as he scrolled down his huge list of contacts. *There!*

A few hundred kilometres away across the French border, Pierre Melville's phone rang.

"James!"

"Mate, Pierre, I need you to go to the target building with me." Abernethy was getting more and more panicky. He would never call Pierre 'mate', but he had. He sensed events moving too quickly and his team was not ready. "I feel we are moving towards end game and I need an experienced hand. Can I brief you when together?"

"Yes my friend, what is your arrival point and when?"

"I will get Sarah from my office to liaise with you, Pierre. She is on the case now. Thank you. I owe you." Abernethy stopped the call and went to check his messages.

He saw what he needed to see. A text message reply from McCabe.

It read, 'Cheers buddy. Past, here I come. Roy.'

It would take a few hours for Abernethy and Melville to meet up. With no direct flights to Derry from either Geneva or Paris, the two men decided to get to London Stansted and onwards on the scheduled Logan Air flight together from there.

It was late morning, and they would not shake hands in greeting for another three hours. The onward flight to Derry would require a further ninety-minute wait when at Stansted. Abernethy estimated he could not get to the target building for six hours. This worried him. McCabe would be alone with McCann all that time. He could do nothing more.

McCabe decided he wanted to hang out in the pool and sauna area while his wife wanted to go to the local shops. The two separated after agreeing what time they would meet up again. The location was easy, the main bar area.

Reception called a taxi for her and soon she was off down the long hotel drive towards the local shops.

Roy McCabe went back to his room to gather his things for a swim and sauna. Minutes later, he was smiling at the pool guard as he walked in and chose a lounger near the large wall to ceiling windows with a view down the side of the hotel.

God, what's happened large boy, he said to himself as he lay down and saw his growing midriff almost looking back at him. *Really need to get exercising. Perhaps, next time.*

A staff member walked over to McCabe when he saw that he was settled.

"A drink or nibbles, sir?"

"Wife's away so I can have a pint. Lager please," he said with a smile pointing to the pool. "Perhaps crisps, plain. I can work it off later."

The pool waiter smiled and walked off to get the order.

He looked out the window. He was not reminiscing nor was he admiring the plush gardens. He was watching. Proper watching, for signs of unusual movement and possible locations of interest. This part had not left him. This need for information gathered with a trained eye. Indeed, he was a little taken aback when the waiter returned with his drink for he had not seen his arrival in advance.

"Thanks."

Right a swim first, he decided as he dived into the pool and set off on the first of the twenty lengths he had promised himself he would complete.

It felt like an age to Abernethy when he finally boarded the plane to Heathrow. The flight from Geneva was a relatively short one, but he spent the ninety minutes reading flies and documents. Always ensuring their contents were kept away from prying eyes.

Across several borders, almost 1000 kilometres away, Melville was likewise waiting to board his plane. The two would meet soon enough but for now they had started their journey towards the target and perhaps towards the exposure of what they were beginning to believe was a ruthless people trafficking gang.

Abernethy read, occasionally stopping to reflect on McCabe and wondering if he had put his friend into harm's way.

When the two men met, arriving off different planes, they only briefly welcomed each other. Both knew the road ahead would be tricky, and, they had not truly started down it yet.

Sitting in the corner of the departure lounge, they properly caught up.

"Is it just us, James? The others don't know we are going in?" said Melville.

"They suspect Pierre. Miranda has been monitoring the ports especially Rotterdam and keeping me alive with activities of our 'friends'," came his reply.

"Friends?"

"Yes, McCann's lot and Drako," he said reluctantly. "It's more of an issue than we suspected. McCann did the dodgy on Drako with a migrant shipment and now the two have started a war between themselves. Messes things up a bit as Drako is now much less predictable and the teams across Europe are seeing more irregular movements."

"Hmm, yes, I can imagine. We expecting him at target building?"

"No Pierre, I'm not but I am expecting an angry and agitated McCann as a result of Drako's interference."

The two men turned toward the window and watched the newly arrived plane they would soon be on and its current passengers disembarking.

A distance away, racing up a dirt track towards an isolated farmhouse were two PSNI cars, blue lights and sirens abound.

Tipped off by a local postal service worker who had seen the family inside, bound and gagged, the police would find much worse in the nearby barn. Soon enough, word would trickle back to McCann that his friend had been attacked. More, that the attackers had likely come for him. He would suspect Drako and this would make him even more of a loose cannon.

Abernethy walked to his plane just as the 'Flash Red' vibrated on his phone. As he read the 'eyes only' message his heart beat a little faster. He had put McCabe in mortal danger.

To tell him or not? He thought.

He decided not to this time.

McCabe had done his twenty lengths of the pool. He had taken longer than he wanted but was very pleased with himself that he had done it.

Relaxing on the lounger, wet but warm with the steam from the sauna trapped inside the building, he downed the pint quickly.

Looking around for the waiter he lifted his hand to catch his attention. He did not need to. His downing of the pint had not gone unseen and a second one suspected the waiter was already en route to him.

"Was it that obvious, my young friend?" said McCabe with an embarrassed smile on his face.

"Yes sir, no sorry sir, no it wasn't," said the waiter.

"It's fine, yes, please another when you are able, thank you."

As the waiter moved off McCabe likewise rose.

Hot tub then sauna, then I guess I should send her a message, he thought to himself. *May stop her spending too much,* and again a smile came across his face.

Stepping into the warm water of the pool side hot tub, he chose the back where he could watch the pool. He would not yet be aware that he had sat very close to the vent from the rooms beneath him.

McCann's car sped along the road. Richards while breaking the speed limit, remained close to it, above, but not enough to gain attention.

Soon enough, perhaps early evening as the sun was about to disappear, McCann would arrive at his hotel, unaware that McCabe was a guest.

Years ago, when building his crime empire, Roy McCabe was no guest. Instead, he was the instigator and leader of wave after wave of raids and disruptive measures against the McCann business, and, after many attempts, was the one to put him away in prison for seven years for money laundering.

McCann never forgot or forgave McCabe and had even sent teams out to try to find him when he retired. Neither man would now know that fate was to bring them together again.

Before he had left his team in Geneva, Abernethy had set his team a task. They were to establish the movements of Jack Geddes in and around the hotel and town. They were to establish why the American Secret Service were interested in a luxury hotel in Southern Ireland.

Best chase Roz when I land. Why Geddes and why now? Coincidence that he was at McCann's hotel or are our American friends doing something behind my back, he thought whilst preparing to go on board the plane.

McCabe held his second pint and enjoyed the heat of the hot tub, but grumbled at the plastic glass, *bloody health and safety everywhere,* he thought. When the timer stopped the water calmed and a sort of tranquil silence appeared. There was only one other person in the area swimming, so it became really quite quiet. As he relaxed more and closed his eyes his senses heightened and as they did so noises reappeared. This time, however, it was not of the water moving or splashing. It was not the noise of machinery humming or birds outside. It was a moaning sound. His eyes opened.

Nothing, no one here, he thought. He closed his eyes again and this time held his breath.

What is that sound. It's like someone moaning, someone ill like what you might hear in a hospital ward. Another. A second sound. *Woman this time?*

Opening his eyes, he looked around him for where it could be coming from and as he did so, he accidently pressed the tub's operation button and the bubbles and water sounds came instantly back.

Shit, can't hear anything now. Damn, I will have to wait. He was angry with himself.

He looked around despite the noise of the water.

Vent. Bloody, vent, has to be that, he thought. He climbed out of the tub and started to dry himself while waiting for the timer to kick in again and the water to settle.

Come on, just stop, he kept thinking. *Plug, there must be a power source maybe I can switch it off.*

He noticed the waiter looking at him but trying not to be seen doing so.

McCabe called him over.

"Hello again. Can you get me more crisps please?" he said aiming to have the waiter away from the pool when the water stopped.

With a smile, the waiter did walk off and then out of sight.

Now, come on it's been a while, and as he thought that the noise of the motor stopped, and the tub water hissed a bit as it settled back to its quiet state.

He knelt down low at the vent and pressed an ear against it. Fixing his body position and slowing his breathing he closed his eyes again. McCabe listened.

It came again. The low staggered, often forced, moan. This time he could clearly hear that the noise was coming from a person. He was certain. It felt close as if directly below the floor, but this couldn't be.

Must be carrying along some distance through the ventilation, he assumed. Then the second noise.

Fuck, there's a female as well, he thought as the two distinctive sounds of people ill and in distress seemed to exit the vent back and forth each waiting for the other to stop before exiting painful breath from their bodies.

"Right, this vent cover is coming off." And with that he grabbed his towel and locker key and went to get changed before seeking out a screwdriver.

Their plane flew silently through the clouds en route to a small Southern Ireland airfield when a non-descript car would be waiting for them. They had just under fifty minutes to go.

Everything was in place. They were unknown to McCann so could easily turn up at the hotel as two colleagues, one from Finance, the other from Procurement, and play the part of businessmen over to further their interest in the acquisition of the local golf course. Then, once purchased, it would be revamped into a Championship course.

Abernethy even hoped that when word of this permeated through the hotel staff, McCann himself might ask for a meeting and a future joint venture with his luxury hotel. The plan seemed feasible. After all they were career spies used to all diverse disguises whether storyline or appearance. This plan needed only a watertight storyline.

The owners of the club, Green Lanyard Land Holdings, had been approached the day before, as the story needed to be accepted and confirmed on national security grounds and had agreed to fully co-operate. So Abernethy and Melville had full confidence in their words should any initial background checks be made.

Abernethy had already provided Melville his fake ID, papers and back story which would need to be passed on to McCabe soon so to avoid any blown cover. His team back in Geneva were monitoring the hotel remotely having hacked into its security camera system. However, for two men to go in, with one further unaware retired NCA officer, the odds were still stacked against them.

Abernethy knew he would need the local Garda to be exact in their timing and execution. This scared him a little for it did not take a moment for a plan to go disastrously wrong once the first bullet is fired.

The plane landed and was taxiing along the short runway when the reply came back from Cherrie about Jack Geddes.

'Geddes at the hotel in a non-professional capacity. Was staying as a guest and gave false name and address as is procedure. Not sure I believe this, James, but it is what I have established to date. Do you want me there? R'

Abernethy read the encrypted message twice.

He quickly texted her back.

'Thanks Roz. No to attendance, have it covered. Please keep looking. Geddes feels wrong. Cheers.'

What he did not say in the message was that they would soon be joined by another.

He had earlier asked his former Interpol colleague to join them and help extend their cover story and be an extra pair of eyes. Miranda had accepted immediately and was already making her way to the target building. She would arrive before the two men as a result of an easier travel route.

When McCabe returned to the pool side, with a screwdriver he borrowed from housekeeping, he did not care about being watched. He knew he may need a story as to why he was taking a vent cover off and had one ready. It would be needed.

He started unscrewing the vent and within a minute. he had a suited man approach him.

"Sir, can I help you?" But this was no offer regarding the removal of the cover.

McCabe looked up.

"No, thank you, I dropped a ring, and this must be the only place it could be as I can't see it anywhere else," came the reply.

"Small ring, sir, to fit through the slits in the vent."

Cover now off and McCabe trying to see the direction of the shaft, he replied again with a second bluff, "Yes, it was my daughter's. I hold it as a lucky charm when she is so far away from me."

Did that work? He thought. *Seen what I need to see let's not act weird, Roy.*

"Right sir, I understand. Why don't I get someone to thoroughly search the vent and below so you can just enjoy your stay with us," said the man.

McCabe knew this was not a question.

"Super, yes. Emm it's gold in colour," he said trying to remain sincere and with that he handed the cover and screwdriver to the man and left the pool area.

McCabe went back to his room and called his wife. After a small catch up and being told she was staying in town longer, he decided to explore the noises a little more and prepared to go outside and around to the pool side wall to see what he can see.

Abernethy took the front seat of the waiting car and gave the driver instructions. Melville sat in the back and caught up with the multitude of emails and messages waiting for him. None spoke.

The journey would take just under an hour. Abernethy was anxious to get to his friend.

McCabe smiled at the receptionist when he passed and wandered out the main entrance. He gave way on the stairs to a tall blonde attractive lady wearing very tight jeans and T-shirt. She was very casual but very fashionable.

"Thank you," she said.

What accent is that then, he thought to himself.

He wasn't to know that Miranda had arrived. He had never met her and had not been told there was more cavalry arriving. He walked on.

"Good afternoon, madam," said the receptionist as the latest guest arrived.

"Hello, I have a booking for a couple of nights. It's under the name of Wolf, Miranda Wolf," she replied. *Thank you boys for my fake surname. No doubt you had a laugh thinking this one up,* she thought as she retrieved the hastily made fake ID if required.

"Yes here we are, Miss Wolf. I have you down for two nights in a suite at the back. You requested to be away from the front entrance area," came her confirmation. "Any luggage to be taken to your room?" she continued.

"No, just this bag and I can manage it, thank you," said Miranda.

"May I take an imprint of the card for any expenses please? I see the room is already paid for."

Miranda handed her the card especially made in her new surname and waited for it to go through.

Hate this bit, every time, it's the will-it-work anxiety, she thought.

Then, green light.

"There you go, thank you. Do you want my colleague to show you to your room?"

"No, I will find it, thanks." She picked up her bag and stepped away only to stop after one pace and turn back to the reception.

"Oh, I am here with colleagues. Can you check if they have arrived or left a message please?"

"Sure, their names?"

"Yes, Mr White and Mr Cochon."

A moment later, she confirmed.

"They are both booked for tonight although neither have arrived yet."

"Thanks," Miranda replied and this time disappeared into the lift and onto her room.

McCabe walked around the outbuildings and on towards where he assumed the pool would be situated. Trying not to look conspicuous he would occasionally stop, look at his phone and start walking and studying the building again.

"There's a guest walking the hotel perimeter, boss," said the first man to another.

"Yes, I see him in the cameras," came the reply. "Do we know who he is, what he's doing?"

"No boss, on it boss, will get someone to bump into him and ask."

It was not unusual for a guest to wander the manicured gardens. It was, however, unusual for one guest to wander so close to the hotel building with little attention towards the beautiful gardens. This raised the security team's suspicions and moments later two were en route to intercept McCabe.

He walked past refuse bins and the din of large air conditioning units.

No back story possible if I am found here, he thought.

McCabe kept looking but for what he was not exactly sure. Then, around one further corner he saw the pool windows, so he knew he was close to something.

The vent by the pool moved down and away in an Easterly direction, he thought pausing for a second. *So any door or entrance should be short of the windows my side.*

A few steps later he saw a doorway.

Fire exit, right this must be the place where the noises came from.

He went over to the door and saw it was ajar. Straight away, he got suspicious. His background made him immediately suspicious. Then his suspicions gave way to acceptance.

We are not great at abiding with health and safety in this country so perhaps it is always pinned open. Staff smoking door, perhaps.

As he went to pull the open door he heard the noise of pacing feet on gravel.

Shit, someone's coming, he thought and instinctively opened the door and went in carefully leaving the door slightly open as he had found it.

Inside was dark and it didn't smell pleasant. McCabe slowed his breathing and let his eyes get used to the dim light. Just as his eyes adjusted the fire exit door flew open nearly slamming into him. The inside light came on and he could see two men standing in the entrance. A third man was already inside what he now saw was a corridor with a few doors coming off it.

"Hello, Mr Nosey Parker," said one of the men at the door. "What the fuck you doing in here then?"

All three men walked closer to McCabe, right up close and into his personal space.

Standing in her room on the second floor and looking out across the countryside, Miranda had seen two men, both looking menacing, walking fast down below her and strangely close against the hotel wall.

Wonder what's pissed them off, she thought. Soon enough she would fit the piece into the puzzle but for now she let that go and looked out the window.

"I lost my ring in the pool earlier, down a vent, and I thought I'd look to see where the vent might end. Also, I'm a bloody guest here so I don't like this bullying," said a defiant McCabe. His law enforcement attitude rose to the top. It would do him no good, however.

"I don't give a flying fuck about being a guest or any fucking ring, my nosey friend, why are you snooping around?" The first man said again.

"Likely pig," said a second, making an oinking sound.

"We don't like pigs around here," said the third man.

"I'm a bloody guest, you muppets, not police," McCabe said again.

"Enough," demanded the first man. "Bring him," he said as he walked off down the corridor.

McCabe was grabbed and struck in the face. His nose broken instantly. He was no match for these two younger thugs. A second strike, this time to his stomach knocking all the air out of him. He slumped down into the grasp of the two men.

McCabe was half dragged, half marched down the corridor.

As he was taken past one room he glanced inside the open door.

Fuck, what is happening in there, Jesus, he thought but was sharply brought back to his own situation with a firm hand across his face.

"Lucky you're too old or we would be cutting you up into pieces and selling parts to the highest bidder Mr Nosey," said the first man.

That was the moaning, mutilated but alive. Poor fucks, thought McCabe not really aware of the dire situation he was in. It was happening so fast.

Miranda received a text message.

'Checking into the hotel now. Where you?' It read.

She replied, 'In my room second floor waiting, James. Let me know when and where to meet' and with that she placed her phone on charge and sat back watching the local news on the room's TV.

Abernethy and Melville took their keys from the receptionist and temporarily parted as they made their way to their rooms, but not before agreeing when to meet up.

"Pierre, let's meet in the lounge bar in thirty. I will let Miranda know," Abernethy said.

"Roger that James," came the reply.

As Abernethy waited on the lift to arrive he texted his friend McCabe.

"Hi, Roy, James here. Hope all is well. Just checking in, mate."

The message was deliberately bland and nondescript so as not to give anything away that doesn't need to, while telling McCabe he had arrived at the hotel. It would be received and read but no reply would be forthcoming.

McCabe was manhandled into a chair in a room next to the room of horror he had just seen, and his hands and ankles tied to it. Strong black tape was placed firmly across his mouth. He was afraid, very afraid. He thought of his wife and where she was.

The room went dark as the third man exited and switched the lights off.

Abernethy was not worried that after an hour he had not yet received a reply from his friend but did look about the hotel lounge hoping to catch a glimpse of him.

The three sat and spoke quietly about what they would be doing next and who would do what. Much more experienced than McCabe at sneaking around they would let themselves be seen during the day and take initial action that night. For now, they would watch and wait.

McCabe too would wait. He would not be aware that his phone had rung three times since it had been taken from him. It was his wife informing him she was heading back to the hotel, and then wondering where he was when he did not answer.

"What to do, boss?" said one man to McCann up in the main suite where he kept himself busy and out of sight. "His Mrs is heading back, and we don't know who the snoop is."

"What did his phone give up?" said McCann.

"Not sure, boss. No obvious names or numbers. His wife kept calling clearly. She's going to be an issue at the hotel," he replied.

"No, she is not," McCann shouted back, the frustration now clear in his voice. "You will look after her when she gets here. She will no doubt ask front desk where he is. Get them to send her down below and secure her."

"There was one number that called and texted four times, boss. It is simply registered as 'James'."

"No surname, no location indicator just James?" asked McCann.

"Yup."

"Fucking suspicious, no? Regular contact from James since he has got here and nothing to identify this man?" McCann stood. "Right, let's go chat with him," and with that McCann and two others headed down to the lower level. The fourth man headed to Reception to pass on the instruction.

The room filled with light from the corridor as the men stood in the doorway. McCabe struggled to focus but when he did, he did not like what he saw.

"Take his gag off," McCann said. "I know this man and I wish to speak with him."

The thick black tape was ripped off. It left a red mark across McCabe's face.

"Roy fucking McCabe. Long-time, my old friend."

There was a pause. The two other men were a little taken aback.

McCann continued.

"I sent teams out to kill you, years back and nothing. We couldn't find you. First the RUC then MI5 was it, kept you well hidden from me they did? Now though," he said with a grin now appearing on his face, "you walk into my place. The chances of that…"

"McCann, I see you're still a thug and a waste of space, although the guns and the cigarettes have bought you a grand place here." McCabe knew he was in for it but did not want to show any fear or weakness. Instead, his sarcasm cloaked his fear…

"Yes, I was bored with hiding so I thought I'd come for a wee break and relax in your spa hotel."

McCann smiled back.

"Why don't we both deal with this like men and me and you take a walk out in the gardens?" McCabe tried, already knew the answer.

"Me, waste my knuckles on you and perhaps get my clothes dirty? No chance my troublesome memory from the past. I will just let the boys deal with you while I take care of your misses. Nice she is if I remember correctly."

He stopped. He was enjoying himself now. With his back to McCabe, he lifted his shirt all the way up.

"You see this lovely cut, my friend. The one running all the way up my back. That's where your friend's girlfriend helped me with her kidney. She didn't know she was helping me but her good efforts wasted on an old man like me prolonging my life so I can profit from others."

He let his shirt drop.

"See, apparently I have an unusual blood group and apparently she was a perfect match, it took years off me having some young flesh stitched inside me." He laughed with a guttural laugh, one seeping up from the depths of depravity.

McCabe sat in silence. He knew what he had seen and who McCann was referring to, Abernethy had spoken of her many times, and her work in Vukovar. He felt a pang of shock and sorrow for his friend's loss and that he now knew what had happened to someone who had left one of life's indelible marks on someone. He had to stay alive to tell him, he had to kill this bastard. As McCann left the room, McCabe grew anxious for his wife.

"You fucking coward, you leave her you hear, you leave her be." But it would fall on deaf ears.

The door closed and McCabe was left tied to a chair with two of McCann's killers.

Chapter 17
The Coming Together

Abernethy was worried. Very worried. Something was wrong. McCabe was not responding, and he had not yet seen his wife either.

Christ, what have I done? He thought.

He stood firm and barked out his instructions.

"Right, we may need to accelerate things. I worry about Roy and we know McCann's around somewhere. Miranda, will you get in touch with Interpol and check the latest. Pierre, go chat to reception and the bar staff. Let it be known that we are here to buy a golf club. Let's see if we can get McCann interested. I will chat to the local law enforcement and get them to up their planning. Let's meet back here for a late lunch, say perhaps three."

Without waiting for a reply, Abernethy took out his phone and made a call. The others left the table to carry out their instructions.

McCann paced his room. Richards sat in an armchair by the window watching both his boss and the outside activity as guests came and went. Richards knew this was a key day and nothing had to go wrong. Richards knew that Geddes was arriving to run over the final instructions. He also knew that his team had an issue in the basement and a complication with a wife pending.

Abernethy received a text.

'James, need you to call me pronto. Drako shipment stopped in Denmark. Suspect new smuggling route? Or Denmark? Now their go to spot prior to the UK? Greg.'

Greg was one of the team in Geneva and would only interrupt Abernethy when on a target location if he felt it absolutely necessary. This was one of those moments.

'Right, could be, Greg', he texted in response. 'Will call you soon', he added, knowing Greg would be awaiting further instruction.

Abernethy then went to his room to call his contact at the Garda.

McCabe was losing consciousness.

The bruising around his face had swollen so badly he could not see out from either eye. He knew he would be dead soon and tried to ignore the pain and think of the memories with his wife, only for his mind to be brought back to the present when yet another blow piled down on him.

He had given his aggressors nothing. He had resisted the desire to bargain information for a more speedy end and he was proud of that.

James will fuck this lot, he thought as his mind and consciousness went blank. It would not return to him.

Moments later, McCann received a call in his room.

"Boss, he's gone. We got nothing, sorry boss," said the man on the call.

McCann ended the call without speaking. He looked at Richards. Richards knew what that meant. It was not coincidence that a former adversary of them both ended up in their hotel yards away from the operating tables. The anxiety levels of both men rose slightly.

What had McCabe found and had he told anyone?

Then a second call to McCann. Reluctantly, expecting more bad news, he answered it.

"Yes?"

"We have the woman," said this voice. "No one saw. She's secure in our quarters. What next, boss?"

McCann thought for a moment.

Richards heard the voice on the call.

"Brenden, let me deal with this," Richards said as he rose and left without waiting on acknowledgement or acceptance.

For the next thirty minutes, Abernethy spoke in detail with the Deputy Commissioner of the Garda and together they firmed up the timing and method for the next and possibly final phase of the operation. The covert surveillance now done, and intelligence gathered, it would soon be time for full blown action.

In a different part of the hotel, she sat on the bed and listened to the voice on the other end of her encrypted cell phone.

Miranda focused on the female voice that told her of the latest capture of a lorry with twenty-three Chinese Uighurs, Syrian and Ethiopian migrants swindled of large sums of cash and stuffed in like sardines hoping for a new start in life. Most had survived to reach Denmark but would be going no further. Now safe in a detention centre, they would at least get shelter and food. None would know of the gruesome mutilation and pain that would have awaited them in a five-star spa hotel in Southern Ireland had they got through.

Soon enough, McCann would know that the net was tightening, and law enforcement would be closing in. As for Drako, the driver of the stopped lorry would unwittingly speak of a village in Estonia where a man bragged of his exploits and riches moving migrants around Europe for money. When he too was brought into custody, he would volunteer information on Drako's operation and whereabouts in exchange for a shorter jail sentence.

He would somewhat brag about the planned death of an American charity worker with links to the CIA later identified as Richard Livingston and that of a female UN worker, Fleming. She had disappeared amongst the streets of Vukovar and how 'her organs had helped save the lives two of his glorious soldiers from battlefield wounds'. This last point would make its way to Abernethy soon enough.

McCann's day would get worse still. In a matter of moments, his phone would ring again.

This time, it was Richards. Expecting an issue with the newly captured guest, he exhaled deeply in despair. It was not McCabe's wife that was the issue, but it would not be good news.

"Brenden, it's the farm. Just had word that when we left, our place was taken up by Drako's mugs. Seems he is pissed off with us and the Rotterdam operation. He is still operating despite the law all over him. No idea how he found out but our friends at the farm had an uncomfortable visit. They are all alive but beaten badly and in shock…"

Again, McCann didn't reply but instead ended the call. He sat in his chair and poured himself a large whisky. Today was not a good day.

Richards was in dialogue with the two members of his team in the room next door to where McCabe's wife was being held when his phone rang.

"Fuck, it's all happening at once," he said out loud to himself.

It was his inside man at the airport who, for a few hundred Euros a month, kept him updated on the comings and goings of key individuals.

The call was answered with a "Yes?"

"It's the American you asked me to watch for."

"Shades. Tall. That one?"

"Yes, the one in the picture and he's wearing shades without any sun in the sky."

"Right, good job." And he put the phone back into his jacket.

Geddes had arrived a little early.

Right, I still have over an hour to sort her and get the place ready for the Secret Service Yank, thought Richards and he turned back to the two men and finished up.

When he had done so, he walked to reception to prepare them for Geddes's arrival and sent a text to McCann informing him of the pending new guest.

Abernethy was finishing up with the Garda when there was a knock on the door. He ended his conversation and went to open the door.

"James," said Pierre, "we have a meeting to go to in thirty minutes."

Behind Melville was Miranda, she was smiling.

"Meeting?"

"Yes, with the owner of the hotel, a man called McCann," he said sarcastically. "Seems putting the word out worked and he wants to meet the businesspeople planning to buy the local golf course."

"No way!" Abernethy exclaimed in part disbelief.

"Yes, true. He wants to explore options for spectators and participants of events to stay here. He wants in at the start," Melville said in a reassuring tone.

"Right then team, we have a meeting to plan. Come in. I will order coffee."

The two entered the room and Abernethy released the room door. It swung close.

Chapter 18
No End Game

There was a knock on the room door. It was probably just the coffee arriving but the three inside stopped talking and looked up.

Instinctively, Melville felt for his gun.

The door was opened, and the coffees were placed on the table near the window. Nothing was said by any of the four. The room had a strange electricity that even the room service member could feel.

They waited for the room service man to quietly close the door behind him then carried on with their planning…

Abernethy's mobile vibrated on the table, catching everyone's attention.

He read the message and then turned to Miranda showing her the screen.

"Can you check this with Interpol, likely Europol won't know," he said. "I believed John Magere was linked but who is this guy?"

Miranda studied the name provided in the text.

"Geddes. Jack Geddes. Let me flip this while we are here and see what my lot can find," she replied focusing instantly on her own mobile only returning to the conversation when the message was sent.

None of the three would see or hear the refuse lorry pull up to the rear of the hotel. Had she been in her own room Miranda might have but she was not there. Moments after it had reversed back close to the commercial bins, the shutters came up on a delivery position. The driver and passenger never left their vehicle, choosing instead to wait and watch for the signal from the three men at the rear throwing refuge bags into the rear. Each one took a toll on the carrier. They were heavy and cumbersome and difficult to get a proper grip of. When one bag was dropped to the ground, and the security member jumped down the short distance to retrieve it, again, neither man inside the vehicle exited to assist.

Three minutes passed and the signal was given. The engine sounded and the refuse lorry drove off.

Destination, a private incineration scheduled and paid for by an unknown and unchallenged individual.

"Get that washed and brushed, just in case," said one man to the guard who had dropped the bag onto the ground.

"Sir, of course, straight away."

"What do we know about these city clowns that want to buy the fucking golf course?" McCann said down the line to his solicitor. "Tell me what you know about the sale price and contract."

For the next few minutes, his solicitor scrolled his online system and interpreted the jargon into normal speak for his client. What neither man knew was that the wording and the contract were both fictitious and designed in a manner that McCann could see as favouring himself.

Just as the rented SUV pulled up to the hotel main doors Miranda received a call.

"This is my man with the answers, guys," she said, accepting the call and assuming the other two knew what she meant.

They did and while they could only hear her responses, they stayed silent and waited for the conversation to end.

"Geddes is the current number one guy. Seems Magere was shipped out to graze, despite the President's links to the Irish. Seems the President is trying to look clean so now this guy's the lead."

Neither man had any interruption pending. They knew there was more coming from her.

"Seems he was Special Forces and was assigned to the Presidential detail years back in and out of the Middle East covering Ambassadors including Israel. More though, until Magere he was bodyguard to the President's closest family!" she exclaimed, now looking directly at Abernethy. "James, I think this guy is the real deal."

"What you mean real deal, Miranda?" said Melville.

"I mean, Pierre, he is the primary. Geddes is solely assigned to the President and cannot be taken off that detail by anyone other than the main man himself."

Abernethy jumped in.

"Meaning the President's bodyguard has left him with others while he visits a five-star hotel in Ireland," he said firmly pondering his own words, "and this visit is not social."

The three in the room stayed silent, the tension in the room tangible. They knew what the implications were of the words just spoken.

Many miles away from the Irish countryside, a helicopter landed at a refugee camp. Its tail identifier had been removed but the occupants were not arriving to take any occupants away. Instead, the two women that exited were on a fact-finding mission. One that would eventually lead to the full and total downfall of the Estonian people smuggler and the network.

The local town was filling with vehicles from outside the area. Most had darkened windows and hardened plastic fitted around the bottom edges to limit unwanted devices from gaining access to the underneath. Inside each, there were officers from both the Garda and unidentified armed response units. None were locals.

The hotel environment was such that all activities outside the grounds went unnoticed. Even the local paid-up snitches were not yet alerted by this activity. Most were home or had seen this before and were thinking it just another dull raid pending in some nearby farm or hostel centre. None expected what was going to happen next.

Those outside for a stroll did look skyward and wonder about the more frequent passing of planes. The town was not usually this popular as a flight path.

The sky was noisy.

But the noise would soon enough dull the blades of the approaching helicopters.

Abernethy believed he had thought of everything. Even down to the actual positioning of the drone that would periodically cover the grounds and feedback movements and activities to the Garda control room. Small enough not to be seen or heard, yes Abernethy had considered everything.

The moment was approaching but Abernethy felt relaxed. He felt ready. After all, he had a coffee meeting to go to.

Geddes locked his rental car and refused to give the concierge the key to allow him to move and park it.

"Reception? Here?" he said as he gestured towards the stairs and the impressive doors at their top. He was answered with a nod.

Geddes entered the building and stormed to reception ignoring the two guests already there.

"I want a man called Richards," he demanded. "Richards." And he walked a few steps to a sofa and stood by it, raising his hand towards the two guests in a sort of apologetic manner.

216

Richards knew Geddes had arrived. Not because of the airport notification or even the stubbornly parked car right outside the main reception but because he heard his own name being called. He was several yards away and arriving to greet his demanding guest.

It was more of a confrontation than a greeting.

"I'm Richards, I came when you barked at my receptionist," he said, firmly setting out his position to the new American guest in front of him.

"Right, I gathered," said Geddes turning to walk back out the main door he had just came in from. "Let's go."

The initial battle had been lost. Richards followed.

Inside the security room the two operators watched as the men began their perimeter walk. Neither seemed to talk.

Miranda and Melville entered the lounge area at the time agreed for their business meeting about a golf course. They had agreed that Abernethy would enter late and after McCann just to try to put him at unease.

"Pierre, I need to talk to you about the mole again," said Miranda, "I know not now but in private, not with James. It is his former boss McKeown and my side want to expose him now."

Melville looked at her. "Let's get through this now and then agree what to do."

McCann was waiting for them. Both walked over to him, they shook hands and pleasantries were exchanged.

McCann had done initial due diligence and the three 'purchasers' back story had seemingly held up. He was satisfied they were whom they claimed to be.

"Are we missing one?" McCann asked as they sat down together.

"Yes, he is on a call," said Miranda. "Won't be long. The bank I think."

"What's the accent you have there?" he asked.

Miranda took pleasantries with a ruthless killer and thug only so far. She chose to smile at him rather than answer. Sipping the recently delivered coffee, McCann knew this would be a formal meeting.

There followed a short moment of uncomfortable silence and stillness only broken when Miranda decided to cross her legs again. McCann noticed. Everything was working well.

Abernethy walked in and chose a route that would mean he would approach McCann from behind where he sat.

The tone and approach was designed to change drastically and again put McCann off balance.

Abernethy placed a hand on McCann's shoulder as he joined the group.

"Mr McCann, so very sorry, I am late," he said with a fake smile ringing across his face…

"Is the coffee still warm?"

McCann went to stand.

"Please, stay down," and Abernethy sitting on the chair close to McCann, very close to McCann.

Now all three were smiling at McCann.

"So, we have Miss Wolf and Mr Cochon here so I am guessing you are Mr White then?" said McCann.

"Correct," Abernethy replied.

All three could not believe that their surnames had been so easily accepted by McCann.

Had he never watched a murder mystery or bloody Bond film, thought Miranda, smiling at this man in front of her…*It's obvious.*

Their exploratory meeting kicked off in now an 'open' and friendly manner. One side wanting to know timescales and volumes aligned to the purchase of expensive dirt. The other side exploring options to get sight of the darker sides of the hotel. It seemed to Abernethy that McCann was just interested in the cash rewards of a partnering with the local Championship level golf course. Advantage Committee.

The two men had walked half of the grounds together and were now more cordial towards each other. Every ground level window was checked for adequate security locking while each and every door and fire door was likewise discussed and notes spoken into Geddes's handheld recorder.

"We will need to discuss the landscaping and the roof layout. Some of the trees and bushes over there are ideal for snipers or cameras or both," said Geddes.

Richards smirked and this was noticed.

"Snipers, funny Richards. I thought you knew and accepted the importance of this guest," barked Geddes.

Richards was thinking about the journalist who thought he was invisible but all the time known to the staff and carefully watched by them. He decided not to raise this.

"Yes, of course. It was that I have always claimed that the plant line was too close, but the boss disagreed," he said on the spot. "I will get this sorted once we agree the new shape."

"The roof?"

"Yes we will go up top later today and you can review for yourself where best to site your guys, but now let's get going around the rest of the building." And this time, off walked Richards.

Got the bastard this time, he thought.

Abernethy got a call on his phone. Looking at the screen it was the code name agreed for his Garda assault team leader. He couldn't take it right now.

Can I ignore this? Has something happened? He thought wondering what to do next.

"Is that the bloody bank again?" Miranda stalled, desperately trying to remember if they had fake Christian names agreed, then out came "James."

McCann noticed the stall.

"You forget your colleague's name, love?" he joked.

"Em, no two things at once, sorry," she replied.

Fuck, yes I did, McCann, what's your problem? Came her very next thought.

Abernethy knew she was giving him an out to take the call. He took the 'out'.

"Mr McCann, yes sorry it is my bank regarding the money exchange into Green Lanyard Land Holdings. Do you mind if I pop out to take this?" said Abernethy not really waiting on or expecting an answer. "These two will continue with you."

When he reached a corner of the lounge where he could not be overheard, but still had McCann in vision, he spoke. The call had been answered but the caller knew protocol was to wait in silence until the code word was given.

"Blue Falcon. Abernethy here, Peter?"

"Hi, James, yes. I need to let you know something. We have just been informed that a two-man security detail arrived at the airport a couple of hours ago and we have reason to believe they are US Secret Service and making their way to the hotel. Are you aware? Do we hold back?"

"Peter, nothing has changed. I am aware. Just wait for the signal. Anything else?"

"No, James, just checking. Over." And the line went dead.

Abernethy took the chance to check messages. There was one from Roz Cherrie.

'Jack Geddes arriving at the target building. Unaware Committee present. R'

Yup, I bloody know he is arriving. In fact, he's arrived, he thought to himself as he made his way back to the others.

Abernethy returned to his group.

"Sorry team, yes right," he said, deliberately interrupting McCann who seemed to be in full flow, "where are we?" He waited a second then again spoke out. "What have I missed?"

He knew this would annoy McCann. They wanted him off guard and not thinking straight and the team all had their role to play and strategy to throw in periodically.

"Shall I recap, James?" McCann said a little frustrated.

"Recap, em, Miranda you get what was said?" he said to his colleague again ignoring McCann's question and instead focusing on his team.

"Yes James, our host spoke openly. Pierre?"

Melville moved forward to pour the last of the coffee.

"Bugger!" he exclaimed spilling a little on the table deliberately. "Sorry, yes, me also. I got it all James no need to recap," he said wondering what McCann would say next.

McCann was agitated. He wanted to leave these fools and get on with his own business. He knew Geddes was around and wanted to make sure all was as assured. However, he had to stay. He had to be patient and he had to appear to like these people.

The chat went on for around forty minutes longer. In this time, the two sides had agreed to meet once more later that night after each side had had time to speak with their relevant legal representatives.

McCann called Richards as soon as he was out of sight of Abernethy and the others.

"Mate, escaped from those foreign fuckers," was his opening gambit even before Richards had acknowledged the call...

"What muppets. Think we have them interested though."

He was frustrated.

Abernethy's games had worked on McCann. He was not thinking clearly.

So the door was left open to exploit his 'hospitality' and wander around the hotel complex looking for useful evidence before the raid. Useful evidence and his bloody good friend McCabe!

"Going for a shower and a change into casuals so I can look the part, chaps," Miranda said to the other two as she wandered off to her room.

Melville nodded and gestured to Abernethy that he was going for a drink in the small bar with the burning log fire.

"Not for me yet, Pierre, I am going to clear my head and chat to Geneva and the squad down the road. Just to make sure nothing has changed and everything remains ready. We need to be careful with Geddes. See you soon." And he too walked off leaving Melville to seek an exploratory meeting with the hotels exclusive red wine list.

When he reached the small bar and approached the waiter, Melville would be known to the man sitting silently in one corner watching proceedings.

"So Mr Geddes, have you done your rounds with my man here?" started McCann. "No doubt you will agree that we are safe and sound for your client," he went on but was to be interrupted and stopped in his tracks.

"Look, I decide. I do the chit chat and you shut the fuck up and follow my lead. Do we understand each other, Mr McCann?" said the American in a calm yet instructive tone.

McCann smiled an awkward but what he hoped was a defiant smile and walked back towards the main reception. His introduction to the special guest, done.

Back alone in his room, Abernethy thought. He was planning the next phase of the operation. His heart was tugging. It was an emotion he was not used to.

Death was close. Death was imminent and its weight sat heavy on his shoulders.

Directly responsible for the destruction of many family units and the cause of many child's tears at the loss of a father.

Abernethy knew there was more coming.

He did not mind the killing of the adult, the target, the terrorist. He didn't even mind that technically he was nothing more than an assassin. However, something had changed. He had started to wonder about the children, hidden from his view, that would never know why their father never came home that night, or why he had given them that extra firm hug and kiss before leaving for work.

He would accelerate the arrival of sixteen 'golfers', some special members from the club they were pretending to buy, to arrive at the hotel, and to be a distraction. Only Miranda and Melville would know that these were no golfers.

They were instead, armed response officers ready to take down the illegal operation from the inside.

Abernethy walked towards the arriving luxury coach filled with 'golfers'. He suspected that he was being watched.

Geddes and McCann watched the new arrivals but for very different reasons. Geddes worried about his pending arrival. McCann juggled his greed for money and awareness with growing anxiety about the goings on below in the hotel's hidden rooms.

The new arrivals piled into reception.

The operation had begun.

On several fronts, activity began to ramp up. Abernethy knew that with the first 'bullet' came the end of all things organised and chance, perhaps even fate, would run his operation after that.

The reception filled. It was deliberate. The security in the back office could not decide exactly where to look or position their cameras. This allowed two couples from the team to move off unnoticed down their pre-arranged routes towards the kitchens and stairwell areas.

Now armed, Melville met with Miranda and the two moved along the back corridors and would soon exit down towards the hotel's underground complex. Their task, to find and extract McCabe. Then, to assist the rear assault team who were themselves tasked with managing any firefight and escape attempt by McCann and his cronies.

Richards was not happy. He had survived many extraction attempts by the local Garda by being constantly aware and never believing in coincidence. Now, at the hotel, three hotshots from the finance world together with twenty plus golfers had descended upon the place and were seemingly running wild. He was growing more and more suspicious.

"Boss, Brenden, I don't like it. Don't like this one fucking bit," he said when McCann answered the call.

"Stay calm, Paddy. I don't like it either, but they are only fucking golfers," came his reply, "Relax." But Richards was having none of it.

"Golfers, my arse. When I see them on the course and not the bloody nineteenth hole then I might believe. I am going to ready the guys, oh and ready the bloody car while I am at it," he barked back at his boss.

"Fine, Paddy, fine. Do what makes you feel best. I will wander down and speak with those bankers and get this calmed." And then the call was ended.

Abernethy's mobile rang.

He looked down at the screen.

McCann, he can go to fuck, and with that he put the phone into his inside jacket pocket with his right hand and with his left instinctively reached down and to the side and felt the comfort that was his holstered weapon.

He made his way out and to the coach where he had agreed to meet with Kyle Martin, a rough and rather uncultured Scot who had, somehow, made his way into the local Irish police force years back and was now leading the assault team on the hotel.

"Right, Martin, report please," Abernethy said as he walked over to the man with his hand outstretched.

Hands shaken; the reply followed.

"The team know the building plans inside out, sir. We will have a team securing the three access points the guests can arrive from and will stop their movement into the danger areas. When this is done and the signal received from all three, only then will two teams circumvent the property from either side meeting together near the rear to support your team if called upon. They will sit it out and wait for any rabbits squirting out the rear."

Martin stopped for a breath. The movement of a car close by distracted him. He was not sure why but the darkened windows to the rear caught his attention. He stared for a moment, then carried on, as the car moved away swiftly down the hotel drive and then out of sight. Only the faint line of dust falling back down to earth remained.

Inside the vehicle were the two main targets. Martin would not yet know this.

"Two will secure the central hallway and reception, while a third will take down the security cameras in the control room." Again, another halt and a look at Abernethy for acknowledgement.

Abernethy looked up from his phone screen.

"Yes, good, and then?"

"Right sir, then the main team of four will approach the security at the four points around the ground floor we chatted about over the phone recently. We still believe these to be the key pinch points and when secured or at worst neutralised, we can then progress down to the lower ground floor and the suspects."

Again, there was silence. It lasted for only a second or two but Martin felt it to be longer. He wanted to get on with things and stop the talking. His team were moving into position and he wanted in.

Abernethy stared at his colleague. His mind racing.

"Right. Good. All covered then as we agreed. Best you join your team," and as the words came out, Martin was moving past Abernethy and towards the granite stairs leading up and into the main hotel hall.

Hotel guards ran around in the confusion while trying still to act professional and courteous towards the new arrivals. They were not used to such a large party of guests arriving all at the same time. The hotel clientele tended to be few and far between but of high net value.

This group's arrival was not a welcome development.

His phone vibrated.

Opening the message, Abernethy knew events were about to go live.

'Ready. About to go in for target. Police teams in position and ready if required. No further comms possible till end.'

Go get him guys, he thought to himself and then straight after, *fuck, I hope Roy's alive.*

Abernethy took up his own agreed position just inside the main entrance. He wanted to ensure that their American Secret Service guest kept his weapon holstered and didn't get involved in the operation.

Then, around different parts of the same building it started. Each and every member of the assault team received the signal. One long, high pitch tone, followed by a second short one.

Guns out, the team went in.

Miranda rushed in the back fire door with Melville inches behind her. One of the two police teams moved to secure the door area and watch and wait for a signal to support them. The other stayed low covering possible escape routes out and across the fields behind them.

At the same time, the door to the security office was forced open and the guard inside over powered and secured hands tied face down on the floor in seconds.

One further armed police officer jumped the reception and less forcibly but quickly secured the hands of the receptionist pushing her down into a sitting position and out of sight of any gunfire that may begin. The same guard then pulled the cables below the desk out of the wall sockets in an attempt to cut any communication lines from rooms to the outside world.

Abernethy could no longer just wait. If he was responsible for the overall success of the operation now in full swing, he was himself getting more involved.

He looked outside and up to the heavens not looking for any divine inspiration but instead to reassure himself that his request for rerouting the flight path from the coast to overhead and the noise that would create, was in fact happening.

Geddes, go get the yank, he thought to himself. He knew that to extract him without fully explaining what was happening, or worse still, to not have given the 'special relationship' a heads up on the operation, would not go down well. *Fuck it. It is what it is* and off he went to his room on the first floor near the rear of the building.

Miranda stopped dead in her tracks.

"Pierre, what the fuck is that? Do you see this?" The colour drained or actual blood from Miranda's face at what she was staring at.

Melville was right behind her. He saw what she saw. He touched her shoulder to acknowledge her question.

Both operators stood in silence. The only noise above the quiet beeping of many monitors being their raised level of breathing.

Both had seen horrors before. Both had accepted and subscribed to the adage that once seen images can never be unseen. Both knew, there and then, that these images, these horrors, yards away, would leave them only with death.

The tip of her gun had pushed the door open and allowed the little light that lit the corridor enter and mix with the strange hospital aesthetic lighting inside.

"Bodies. Christ, just everywhere. And…they are still alive but shouldn't be," she said.

"Yup, see it. Not sure what it is, but I see it," came his reply.

Very quickly they became aware of more noises not just their breathing.

Dying faces stared back at them in the doorway. Mutilated and roughly patched up bodies were everywhere. Slumped on metal beds and large recliners. The new light from outside the pungent and vile room had awoken what life and will that remained and now a dozen eyes looked at the two new faces in the doorway.

Miranda saw one face change from a deathly stare quickly into fear.

"Her," she said. "Look at her." Miranda pointed to one of the macabre audience in front of her.

"She's afraid. She's afraid of us, of what we do to her. She doesn't know who we are. Christ what is this," she said. Her voice raised, her heart beating way too fast.

"Go back. Get the first team here now. They will secure this. I will go forward for McCabe," said Melville.

She stood. Unresponsive.

"Miranda, do it now!"

Then, with a helping hand, Melville turned her gaze away from the faces of horror and towards where they had come. In a second, she was back and then running down towards the fire-door they had entered in from.

Moments later, she was back at the same point. Melville had moved further up the corridor, and she was desperate to join him to give him support but she stopped. Turned back to the offices behind her and spoke.

"This is now your tasking. Protect what is in this room but do not enter and perhaps you do not want to look inside," she said.

Perhaps, it was adrenaline but the first officer, gun raised, stepped up past her and saw inside the room. As he did so his stomach emptied violently onto both his legs and boots and out across the room floor with splashes landing on one half alive body, lying on a lowered metal bed, and for whom this additional event meant nothing. He was hoping for death and the new smell of sick meant nothing.

Mutilated bodies lay everywhere. Many seemed alive and moving painfully. Machines whirred and stopped then whirred again. Tubes, inserted into arms and chests dangled twisted together like spaghetti. The two police officers could not now un-see what they had just seen.

I bloody warned them, she thought as she ran further into the complex looking for her partner.

"There he is, Christ," said Abernethy as he happened to see his target coming out from the gym area and presumably make his way back to his room to freshen up.

"Hello, you, Geddes," he called out. "You, yes, a word please," Abernethy repeated in a firm tone.

Geddes stopped and waited, turning his body slightly sideways instinctively to make it a smaller target. He never took his gaze of the fast-approaching man.

"We need to talk. There is something you need to know, Geddes," he said now much closer.

The two men spent a moment eyeing each other up. Both were highly skilled at reading body language and the environment around themselves often at the same time.

"Right, the new guests?"

Abernethy nodded.

"OK, golfers, my arse," he said with a smile. "Don't know their tee from their driver."

The lift door opened and Geddes entered.

"You have until the door opens again to say what you need. That is if you're getting in."

Abernethy entered the lift and the doors closed automatically behind him.

When he wandered back down the stairs to reception rather than wait on the lift that had gone further up, Abernethy was more relaxed. The American guest was pleased that he had now been given the heads up and could leave discretely without risk to reputation to anyone that might have been planning a visit.

He promised to be out and away within twenty minutes. Abernethy had promised him speedy safe passage should he be accidently caught up with events around the hotel.

Miranda had now caught up with Melville who had waited on her just a little further along the corridor. He had seen a bottle neck and decided to secure the location and wait on her. Now together, they moved on further into the underground part of the complex. McCabe was their target now and soon enough they found him.

"That door, Miranda," said Melville and it was forcibly opened. Both guns pointing inside on entry.

"No, here," he said quickly turning and moving on towards the next door.

"Mine, ready?" he continued. Both knew the routine well. They had practised 'door kicking' many times with their respective special forces operators back home and now the training was being utilised for real.

In they went again.

Two seconds passed, and "not here" Melville said again as he turned to move out. Miranda was closer to the exit so now she took the lead.

There were three doors left to open and three rooms to clear when she went up to one of them.

"Mine," she called as she grabbed and put pressure on the handle, but this door did not open.

"Leave, next," came the command from behind her but Melville had already moved on to the next door.

"Mine, ready!" he exclaimed as he grabbed the handle and pushed.

It opened and both piled in.

"There!" she exclaimed pointing her gun instinctively down towards the figure on the ground.

In one corner lay a body next to a broken chair. The body appeared bound and motionless.

She knew to check the body before leaving. They both knew they had to check the remaining two rooms before returning to what they believed was McCabe. The room was dimly lit but both knew they had found him and he wasn't alive.

"Mine," came the call from Melville as the final open door and room was considered safe then moving past the room with their target in, and without looking in, they went back to the door that Miranda had failed to open first time.

Still firm, she moved back and then raising her leg kicked at the handle. The lock moved some in its locked position which both knew meant it was now weak. Melville touched Miranda on the shoulder and she knew to move aside.

He lunged shoulder first at the door, and it fell open with him stumbling into the room gun still in the ready position. She followed behind him quickly.

"Nothing here, out and let's get him up top," she yelled. Her voice pumped with adrenaline.

Melville lifted the dead body as much as he could. It was dead weight and as such was extremely heavy to move. There was no support or partial assistance as can happen with some still alive. Miranda knew to let Melville struggle along with the body as she went first back along the corridor towards the police team.

She needed to be ready just in case an unwanted surprise came towards them and Melville was now unable to defend himself.

"You, here now, give him a hand," she called out as she saw the armed police still loitering outside the macabre room of mutilated and stitched up bodies. They had seen enough and now stood outside guarding the near dead.

Two officers willingly came to assist Melville. It was a chance to get out and up into the light and they grabbed it.

"Take him outside and secure the body before getting back to watching the rear for snipers, OK?" barked Melville.

"Yes sir, right sir." As McCabe was now carried with more care back towards the light and the rear hotel exit.

"You two can move back to the exit but stay inside and watch the corridor for new movement, OK?" came the second command.

Both remaining police officers moved back behind Melville and Miranda a short distance and took up position at the fire door exit.

Leaving the officers to take control of the back of the building, Miranda took the lead in returning back along the corridor and towards the stairs up into the main body of the hotel and back into the pending firefight. Melville ran close behind.

When they reached the ground floor landing, they both stopped for a moment.

"Gun away but safety off. I hear no shooting so lets us not start it, agree?" she said to Melville.

He nodded and both returned their weapons to their holsters and out of sight.

The door closed automatically on his room and Geddes walked the short distance to the lift. His luggage making no noise as he wheeled it behind him.

Fourth floor, stairs then, he thought to himself.

Then, seconds later coming out into the main reception, he saw Miranda.

He walked past her and without knowing, had looked her up and down. She, on the other, had had noticed his attention on her but let it go and turned to face her partner and send Geddes an informal signal.

"Leaving now," he said as he handed the key to the officer behind the reception counter and Geddes simply turned and walked towards the exit doors.

Yes, leaving now not checking out, he thought with a smirk on his lips. He exited the building and made two calls on his phone a short distance away. The second call was for a taxi to take him back to the airport.

Abernethy ran to reception.

"The tall American, Geddes, has he checked out yet?" he demanded of the officer watching the reception area.

"Sir, not exactly checked out but he has left. Left the hotel, sir, with his luggage yes," came the reply.

Good, one less cluster fuck likely, he thought.

"James, we found him."

It was all happening all at once and Abernethy was close to losing control. He turned and saw Miranda slightly out of breath coming towards him. Melville nodded from a distance but headed towards the reception and the officer. He wanted to know how it was going and asked for the lead officer Kyle Martin to come and report.

229

"James, Pierre and I found your friend. It isn't good, James. These mad men had hurt him bad but he feels nothing anymore."

Abernethy looked straight into her eyes. She could see the hurt in them.

Her lips moved as she was about to speak again.

"Good job, Miranda. Now make sure that the guests are secure and we get all these bastards," Abernethy said as he walked towards the stairs. "I am going to have a word with the hotel owner."

She knew what he meant. "Be careful James," she called back and then went to join Melville again.

Abernethy stormed off towards the closest stairs that would take him to the master suites and McCann just as she shouted back again at him. For a moment, he contemplated ignoring Miranda believing she could look after herself. Then, however, his professional self, bullied its way into his conscience and he stopped and turned to face her.

"James, it's the brass in London, at the NCA, they have the mole, it is McKeown and he is fully hooked and they want to know if we are pulling him in," she said holding her phone aloft as if to convince him of the sincerity of the call.

Just then, Abernethy forgot what he was about to do. A sinister smirk came over him and his eyes seemed to darken, sweet revenge for the past, *I hope the bastard rots,* he thought. "Thanks Miranda, some good news for once."

"Pull him in, right in and when you have done that pull the plug on everyone around him, associates and colleagues. 'Fishers of Men' my arse, this is for the JSGNI back in the day and for Mo Mowlem, you fuck!" he exclaimed triumphantly.

She didn't understand all that he had said but Miranda got the gist of it and took a little pleasure herself knowing that while her good friend had lost McCabe, he was having some sort of revenge with McKeown. Further still, they would all benefit when he talked and the network of smugglers appeared as sitting ducks for the enforcement agencies across Europe.

Neither said anything further. Miranda spoke down the line to the caller and Abernethy turned back towards the stairs.

He reached the top of the stairs and checked the compass feature on his phone.

Hotel is South to South East facing at the front. McCann's room is just offset over the main entrance so that is South to slightly West, he thought. Then looking up at the two options available he knew where to go.

Fucker's in there, and checking that the safety was off on his 9MM Glock he moved towards McCann's door.

Wasting no time or adrenaline, he let off one round at the lock and followed the bullet in gun still primed for action.

"McCann, I don't want to talk to you about fucking golf," he said at first. "Show yourself and let's be doing this, you scum bag."

Abernethy didn't know if it was the adrenaline or the loss of his friend that was making him so ready and willing to have the gun fight but, either way, he was ready for it.

Room by large room, Abernethy searched for him, waiting, and wanting movement and a target to shoot at but in the end he conceded that there was no one in the suite. McCann was not hiding in his suite and yet he was not obviously out of it nor had he heard any radio confirmation of his sighting.

Where is he? He can't have got out already.

He sat on the edge of the bureau and wondered what could have happened.

The meeting in the bar and the agreed follow up. He couldn't have suspected anything.

Then it began to dawn on him.

The coach load of guests. He doesn't stay when guests arrive, but there was still something troubling him.

He started to retrace his steps over and over in his mind.

Then, when he had arrived back at the conversation with Kyle Martin, it struck him.

The car with the darkened windows. The bloody SUV that had caught Martin's and then his attention. That must be it, he thought. *Timing is perfect.*

Trying to think if he had caught the registration plate something else came over him.

That fuck was getting out, probably smiling as he did and would have been staring straight at me. Bet that fucking doctor was in there also. Shit and this made Abernethy's blood boil for a moment.

"Right," he said out loud. "Too late for now, later, back to the task at hand," and with the noise of his voice and the confirmation of action, Abernethy stood and rushed back out of the room and back towards the stairs.

Abernethy had reached the top of the stairs back down to the main reception when it started. Slowly at first, one 'bang' then seconds later a second. 'Bang.' Then it all seemed to happen at once.

As he ran down, he heard shot after shot. Gauging the tone and the regularity of the firing, Abernethy considered it to be more than just random and that it was his team firing in a suppressive controlled manner.

Bursting through the ground floor doors, Abernethy slid down and towards the left to cover. He had surveyed the area meticulously as he always did and had already chosen that specific vantage point should the need arise. It had.

Controlled shots were being taken all around and very quickly Abernethy realised that this was suppressive fire only to keep McCann's men away from the central area of the building and force them towards the rear and the waiting police reinforcements. It also allowed officers to secure the guest areas and instruct the frightened to remain in their rooms.

"James, they are escaping out the back," shouted Miranda. "No sighting of the primary target however, or the doctor."

Melville then appeared.

"Hey, this way," he shouted just as the firing stopped.

The operation had been a huge success and was over in minutes. None of McCann's men had been up for the fight and had surrendered as soon as they had come across any armed police.

"Down in the basement area, you may not want to see what they found, James," he said.

"The bodies?" he replied.

"Em, well it would be bodies if they were dead," and the look on his colleague's face told him that something very gruesome awaited him down in the basement.

"Ok, lead the way, and, I assume then, that medical help is on the way?" Abernethy questioned.

"James, the best help for those we have found is to be." Melville paused for a moment, initially thinking better not to say what he was thinking but then said it anyway, "well to be put down like an old dog."

Both men just then stopped and looked down the stairs.

Melville then released the door to Abernethy as he started down. Abernethy followed. Neither spoke any further.

Both men were highly trained. They had seen horror many times before and knew that the last thing victims needed to see was the rescuers' reaction of shock. Melville took over.

They looked inside at the mutilated bodies, moving slowly like worms across a slab in the rain, trying to find shelter and solitude. These 'worms' did not seek solitude but instead longed for death and the 'rain' was red in colour on the floor beneath them.

"Medical is imminent and have been primed for multiple casualties. A heli is en route for those that might make it to proper attention at the General Hospital." He looked down at Abernethy's boots as he spoke knowing he was not able to give the operational situation without being distracted by the morbid and putrid sight of these former human beings now hardly recognisable as the same species as himself.

The training was working but it was getting harder to focus.

Abernethy stared at one victim.

A young woman, perhaps in her early thirties with the remnants of long auburn hair.

He thought of Victoria Fleming and in a moment of weakness, he wondered if this had been her fate. She had disappeared many years back in Vukovar at the hands of human traffickers now confirmed as organ selling criminals.

"James," he said out loud to himself and then he was back.

"Right, please stay here and manage their comfort as best you can. You," he said looking at one of the younger looking officers assigned 'guard' duty over the finding, "you support Pierre and try to make them comfortable and await the medics."

"Sir, me sir, but what if one comes close, sir?" said the officer clearly going into some form of mental shock.

"Then," Abernethy said firmly, "I suggest you remember that what you see are human beings who did not choose this for themselves, and," now in a temper, "remember why you wear that uniform. To 'Serve'!" and with this, he laid a firm hand on the officer's shoulder before retrieving it and walking out into the corridor and towards the rear fire door.

He knew it was over. There was much still to do, however, Abernethy knew this monster of a hospital was dead and buried. He knew that the Irish legal system would start up and try to negate the horrors of what had been happening on its doorstep. He knew that more desperate and war traumatised innocents would get caught up in the trafficking circle and he knew that McCann was still free.

Most of all, he knew that with McCann still free he still had much work to do to avenge the innocent victims and the death of his good friend whom he had put in danger's way.

The success of the mission lay heavy on Abernethy's shoulders. In his line of work, success means not casualties. Success means evil is defeated. His success felt like defeat, yet again.

Geddes's phone received a text message.

It was McCann.

McCann had been informed that the 'tall American with the sunglasses' had passed through security and into International departures by his man on the inside.

Geddes's read the message.

Reassured a little that the doctor had escaped with McCann, he finished reading the message and allowed himself an inner smile.

He took another sip of his tea. He had grown accustomed to drinking tea when he finished his third tour of Afghanistan and now, sitting in an Irish airport, waiting on boarding and a return to Washington DC, he sat and drank tea.

He returned to his phone and made a call. When it was answered, he spoke.

"Sir, sorry to bother you."

Then he waited.

"There has been a slight delay," and again he waited and listened to the reply.

"Yes sir, we have a match but she is currently being driven to a new vantage point by my Irish contact. The plan needed to change, sir."

Geddes looked at his phone.

"No, Mr President, we do have a match, we just need to get it to the new location. I am en route back and will fill you in properly, sir."

Geddes then ended the call.